Arthur Tappan Pierson

The Divine Enterprise of Missions

A series of lectures delivered at New Brunswick, N.J.

Arthur Tappan Pierson

The Divine Enterprise of Missions
A series of lectures delivered at New Brunswick, N.J.

ISBN/EAN: 9783337298296

Printed in Europe, USA, Canada, Australia, Japan

Cover: Foto ©Andreas Hilbeck / pixelio.de

More available books at **www.hansebooks.com**

THE
Divine Enterprise of Missions

THE DIVINE

Enterprise of Missions

A SERIES OF LECTURES

DELIVERED AT NEW BRUNSWICK, N. J., BEFORE THE
THEOLOGICAL SEMINARY OF THE REFORMED
CHURCH IN AMERICA

UPON THE

"GRAVES" FOUNDATION

IN THE MONTHS OF JANUARY AND FEBRUARY, 1891

BY

ARTHUR T. PIERSON

———◆———

NEW YORK
THE BAKER & TAYLOR CO.
740 AND 742 BROADWAY

TO

NATHAN F. GRAVES, Esq.

OF SYRACUSE, NEW YORK

TO WHOSE DISCRIMINATING MUNIFICENCE THIS LECTURESHIP

OWES ITS FOUNDATION;

AND TO WHOSE DEVOUT AND INTELLIGENT INTEREST IN THE

GREAT WORK OF A WORLD'S EVANGELIZATION

SO MANY OF

THE FRIENDS OF MISSIONS TRACE THEIR OWN INCREASED ZEAL

FOR THE COMING OF THE KINGDOM

THIS VOLUME

IS AFFECTIONATELY AND MOST RESPECTFULLY INSCRIBED

By the Author

INTRODUCTION.

BY REV. D. D. DEMAREST, D.D.,

PROFESSOR OF PASTORAL THEOLOGY, NEW BRUNSWICK, N. J.

N introducing to the Christian public this volume of Lectures on Missions, delivered before the Theological Seminary of the Reformed Church in America, at New Brunswick, N. J., it is proper that a brief account should be given of the origin of the lectureship.

On the 16th day of April, 1888, Mr. Nathan F. Graves, an Elder in the Reformed Church of Syracuse, N. Y., and an active member of the Board of Foreign Missions of the Reformed Church in America, addressed the following letter to the Rev. Prof. Mabon, of the Theological Seminary:

"Syracuse, N. Y., *April* 16th, 1888.

"*Rev. Prof. W. V. V. Mabon, D.D.*

"My dear Sir—I understand that there is no Seminary or Professorship of Missions in the United States. I may be mistaken, but I am quite sure that there is no adequate provision made for a service so important. I have noticed that the missionaries that are instructed at Basle have quite an advantage over those who receive

no special instruction to fit them for their important
work.

"I write to enquire if the subject has ever been considered in the Seminary; and if you consider it desirable
and practicable to establish such a professorship, I will
be greatly obliged for a reply at your convenience.

"Very sincerely yours,

"N. F. GRAVES."

The Faculty having declared that, in their opinion, it was desirable and practicable that some
agency for missionary instruction should be established in the Seminary, conferences were held by
Mr. Graves with a Committee of the Faculty, with
Rev. John Mason Ferris, D.D., for many years
Secretary of the Board of Foreign Missions of the
Reformed Church in America; with Rev. Henry
N. Cobb, D.D., present Secretary, and with various friends of Foreign Missions. The result was
a proposal by Mr. Graves to provide liberally the
means for a course of lectures for the year 1888–
89; the lecturer or lecturers to be appointed by
the Theological Faculty in connection with the
Secretary of the Board of Foreign Missions of the
Reformed Church in America, while further action
of a more permanent nature was to be left for
more mature consideration.

Accordingly, a course of six lectures was delivered in the S. A. Kirkpatrick Chapel, the use of
which was kindly granted for the purpose by the
authorities of the College. The lecturers and
subjects were as follows:

1. Rev. Henry Stout, of Nagasaki, Japan—The Unique Characteristics of the Missionary Work in Japan.

2. Rev. Cyrus Hamlin, D.D., formerly of Constantinople—Fifty Years of Missionary Education in Turkey.

3. Rev. Leonard W. Kip, D.D., of Amoy, China—A Heathen Stronghold.

4. Rev. E. M. Wherry, D.D., of Saharanpoor, India—The Religion of Islam.

5. Rev. F. F. Ellinwood, D.D., Secretary of the Board of Foreign Missions of the Presbyterian Church—The Undesigned Testimony of False Religions to the True.

6. Rev. John H. Wyckoff, of the Arcot Mission —Brahmanism and Christianity.

In their report made to the Board of Superintendents, May 20th, 1889, the Faculty said: "These lectures were able and instructive, and the impression made was so salutary that we earnestly hope that the thought so generously conceived by Elder Graves will be matured in permanency, and that hereafter our students may be able every year to receive instruction from men of wisdom and experience in this great subject. The thanks of the Seminary and of the Church are due to the Elder whose heart, in its deep sympathy with Christian effort in evangelizing the world, has projected the scheme, and inclines him to provide liberally for its accomplishment."

Mr. Graves being satisfied with the experiment, very promptly and cordially expressed his wish and readiness to provide for a course of lectures for the year 1889–90, and also for one for the year following, so that the lecturer might have two years for preparation. He has since made provision for the future, including the year 1892–93.

The second course was delivered in the winter of 1890 by the Rev. John Hall, D.D., LL.D., of New York City, embracing lectures on the following subjects:

1. The Bible Basis of Missions.

2. The Missions of the Early Centuries of Christianity.

3. Missions Previous to the Reformation.

4. Missions and the Reformation.

5. Missions from the Reformation to the 19th Century.

6. Modern Missions, their Difficulties and Encouragements.

The Faculty, deeming it to be right and wise that the Christian public should have the benefit of these lectures, and that ample opportunity should be afforded for the attendance of the largest number, obtained from the Consistory of the Second Reformed Church the use of their house of worship for the purpose. The spacious building was crowded every evening with attentive listeners.

The third course, by Rev. Arthur T. Pierson, D.D., comprising the lectures contained in this volume, was delivered in the winter of 1891,* in the First Reformed Church, which was kindly granted for the purpose. The lectures were heard by large congregations with increasing interest to the end of the course.

At the close the following resolutions, offered by Rev. Prof. T. Sandford Doolittle, D.D., of Rutgers College, were heartily and unanimously adopted by the large audience present :

Resolved.—1. That our hearty thanks are due to Rev. Arthur T. Pierson, D.D., for the zeal and efficiency with which he has presented so much valuable information in regard to the mission field and the claims of the Master upon us to act as missionaries in spirit, if not in person.

2. That thanks are due also to the Faculty of the Theological Seminary for not limiting these lectures to their class-rooms, but for making them public in one of the churches of the city, so that the people of various denominations are allowed the privilege of hearing them.

3. That we take a special pleasure in exhibiting a grateful recognition of the wise and noble generosity of Mr. N. F. Graves in establishing this annual course of lectures for enlarging the knowledge and intensifying the interest in Christian missions.

While the students of the Seminary for whom these lectures were especially intended have derived inestimable benefit from them, it is gratifying to know that many Christian people of all denominations have been sharers in the benefit. It is believed that announcements of future courses

* In January and February.

will be received with great satisfaction by the Christian public. It is hoped that they may prove to be a great stimulus to missionary zeal, be promotive of unity in Christian faith and work; and of intelligent and untiring service in the kingdom of our Lord Jesus Christ, to whom be all the glory.

D. D. DEMAREST.

AUTHOR'S INTRODUCTION.

IT was a wise maxim of Cicero, that, in the opening of an address, the speaker and his audience should come to a mutual understanding. Let the author thus early acquaint his readers with the supreme aim which has controlled his utterances.

In the preparation of these lectures two paths lay open before the lecturer. He might, acting as an annalist, trace that march of missions, which is the marvel, if not the miracle, of this modern age; or, like the historian, he might seek to examine into those fundamental laws and philosophical principles which are the keys of history. In the Books of the Kings, for example, we have the historical annals of the Kingdom; in the Books of the Chronicles, the ethical survey of the Theocracy: in one case a simple record of events; in the other, a lesson on the faithfulness or faithlessness of the kings toward the King of Kings, with the rewards and retributions consequent upon such opposite courses.

I have chosen, as the theme, *The Divine Enter-*

prise of Missions; and shall modestly attempt a
Philosophy of History, dealing with the "Theocracy" rather than the "Kingdom." The annals,
both of ancient Israel and of the modern Church,
record mingled success and failure. Whether it
be the one or the other cannot depend on any
chance or accident. There is no fatalism in history. Our instincts tell us that success must be
the consequence and crown of conformity to the
pattern shewed us in the mount; and failure, the
result of departure from the divine standard.
Some golden calf which some Aaron may have
cast, out of unhallowed offerings; some carved
altar, which some idolatrous Ahaz may have set
up in place of the unhewn altar of the divine
simplicity that is in Christ—in a word, some dis-
placing of the pure and perfect type of doctrine
and method, prescribed in the Word of God, may
account for the withholding of blessing, and for
defeat and disaster in our missionary work.

We have need, perhaps, to begin again, and lay
anew the basis of missionary enterprise; or, if we
find the former foundation firm and sound, we
may need at least to see whether, on that foundation, we have been building gold, silver, precious
stones; or wood, hay, stubble. Possibly, into the
structure of our mission work some errors have
been built, which are serious if not radical. To
get God's own conception of missions informed
and infixed in our minds, our hearts and our prac-

tical methods, might lead to the partial and even total revolution of our present mission work.

Feeling the solemnity of this trust, as the incumbent of this lectureship, for my own sake and that of my readers, and for the sake of a cause wider and broader than all, I have given myself, Bible in hand, to a careful, prayerful study of this theme, seeking to be rid of all bias, either of prejudice or prepossession, and to be led into all truth. And, as the studies which, for more than a year before the delivery of these lectures, were largely limited to this one subject, have rent the veil from much that was hitherto hidden or at best obscure to my own mind, it will not be strange if some things which found utterance in the lecture-course may strike other minds as new, and even as untrue. The lecturer ventures to ask the confidence of his indulgent readers and, on their part also, patient study of the principles laid down. Let there be applied to them, not the test of human authority or opinion merely; but the touchstone of the Word of God, and of His manifest working in the History of Missions.

Human tradition is a dangerous ally of the Bible, for, too often, it "makes void the Word of God." At first only a vassal, it becomes a consort, and finally a sovereign, usurping all authority. And, as Luther found it necessary to question even the venerable traditions of the elders, and separate the infallible Scriptures from all the chaff

and alloy of mere human teaching, it behoves us
to pray for grace to go back to the very beginning,
and inquire of the Master himself what are the
eternal and immutable principles of mission work.

ARTHUR T. PIERSON.

2320 SPRUCE STREET, PHILADELPHIA,
     October, 1891.

I.

THE DIVINE THOUGHT OF MISSIONS.

HEN, on the 15th of May, 1618, after more than twenty years of patient experiment, Johann Kepler completed his discovery of the so-called " Harmonic Laws," or the relations of the planets ; when the secret doors, that had waited six thousand years for a key, were at last unlocked by the theory of an elliptical orbit, the great astronomer of Magstatt, no longer able to contain his rapture, cried, " *O Almighty God, I think Thy thoughts after Thee !* "

What the " Legislator of the Heavens " did, in the department of astronomy, we seek to do in the department of missions—think God's thought after God. The words " *idea* " and " *theory* " are, to some linguists, sacred, because of a possible derivation of the one from the Latin, *deus*, and of the other from the Greek, θεος ; and of a possible design by those words to express conceptions as they lie in the mind of God. If such be the real roots, the word *idea* (*in deo*) would mean a thought first conceived in God, and then expressed to men —a *theory* would be a sacred image, pattern, or plan of God. The ancient Platonists used the word ιδεα, of an eternal immutable and immaterial form or model of an object, an archetype, a pattern.* In this sense, ideas were the pattern according to which the Deity fashioned the phenomenal or ectypal world.†

An *idea*, therefore, properly implies a *perfection of image*. If we can, at the outset, get before us the divine conception of missions, what a starting-point will that be, and to what an advanced goal might we hope to reach, if, true to our starting-point, we keep on our course without deviation !

The four Gospel narratives have, at the close of each—as has also the Acts of the Apostles, that "Fifth Gospel," at its beginning,—certain words of our Lord which are evidently meant for the guidance of His disciples, in all time to come, as to their great mission and commission. Each of these accounts contains something, different from the others, yet essential to the full and complete expression of our Lord's will and our duty. As, in a composite photograph, various facial forms and features blend, combining individual peculiarities in one collective result, so, if we may project, as upon one sensitive plate, these five forms of the Great Commission ; and, instead of looking at them separately, behold them all, blent in one composite view, we may at one glance see the mutual relations of these various words of instruction and get the grand total.

* Worcester's Dictionary.   † Sir Wm. Hamilton.

With this aim, we may reverently venture to combine these five fragmentary utterances into one, without implying that, in our Lord's original teaching, they were thus blended; or that it is possible to determine either their logical or chronological order. We seek simply to frame a general summary, without omission of any particulars; and to group together words of instruction or promise which, by affinity, belong together. The attempt so to arrange and combine has been attended with such profit to the writer, that he cannot but hope it may at least prompt abler students of the Word to improve upon the imperfect result. Close study of these farewell words of our Lord will reveal an exquisite poetry of thought, a certain rhythm and rhyme of conception, which need the aid of parallelism to convey this correspondence.

I.

And Jesus came and spake unto them, saying:

"PEACE BE UNTO YOU!"

And when He had so said He shewed unto them His hands and His side. Then were the disciples glad when they saw the Lord ; then said Jesus to them again :

"PEACE BE UNTO YOU!"

II.

"ALL POWER IS GIVEN UNTO ME

IN HEAVEN AND IN EARTH.

AS MY FATHER HATH SENT ME,

EVEN SO SEND I YOU."

III.

Then opened He their understanding that they might understand the scriptures; and said unto them:
" Thus it is written,
And thus it behoved Christ to suffer
And to rise from the dead the third day;
AND THAT
REPENTANCE AND REMISSION OF SINS SHOULD BE PREACHED IN HIS NAME
AMONG ALL NATIONS,
BEGINNING AT JERUSALEM.
AND YE ARE WITNESSES OF THESE THINGS."

IV.

"GO YE THEREFORE INTO ALL THE WORLD AND PREACH THE GOSPEL TO EVERY CREATURE.
GO, MAKE DISCIPLES OF ALL NATIONS,
Baptizing in the name of the Father, and of the Son, and of the Holy Ghost ;
Teaching them to observe all things whatsoever I have commanded you.
He that believeth and is baptized shall be saved,
But he that believeth not shall be damned.

V.

AND, BEHOLD I SEND THE PROMISE OF MY FATHER UPON YOU.
Depart ye not from Jerusalem,
But wait for the promise of the Father
Which ye have heard of Me.

Tarry ye in the city of Jerusalem,
UNTIL YE BE ENDUED WITH POWER FROM
ON HIGH.
For John truly baptized with water,
But ye shall be baptized with the Holy Ghost not many
days hence.
Ye shall receive the power of the Holy Ghost
Coming upon you;
AND YE SHALL BE WITNESSES
UNTO ME
Both in Jerusalem and in all Judea,
And in Samaria,
And unto the uttermost part of the earth."
And He breathed on them
And saith unto them,
" Receive ye the Holy Ghost."

VI.

"AND LO, I AM WITH YOU ALWAY,
EVEN UNTO THE END OF THE AGE.
And these signs shall follow them that believe :
In My name shall they cast out demons ;
They shall speak with new tongues ;
They shall take up serpents ;
And if they drink any deadly thing it shall not hurt
them ;
They shall lay hands on the sick and they shall recover."

VII.

And He led them out as far as to Bethany.
So then, after the Lord had spoken unto them,
He lifted up His hands and blessed them ;
And it came to pass, while He blessed them,
He was parted from them ;

And while they beheld, He was taken up,
And a cloud received Him out of their sight.
And He was carried up and received up into heaven,
And they worshipped Him
And returned to Jerusalem with great joy,
And were continually in the temple
Praising and blessing God.
AND THEY WENT FORTH AND PREACHED
EVERYWHERE,
THE LORD WORKING WITH
AND CONFIRMING THE WORD,
WITH SIGNS FOLLOWING.
AMEN !

Thus, combining all these farewell words of our Lord, and grouping together sayings that bear to each other a peculiar relation, we find that the whole naturally falls into *seven parts.*

First, we have a double salutation of Peace.

Secondly, a declaration of Divine Authority, and a distinct, authoritative Commission—sending the disciples forth,—a transmission of this authority.

Thirdly, an unfolding of the essential truths of Redemption, the Atoning Death and Resurrection of Christ, and the substance of the message to be borne in His name. And here occurs that phrase central and vital to the whole commission, "*Ye are witnesses of these things.*"

Fourthly, we have the universality of the commission indicated in three unmistakable terms: two of which are collective,—" all the world," and " all nations,"—and the third of which is distribu-

tive,—" every creature,"—showing us that while
the message is universal, it is also individual.

Fifthly, we have the great qualification for the
proper discharge of the commission ; the Enduement with Power by the baptism of the Holy Ghost.

Sixthly, we have the assurance of the Saviour's
personal presence, and of signs following those
who believe.

Finally, we have the Lord's parting blessing
and ascension and the brief record of the fulfilment begun, both of the duty of the Church and
of the promise of her Lord.

In this whole body of instructions there is *one
word*, so central, so vital, so emphatic, that it is
the only word which is made especially prominent
by repetition ; it is the word WITNESS. " Ye are
witnesses of these things " ; " Ye shall be *witnesses*
unto me." The only other word that rivals this
for prominence is the word "*preach*," which really
conveys essentially the same meaning, since the
soul of preaching is witnessing.

It seems, therefore, that if, at the outset, we
desire to grasp the divine idea of missions, here
we shall find our starting-point toward the most
advanced goal. It is like God to be simple ; and
in that one word, *witness*, is condensed the whole
wisdom of God as to this world-wide work. We
are to be witnesses unto Him. Let us seek to
enter more fully into this thought of God as conveyed in this word.

The race of man is lost in sin—lost to God, and to holiness and heaven. Beside the generic, federal fall of the race in its head, there has been a voluntary and personal fall, each sinning soul for itself, in departing from the living God. Jesus Christ, the second Adam, takes man's place. He obeys the law which Adam transgressed, and proves obedience possible ; then He dies in the sinner's place to make his redemption also possible. We do not here tarry to consider the *philosophy* of the plan of salvation : the *fact* is enough that, in some way and sense, "He bare our sins in His own body on the tree, that we, being dead to sin, should live unto righteousness," and that "by His stripes we are healed." While the Word of God repeatedly and constantly affirms this fact, it never attempts to exhaust its philosophy. Nor need we.

The only condition of salvation is the *acceptance* of God's free gift of eternal life through Jesus Christ our Lord. As Chalmers taught, this is the supreme glory of the Gospel, that it is simply to be *accepted*. Repentance is only that godly sorrow for sin and that sense of need which dispose us to faith ; obedience is only the natural fruit of that new life begun in believing. And so *faith* is central and all-inclusive, and faith is believing, and believing is *receiving*. "To as many as *received* Him, to them gave He power to become the Sons of God, even to as many as *believe* on His name." That one verse proves that to *believe* is to *receive;*

and, in all the instances in the Gospel according to John where that word, believe, occurs, we may substitute the word, receive, and find the sense unaffected.

We need to take one step further, and we reach another equally simple but equally vital truth. "God would have all men to be saved and to come to the knowledge of the truth." The salvation is broad enough to cover the sin of all mankind. The rescue is ample for the ruin of the race. How shall the unsaved be reached? Behold again how divinely simple is the thought of God: let every believer become a witness—let every man, who is saved, seek to save. It is no irreverence to say that God's whole idea of missions may be found, in essence, in that one word, *witnessing.* The salvation of God is full and free. To accept it freely is immediate *justification;* to accept it fully is complete *sanctification;* to witness to it fully and freely is complete *service*—it is to be a missionary wherever we are.

Let us dwell a moment on the *simplicity* of witnessing for Christ. Nothing can be more primitive and simple. The word itself has a lesson: it is from the Saxon, *witan,* to know, the root of many kindred words, "wit," "wist," "wisdom." A witness needs, therefore, but two characteristics: knowledge and utterance. To know and to tell makes a witness, and hence even a little child is now admitted to our courts of law as competent to testify. And in the higher Court of Humanity, the Parliament of Man, even a little child is admitted, to bear witness to Jesus and the great salvation, before the tribunal of public opinion; because a child can sin, can repent, can believe, and can therefore tell what he knows of salvation by faith. In fact, no testimony is more convincing than that of a guileless child.

This simplicity is in order to *universality;* for it brings the privilege within the range of all believers. As the Gospel is marked by its universal adaptation to man as man, so the missionary charge is peculiar for its universal adaptation to believers as believers. It requires but the least measure of capacity, to sin, and whoever can sin, can be saved from sin; and so it requires but the least measure of capacity to be a witness, for whoever can sin and can be saved, can tell of salvation.

We repeat, it is simple that it may be universal. This duty, this privilege, is committed to all believers, and has reference to the whole race of man. It is therefore doubly universal; all believers are to witness, and are to witness unto all. All who are saved are to bear testimony, and all who are unsaved are to hear that testimony.

Here we meet, at the outset of this discussion, the first of those traditions of men which have practically made the Word of God of none effect. Believers commonly have no sense of either *personal duty or responsibility toward lost souls.* Whatever be their duty, it is believed it may be done indirectly and by proxy. Nay, during the ages, the Church of God has come to recognize a dividing line, not found in the New Testament, between the *clergy* and the *laity*, so-called. A small minority of church members are set apart for the preaching of the Gospel and the care of souls. The very terms "preacher," "pastor," "curate," have come to embody this conception, that these men are especially ordained to preach the Gospel, shepherd believers, and care for souls. What, then, is the duty of the "*laity*," but to take care of the "*clergy*," hear the Gospel which they preach, keep in the fold, or follow with the flock where the pastor leads; and to see to it that, while the "curate" is caring for souls, he shall be paid for his professional work? This is the theory, judged by the practice. The great bulk of professing Christians have no systematic work for unsaved souls; many of them have never yet even looked upon it as a duty to seek and to save that which was lost. In their conceptions of the Christian life this does not enter as a necessary integral factor. To go to church with reasonable regularity, to pay pew-rent punctually, to be honest and honorable and charitable; to behave like a Christian in the church, in the home, and in society, especially if, to all else, be added a generous gift now and then to missions at home and abroad; this is —to most professed believers—to live the life of a

disciple. O for the trump of Gabriel, to peal out
this truth as with the voice of the thunder !—*in
all this a true child of God sees but the beginning,
not the end, of holy living!* Where shall we find
adequate room for that grander thought of *direct
service* to God in witnessing to souls in Christ's
name ?

We here unhesitatingly affirm that the conception of Christian life which leaves out personal
labor for lost souls, is as radically wanting as that
conception of salvation which leaves out faith : for
believing is not more prominently connected with
salvation than is witnessing connected with service to God ! And, because all new energy or
enterprise in missions hinges on a revival of this
apostolic faith and practice, we give it intensest
emphasis here at the outset of this discussion.

Careful comparison of the various accounts,
given by the evangelists, of our Lord's last inter-
views with his disciples, has led Rev. Dr. Robinson
and others to conclude that the gathering on the
"mountain in Galilee" was the occasion when, as
Paul says, "He was seen of above five hundred
brethren at once." * It was not needful that He
should go into that northern province simply to
meet the eleven, whom He repeatedly met in Jerusalem ; nor could it be any of them who "doubted,"
since even the sceptical Thomas had ceased to
question. But Christ had spent the bulk of His

* Cf. Matt. xxviii. 16 ; I. Cor. xv. 6.

active ministry in Galilee: there He had spoken most of His wondrous words and wrought most of His marvellous works; and there most of His disciples were found. That parting interview in Galilee seems meant to commit formally and finally to the great body of His followers the work of witnessing for Him.

To clothe that closing scene, depicted by Matthew, with such an environment, is to invest it with a new grandeur. Not to a few apostles alone, in some secluded chamber in Capernaum, but to a multitude numbering upwards of five hundred; His pulpit a mountain peak; His audience chamber bounded only by the horizon, and roofed in only by the canopy of heaven, the cathedral of nature! How fitting that the world's Redeemer, stretching out His pierced hands as though to touch the farthest limits of the globe from sunrise to sunset, where no narrow walls could confine His voice, should say to all His disciples: "Go ye into all the world and preach the Gospel to every creature!"

This ought to be granted, as beyond all dispute: preaching the Gospel, in its original and proper sense, is the privilege and prerogative of no exclusive class: it inalienably belongs to all believers. Those terms, "clergy" and "laity," are the invention of the devil in the Dark Ages. The former, from κλῆρος, a lot, is an Old Testament conception brought over into New Testament times. The

tribe of Levi was the "lot," or heritage of the
Lord; and the "clergy" have been conceived as
being specially and exclusively chosen, like the
Levites, to perform this ministry. On the other
hand, the term "laity," from λαος, the people, in-
dicates the current impression that the body of
believers—the people of God at large—are shut
out from the exercise of ministerial functions.
As Gibbon says: ' The progress of ecclesiastical
authority gave birth to the memorable distinction
of the laity and clergy which had been unknown
to the Greeks and Romans. The former of these
appellations comprehended the body of the Christian people; the latter was appropriated to the
chosen portion that had been set apart for the service of religion."

The introduction of this distinction into the
Church of Christ was not only an invention of the
devil, but a master-stroke of Satan-craft. Where
in the New Testament is to be found a trace of
that rigid line that so sharply separated priests
and people in the days of Judaism? The older
conception of a kingdom of priests,* which ante-
dates the separation of Levi's tribe for the service
of the Tabernacle, now comes once more to the
front. No believer finds himself fenced into an
outer court,—even the veil that hid the Holy of
Holies is rent in twain; and, without priestly or
high priestly mediation, every child of God comes

* Exod. xix. 6.

boldly to the mercy seat, having access through
Christ by one Spirit unto the Father. Every believer is, therefore, by right a preacher. No
sooner does Andrew find Jesus than he goes after
Peter; or Philip, than he seeks Nathanael. Nay,
even a woman, and she a Samaritan and an outcast, when she finds the Messiah at the well,
immediately leaves her water-pot, in her haste to
impart, as from an inner spring, greater than
Jacob's well, a life-giving draught to thirsty souls
in Sychar!

No more significant statement can be found,
even in that great book of missions,—the Acts
of the Apostles,—than that which follows the
account of Stephen's martyrdom: "There was a
great persecution against the Church which was at
Jerusalem; and they were all scattered abroad
through all the regions of Judea and Samaria,
except the Apostles: therefore they that were
scattered abroad went everywhere preaching the
Word." *

With what divine care is this fact framed into
sacred history! The Spirit of God records a general scattering abroad, but records also that, in
that scattering, the *Apostles are not included;* those,
then, that went everywhere preaching the Word,
were simply ordinary believers. Behold them—
the elect dispersion, driven by the red hand of
persecution into the remote parts of Judea and

* Acts viii. 1-4; xi. 19, 20.

Samaria, and afterward to the Phœnician coast, to Cyprus, to Antioch. Without one ordained apostle, even to lead the way, they preached the Lord Jesus; and God, who by His Providence dispersed them, by His grace set His seal upon their work, for "the hand of the Lord was with them, and a great number believed and turned unto the Lord." *

Thus far, certainly, we find no rigid line separating and dividing disciples in proclaiming the good news.

Those who are infected with the "High Church" tendencies of our day may do well to note that, in the Acts of the Apostles, there is not found any sacred line of limitation *even in the administration of the sacraments.* Philip, who acted as an evangelist, and went down to Samaria and preached Christ with such power, also baptized both men and women, as he did the eunuch of Ethiopia; † and yet this Philip was at best only a deacon, set apart, it is true, but not set apart as a preacher, but as a server of tables; and one case of such exercise of sacramental rights is enough to break down the limiting line. The whole trend of New Testament teaching is in the direction of the universal priesthood of believers. In this divine Charter of the Church, these truths are self-evident, that all believers are new-created and equal in their inherent privileges, endowed with certain

* Acts xi. 21,   † Acts viii. 5, 12, 38,

original, inalienable rights, among which is witnessing.

It would be unfair to interpret these words as
a fling against an ordained ministry. There are
many good grounds for setting apart godly men to
the service of pulpit and pastorate. We cordially concede this, in the interests of law and order,
of sound doctrine and good government, of organization and leadership, of aptness to teach and
wise, systematic curacy of souls. But to erect
Christ's ministers into a clerical *caste*, to build a
barrier between them and the rest of God's people
in the matter of witnessing for Christ and winning
souls—that is both false to Scripture and fatal to
missions! We must turn back and retrace our
steps and get once more upon the primitive apostolic platform. We need another Luther who
shall nail up his theses upon the doors of the
"church of all saints," and assert, in behalf of all
saints, their "Declaration of Independence," with
these original, inalienable rights. We must brush
away the rubbish of human inventions and devices
of the devil, and plant our firm feet on the broad
basis laid down in the Word of God, that, by
right of redemption in Christ, all the Lord's people are prophets, priests, and kings. Whatever
function, inhering in believers, may, in the interests of expediency and for the general good, be
conceded to a certain class, one universal right
must be retained—or if, in any measure, practically

given up, it must be reclaimed and restored, viz. :
*the common right of all believers to proclaim the
Gospel.* This can be surrendered only with disaster to the best interests both of the Church and
of the world. No mistake can be more fatal—
fatal not only to a world's evangelization and redemption, but to the service, growth, and even
spiritual life of the disciple himself.

Often as this great truth has been wrested from
the clutch of ecclesiasticism, it needs to-day again
to be recovered and reasserted—proclaimed as
with the clarion voice of the Apocalyptic Angel.
Three centuries, and nearly four, have rolled away
since the lamp of the Reformed faith lit up the
darkness, and still the subtle foe of Christian missions, both at home and abroad, is clericalism.
The bulk of church members find their strength in
sitting still—it is only the few to whom it is a
necessary part of a Christian life to bestir themselves, and serve—to give alms and minister to
want and woe—to teach others the truth, to win
others for Christ, to bear a dying world on the
heart, and by prevailing prayer and daily testimony
seek by all means to save some.

This witness, which is thus simple and universal,
is also *experimental;* and, in this sense, is not, after
all, either so simple or so universal ; for it demands
knowledge, not that of the schools, but of the school
of Christ—and is based on the high attainment of
experience. It is because so few *know, beyond*

doubt,—because so few reach to the certainties of spiritual things,—that so few are competent to give effective testimony. There should be fixed firmly in our minds this axiom of spiritual life, that *experience limits testimony.* We can *witness* only so far as we *know.* Settled conviction, intelligent and immovable faith, however narrow its bounds, is indispensable to convincing others or developing faith in others. Better—like the blind man whose eyes Jesus opened—to be able to say, " *One thing* I know," than to be half confident on many things; for it is only the certainty of assured conviction that enables us to convince.

This is an age of *doubt,* and not only so, but it is an age when it is fashionable to doubt. It is coming to be a mark of intellectual aristocracy to be sceptical. The first families in the world of intellect have adopted a new coat of arms; their escutcheon is a shield, bearing an interrogation point. Faith is confounded with credulity. The simple confidence of a child-like believer, who takes the Bible as the Word of God, is met by the learned and cultured with a complacent if not compassionate smile—and the Gospel is treated by some with even a lofty contempt, as though it would do for women and children and small men, but not for great minds and highly cultured people.

It is well for us all to understand that, so far as *doubt* invades and controls our Christian life, our witness for Christ is at an end. There may

be a formal testimony, but it is soulless and pow-
erless.   The world, and the Church too, wait for
men of strong conviction, who can, upon matters
upon which others are uncertain, say "*I know*,"
and can give an answer to every one that asketh
a reason of the hope that is in them.   Emerson
declared that we need positive men, not negative
men—affirmations, positions; not denials, nega-
tions.   Goethe, with a despair begotten of habitual
doubt, cries, " Give us your convictions ! as for
doubts, we have quite enough of our own."   And
Mr. Spurgeon quaintly adds : " It may be a great
thing to doubt, but it is a greater thing to hold
your tongue till you get rid of your doubts."
Those who, in this sceptical age, are sowing the
seeds of doubt, may do well to consider whether
one firm conviction of truth is not of more service
to mankind than a thousand denials, or questions,
or uncertainties.

On this subject, Rev. Dr. C. F. Deems has
given young men a wise maxim : " Believe your
beliefs and doubt your doubts.   Never make the
mistake of doubting your beliefs and believing
your doubts."   Faith and unfaith are both sus-
ceptible of nurture, of culture.   He who presumes
that what he has been taught to believe is, for that
reason, to be questioned ; and that what he has
been led to question is therefore unworthy of un-
questioning confidence, and that his doubts are
more trustworthy than his faiths, will find him-

self drifting away from all the moorings of truth
and duty,—on an open sea, where clouds hide
the stars and fogs obscure all headlands; and
where, without compass, chart, or rudder, he is
driving on blindly toward the utter wreck and
ruin of all religious faith.

Blessed be God! it is possible to know God and
the truth, and to find verity and reality even in
the subtle, elusive, evasive sphere of the spiritual
and eternal. There is an unseen world—and we
have senses more subtle than the five physical
senses—which, being exercised to discern both
good and evil, become keen-edged, sharp-pointed,
and acutely discriminating. Reason, which sep-
arates between truth and falsehood; conscience,
which detects the right and the wrong; sensibility,
which discriminates between the attractive and
the repulsive,—these are examples of these subtler,
finer senses, which pertain to the sphere of the
unseen. God has given us physical senses as
media of communication with an external, material
universe; and so He has given us these more
delicate senses, whereby to detect truth, right,
beauty, and communicate with the invisible and
the eternal.

Columbus discovered the New World before
he *saw* it. By the testimony of ancient writings,
by a broad and clear induction from many facts,
by the observations of other navigators, by the
calculations of his own science, he had the evi-

dence before him of a continent not seen as yet
by European eyes.* And so it is possible by experiment to know whom we have believed, and
what we hold as true. Even God needs not to
be "unknown,"—as at Athens. We may "taste
and see" that He is good; "hear and know" the
truth; "feel after" and "find" Him who is not
far from every one of us, "handle" Him in the
closet and "see" that it is He Himself. The
Bible, referring to experiment in spiritual things,
thus uses terms kindred to those that we ordinarily
apply to sense perceptions, and applies them to
spiritual cognitions and recognitions.

When Professor Morse, the electrician, in the
closing part of the session of Congress in 1842–3,
sought aid to the extent of $30,000, to build the
experimental line of telegraph between Baltimore
and Washington, he had reached the last days of
the session in apparently fruitless and hopeless
endeavor, and was preparing for his return home.
The committee appointed by Congress had met,
and, after a morning's discussion, could reach no
unanimous conclusion. During the recess, however, Mr. Morse had taken the chairman to a large
room in the hotel, where a small telegraphic circuit
was erected. Bidding him take a position at one
end of the room, he himself went to the other, and
for an hour the most satisfactory trial was made of
the telegraph. And, when the committee re-as-

* Exeter Hall Lectures, 1854–5.

sembled, the chairman said: "Gentlemen of the Committee—When we adjourned this morning you were equally divided as to the expediency of recommending to Congress to make this appropriation, and it fell to me to give the casting vote. I am now ready to give my emphatic decision in favor of the appropriation, for I have both sent and received messages across the wires! "

The wires are up between this world and the unseen; and he who enters into his closet, and prays to the Father who is in secret, sends to the Throne of God the message of believing prayer, and gets back the answering message of a faithful God! He can give his emphatic voice and vote for the reality of things unseen, for he has come into sympathetic, personal touch with God Himself.

The oratory of the soul is also its observatory —the place of observation and revelation; and, if there were more constant and close fellowship with God, there would be more knowledge of God and more capacity for witness. Answered prayer is the open path that leads to knowledge of a prayer-hearing God. Obedience is both the organ of spiritual perception and the school of spiritual education; for, "if any man will do his will, he shall know of the doctrine."* "To love God and keep His words, is to have the manifestation of God as it is impossible to the world."† It is

* John vii. 17.   † John xiv. 23.

possible to walk with God and be in constant
contact with Him. Our doubts, instead of being
our glory, are our shame—they come from mind-
ing earthly things, from living on a low level, and
walking according to the course of this world.

This witnessing, being thus based upon experiment and experience, *must therefore be confined to
believers.*

Two words we have already found to be conspicuous in the Great Commission,—"preach,"
and "witness." To preach is to proclaim as a
herald ; to witness is to testify from personal knowledge. The two widely and essentially differ, yet
they complement each other. A herald is only
the mouth of a *message;* a witness is the mouth of
an *experience.* The public crier may announce or
proclaim, for hire, tidings in which he feels no
interest, and of the truth of which he has no knowledge. But a witness can speak only what he
knows and testify only what he has seen, heard,
felt. He is a herald, indeed, and a herald of good
tidings, but he is more—he is an example and
proof of their verity and value. And therefore
only a believer can be a witness.

The Gospel ministry is not a learned profession
into which men may go at their own option or at
the beck of avarice or ambition. It is a divine
vocation, to which men are called by the voice of
an Indwelling Spirit, who qualifies them to *bear
witness* for God. No man, however gifted or

learned, is competent to preach, except so far as the truth he proclaims is the girdle which firmly and closely embraces his very vitals and holds in place all his other armor.* In countries where there is an Established Church, the danger always is that unconverted men will find their way into this sacred office, who, as Norman McLeod used to say, preach the truth—truth which is the world's life and which stirs the angels,—but too often as a telegraphic wire transmits the most momentous intelligence ; and who grasp that truth, only "as a sparrow grasps the wire by which the message is conveyed." Let this be engraven on our hearts : that no human being is prepared to proclaim the good tidings, unless, and except so far as, those tidings have become to him or to her the means of salvation and sanctification. If a man could combine in himself the intelligence of a cherub and the love of a seraph, he could not, even then, be a *witness*, if grace had not transformed his own soul.

Doubtless the angels would gladly have been the bearers of these good news. We are divinely told how they stand overawed before such a display of grace to sinners, and, as from the verge of some unfathomable abyss, gazed down into the depths of a love which they "desire to look into," but cannot explore. And, had they been entrusted with this message, on what joyful wings would

* Ephes. vi. 14.

their legions have swept round the world trump-
eting forth the blessed news! It would not have
been nineteen centuries before even one-third of
the race had been practically reached with the
Gospel. But there was one fatal deficiency in
angelic preaching:

> "Never did angels taste above
> Redeeming Grace and dying Love!"

And so God crowds them back, and thrusts
forward, into the coveted place, *saved sinners.*
The poorest, humblest, most unlettered believer,
who has known penitence and faith, can do a work
for God to which Gabriel himself would be unequal. Thus only can we explain the fact that,
while an angel hovers about the chariot of the
inquiring Ethiopian,* he does not himself speak
to the eunuch, but bids Philip approach and guide
him; and, even when the angel appears to Cornelius and announces to him God's acceptance of
his alms and his prayers, he is restrained from further announcing to him the words of life and salvation, and significantly says: "Send men to Joppa
and call for one Simon, whose surname is Peter;
he shall tell thee words whereby thou and thy house
shall be saved." †

How few believers appreciate this great truth,
that while God is thus pressing upon them this
solemn duty of preaching the Gospel, it is a *privi-*

* Acts viii. 26.   † Acts x. 1-5; xi. 13, 14.

lege so high and holy as to be coveted by angels! An archangel himself could not preach the Gospel as you or I can. We can say, I was a lost sinner, but now by grace I am saved—*that*, no angel of any rank in the whole hierarchy can say; and, because God will have *witnesses* for His heralds, only believers are admitted to this privilege.

But there is quite another side to this matter. If believing disciples are essential to witnessing for God, witnessing for God is not less essential to believing souls. In the Sermon on the Mount, our Lord begins by a graphic portrait of a true disciple—and immediately passes from character to *influence*, which He presents in two simple familiar figures: "Ye are the *salt* of the earth," "Ye are the *light* of the world." Salt that has no savor neither savors nor saves; light that has no ray neither shines nor burns. In those very forms of figure our Lord is saying to us that a believer without a witness is worthless as savorless salt, or a rayless lamp. We must get beyond the conception of service to God as a mere help to growth, —it is a condition of life. Salt without saltness is no longer *salt*. A light without a ray is no longer a *light*. It is of the *nature* of the Christian life to witness, and, when there is no witness, is it too much to say, that, logically, there is no life?

When we look abroad and see between thirty and forty millions of professed believers, the major part of whom impart no godly savor to season society, and bear no witness to the power of a saving Gospel to enlighten the world, it is only judging the tree by its fruit to say of such, "having a form of godliness, but denying the power thereof." We shall never reach the heart of the difficulty in our foreign missionary work until, by sharp, resolute, fearless thrusts of the sword of the Spirit, we reach the consciences of many professing Christians; and dare to arouse them from a self-complacent apathy and lethargy by a bold application of the truth. We must dare to use God's own touchstone of piety. Down beneath outward ordinances and formalism thousands of church members are living a life essentially ungodly and unregenerate. They are not "new creatures," in whom "old things have passed away, and all things have become new." There has never been a surrender to God; the will is unsubdued, the heart is unchanged, they are under the dominion of the flesh, the natural man, the carnal mind. Worldly amusements ensnare them because they have no relish for higher joys—they are greedy of gain because they know nothing of the higher gain of counting all things loss for Christ. Their names are on church rolls, but are they on the Book of Life? They cannot be depended on to *work* for God, or even to *give*, because their hearts are not right in His sight.

Such words as these cannot be written or spoken without giving personal anguish to one who is compelled to utter such testimony. But let us remember Christ's own words : " If any man wil come after me, let him deny himself and take up his cross daily and follow me." Cross-bearing is the one condition and sign of discipleship. What is cross-bearing ? In nothing, perhaps, has the tradition of men more made void the Word of God than in the common popular abuse of this phrase. We talk of " crosses," little and great. Every trial of our patience, every vexation of daily life, every-thing that crosses our inclination, is a *cross.* We make crosses so common that we lose sight of that unique and sublimely solitary self-offering which our Lord meant to convey by the phrase.

Let us notice that the word *cross* never in the Scripture occurs in the *plural.* There is but one *cross :* it is the cross of self-abnegation. To Christ the cross meant one thing, and nothing less : *His sacrifice of Himself to save others.* And that is what it must mean to every disciple. To take up the cross and bear it after Christ is to undertake, like the Master, a life of self-denial for the saving of others. It is to lose life and lose self for His sake. It is to be willing to die, if need be, that others may live. When our Lord hung upon the cross His enemies tauntingly said : " He saved others : Himself He cannot save." No sneer ever hid a truth so sublime. In the Christian life, saving self and saving others are utterly incom-patible ; and the one great difficulty with the whole body of professed disciples is that most of them are trying to save themselves and yet be saved. And so it comes to pass that, while thousands go to church, come to the Lord's table, say their prayers, and bear the name of Christ, they live a life essentially worldly, are engaged in no soul-saving work, and have no relish for it; they have no experience of the sweetness of a voluntary self-denial for His sake, and spend a thousand times as much on self-indulgence as they give to feed the hungry, clothe the naked, or even give the living bread to dying souls!

Consider what would be the immediate result, if every professed child of God could burn with Paul's passion for souls—could know the "great heaviness and continual sorrow of heart" for the unsaved, that made it possible for him to wish himself accursed that they might be blessed!

That was cross-bearing; he died daily, he was crucified with Christ, he bore the very marks, the στιγματα, of the Lord Jesus. Could ten thousand, of the thirty or forty millions of professed Protestant believers, burn with such a Christ-like passion for souls as that, for one year, the Gospel would within that year be carried round the globe! But arguments and appeals are vain, while you argue with the deaf and appeal to the dead. Before the Church can "convert the world," the Church must be converted. The remedy for this widespread indifference must be radical.

The difficulty is not in unsanctified purses, or un-sanctified cradles; it is deeper—in unregenerate hearts. "By their fruits ye shall know them." If you have no witness for Christ, have you anything to witness?

We strike here the very bottom of this divine philosophy of missions. We are to conceive such witnessing as a necessity to a truly saved soul. A light that does not shine, a spring that does not flow, a germ that does not grow, is not more an anomaly or a contradiction than a life in Christ which does not witness to Christ. "We cannot but speak the things which we have seen and heard," is the natural utterance of every believer whose eyes and whose ears have been opened to behold the charms and hear the voice of Jesus. He who has thirsted for God as the hart panteth after the water-brooks, who has known the gift of God, who has asked of Him and has drunk the living water, will find not only his satisfied soul thirsting no more, but he will find the water of life springing up within him, a living well. And, if there be a spring within, there will flow a stream without. "He that believeth on me, as the Script-ure hath said, out of his inward being shall flow rivers of living water." If therefore there be no impulse outward, how can there be any life inward? If there be no stream, is there any spring? if no ray, is there any light? if no witness, is there any experience? These are serious and searching questions; and, as Christlieb has hinted, that disciple who has no testimony for Christ, no spirit of missions, is rather himself the subject for Gospel conquest, presenting in himself a field for missionary labor. He who has no passion to convert needs conversion.

This is God's test of piety: "If any man have not the Spirit of Christ, he is none of His." If any one thing marks, above all else, the Spirit of Christ, it is the unselfishness of service. To seek even salvation, for its own sake alone, is utterly repugnant to the whole disposition of a thoroughly regenerate disciple who is recreated in the image of Jesus.

In the Jerry McAuley Mission, in New York City, was a poor victim of drink and of vice who bore in his body the marks of his crimes. Nature herself resented his violation of her laws, and avenged herself in his person. He had become bowed and bent until he was a mere dwarf, and the very fibres and tissues of his throat had been eaten away until there was no palate, tonsils, or vocal chord, and he was without power of speech. When Christ found him, the grace that healed his soul bore help to his body, and, in course of time, the dwarf and cripple, like the woman with the spirit of infirmity that could in nowise lift up herself, was made straight and glorified God. And, though the lost vocal chords were never restored, this old man could not endure to be without his witness to restoring grace; and, night after night, the assembled thieves and drunkards at 316 Water Street would behold him giving his testimony. He would first bend low and bow down, as if hopelessly crippled and crooked, and then raise himself to an erect posture, stretch himself to full length and lift his hands and eyes toward heaven, his face lit up with the radiance of inward peace; and every beholder knew what all this meant. "The lame man leaped as a hart, and the tongue of the dumb" sang praise unto God. It was his witness in pantomime. If he could not testify to the ear, he must to the eye. The saved man was not content to have unsaved men go unwarned, and the saving power of God go unwitnessed. And the superintendent of that mission says that no audible testimony was more effective than that visible witness to Him who had lifted the cripple of sin into the erectness of a saved man.

This word witness has in it a whole world of suggestion and inspiration touching the work of missions. It outlines, in one word, the great purpose of our Lord in connecting His saints with His service. In both Testaments it is one of the prominent and dominant words. Around it the whole philosophy of missions crystallizes and the whole history of missions centralizes.

The idea of such a witness to all men is suggested in the Old Testament, like many other Old Testament truths—a veiled revelation faintly seen and feebly grasped by Old Testament saints. It belongs to the gradual unfolding of that missionary idea, which may be traced like a silver rill back to its spring in that germinal promise that the seed of the woman should bruise the head of the serpent. In the New Testament the veil is withdrawn and the truth clearly revealed, but now it is the eyes of disciples themselves which are blinded; even Peter slowly accepts the lesson thrice given him on the house-top at Joppa, that no man was to be called common whom God had cleansed. But in all ages, however dim the vision or revelation of this truth, witnessing to God has been the grand duty and privilege of disciples; and from the martyr Abel until now every true believer has, by his life and death, witnessed to men the power of faith. This was the basis of apostolic succession and of prophetic succession—yes, it lies beneath priestly and kingly succession as well. It is the golden thread which binds the ages together. God was the first, the original witness to Himself; then He committed that witness to prophets as He more and more withdrew Himself into the secret place; then came the Last Seer, and prophets gave place to Him in whom all their witness terminated and culminated, the Lord Jesus Christ; then He became God's witness; and, when He was received up into heaven, the Holy Spirit witnessed to Him, and qualified saved and sanctified disciples to bear witness, and so carry on the blessed succession until the end of the age,—one chain of many links reaching from a Lost Eden to a Regained Paradise !

This is an "apostolic succession" indeed, in which the goodly fellowship of the prophets, the holy company of the apostles, the noble army of martyrs, Jesus Christ Himself, all take part, with God the Father of all, in testimony to the truth. It may well be doubted whether he who bears no part in this testimony has any part in the salvation. Would that every reader might feel the full force of this paradox of missions :

> " Christ, alone, can save this world ;
> But Christ cannot save this world, alone."

In the plan of God, every believer is a witness. In the wide field of the world, every disciple is needed as a workman. Without him, God cannot do this work, unless He abandons His plan ! The Church must be aroused to this great truth and fact, that both Christ and the world are waiting for disciples, as such, to become heralds of the Gospel and witnesses to Christ ; that a few thousand missionaries, scattered through cities and states at home or empires abroad, can never overtake the awful destitution of a thousand million of souls who know not the Gospel. The only hope of the race is that, as in apostolic times, the whole Church shall become a body of evangelists, and every converted soul consider it a necessary part of discipleship to witness to all men that Christ died for all.

Christian missions originated with God. The commission of the Church is from Heaven, and can be wrought out, only as it was thought out, along the lines and within the limits drawn by a hand divine. Here there is no room for human invention or innovation: all such is interference and interruption to the plans of God. All human accretions forming about the pure thought and plan of God,—like fungus growths and parasitic mosses about a tree, that both obscure its growth and endanger its life,—need to be torn away that we may look again upon the plan of God in its bare simplicity.

Our Lord's chosen definition of the work of His Church in this age, hangs on this same little word, witness: "This Gospel must first be preached *as a witness* among all nations; * and then shall the end come." This was, first and last, His form of statement. The very terms used compel the inference that not only is this work to be carried on to the very end of the age, as a limit, but that the end, as a consummation, somehow *waits* for this as a preparation and preliminary. This we believe —and it is a mighty impulse to a world's evangelization—that neither the complete salvation of the race of man nor of the Church of God can be reached until this condition is fulfilled. To you

* Matt. xxiv. 14; εις μαρτυριον.

and me it belongs to "fill up that which is behind of the afflictions of Christ, in our flesh, for His body's sake, which is the Church "—and so complete, by our own travail, the travail of His soul !

The Gospel witness, that is thus simple in character and universal in obligation, natural and necessary to a new-born soul, essential to the plan of God, experimental, and therefore effectual, is designed to be also *perpetual.*

If the Book of the Acts be carefully examined it will be seen to be the one *incomplete* book of the Bible. At the beginning we read—"The former treatise "—"of all that Jesus began both to do and teach, until the day in which He was taken up." These words, "former," "began," "until," imply something going before in the Gospel narrative, and imply that, in the book which follows, the writer is to give us the *latter* treatise of all that Jesus *continued* to do and teach by the Holy Ghost, *after* that He was taken up. And so the Book of the Acts implies something going before it.

If we turn to the close of the book, we observe equally plain signs of something to come after. "And Paul dwelt two whole years in his own hired house, and received all that came in unto him, preaching the kingdom of God, and teaching those things which concern the Lord Jesus Christ, with all confidence, no man forbidding him." The Gospel according to Matthew ends with a manifest conclusion, that leaves nothing to be added ; the

Apocalypse ends with a special injunction, forbidding any addition or subtraction ; but here the
curtain simply falls on Paul, teaching and preaching, without even bringing to a close the scene in
which he last appears.   And the reason is because
this book is the Book of a Witnessing Church, and
that book never will be closed until that witness
is also concluded ; until the Gospel is borne to the
uttermost parts of the earth and the last witness
has been uttered, and believed or rejected.

Any one of us, any believer to the end of the
age, may write his own name where Paul's now
stands and fill out the record with his own witness
for Christ.   Or, if he be too humble in his own
esteem to venture on a record, there is Another
who, while he is living and working for his Master,
is writing a new chapter to record how he also
passed the years teaching and testifying of Christ
and of the grace of God.

When the Bishop of Ripon read that narrative
of John Williams' labors in the South Seas, he laid
it down, exclaiming, " There is the Twenty-ninth
chapter in the Acts of the Apostles ! "   Every believer has only to take his place among God's witnesses, and in his generation to testify to all men
the Gospel of His grace, to be admitted to a place in
the holy company of the apostles, and have his name
and life history recorded in that unwritten sequel of
the Acts, which is to be read before an assembled
universe in the Day when the Books are opened !

II.

THE DIVINE PLAN OF MISSIONS.

HEN, on the site of Byzantium, Constantine, in the year 328 A.D., was himself, in person, marking out the boundary line for the proposed city of Constantinople; and when his attention was called to the vast extent of the area he was enclosing, and the improbability that the City of the Cæsars would ever occupy it, he calmly answered: "*I am following Him who is leading me.*"

The Church has attempted a gigantic task, in extending and enlarging the place of her tent and stretching her canopy over a world-wide area. The work is so stupendous that it has inclined some to remonstrate, and even to ridicule. But, be it ever remembered, that in so doing we are "following Him who is leading" us. It is He who has bidden us "Lengthen our cords and strengthen our stakes." No task can be too colossal in magnitude if He plans it and entrusts to us the execution of what is really His plan. And here is the threefold dependence of His servants: the *plan*, the *promise*, and the *providence* of God.

The idea, or thought of God in missions, as we have already seen, is this: a Gospel message, received by faith in the heart, and proclaimed, by the mouth of every believer, in the ear of every other human being.

The *Plan* of God is akin to His *Thought;* but though closely related to it, not identical with it. The English word "plan"—from the latin *planus*, flat—originally refers to a representation of any object or conception drawn upon a flat surface, like the map of a country, or the plan of a building. We can all readily distinguish, in our own minds, between the conception of a cathedral, as it lay in the brain of Brunelleschi, and the draught of Santa Maria's Cupola, as put upon paper. Now God has an idea of missions: He projects His thought upon the pages of His Word, and still more clearly defines it by the pencil of History. His idea and ideal become real in the practical plane of action; and that is His *Plan*.

The importance of studying and understanding His plan cannot be overestimated. The late Prince Albert said no wiser word to the younger men of his generation than this: "Find out the plan of God in your day; and then beware that you do not cross it, but fall into your own place in that plan." Sydney Smith expressed the same thought in his quaint way, when he compared men to pegs, and their spheres of service to the holes into which the pegs must be fitted.

Nothing perhaps is more fundamental to a truly
serviceable life than to know what God's plan is,
and knowing it, come into right relations to it.
When His mind guides, no mistake is possible; no
failure is conceivable, when His will controls.
Faber writes truly:

> " He always wins who sides with God,
>   To Him no chance is lost."

To God's chariots two celestial chargers are
yoked: Omniscience and Omnipotence; the rim
of those chariot wheels is so high that it is dread-
ful, and full of eyes before and behind. To set
oneself against God's purpose is to be trampled in
pieces under the feet of those steeds, and ground
to powder beneath those wheels; but it is no less
certain that, to work for and with God is to be
borne along irresistibly toward the goal of con-
summate victory and final glory!

There are two ways of finding out God's plan,
and they are to be pursued along parallel lines.
One is to study His *Word*, and the other, to study
His *work;* on the one hand to search the Scriptures, and on the other, to watch that march of
God in history which is His preceptive teaching
wrought into the form of acts and facts. We say
these two methods should be pursued side by side,
for they mutually complement and correct each
other, or, rather, our understanding of both.

In addition to these, we need also, and above

all, a *receptive mind.* There must be a clear-seeing
eye, otherwise in vain is the plainest handwriting
of God on the pages of the Word or on the walls
of the ages. The "natural man" does not receive
the things of the Spirit of God, neither can he
know them, for they are spiritually discerned; the
"carnal mind is enmity against God, not subject
to His law, neither indeed can be": so far therefore as we search the Scripture with the natural
mind only, we shall not *see* His plan; and, so far
as we approach it with the carnal mind only, we
shall not *obey,* even if we perceive, His will.

Scripture and history are the two books of
God on missions, and each throws light upon the
pages of the other; but one may read both and
still be as blind to their real meaning as is the
Jew, who reads the prophecy of Messiah without
seeing in it the forecast of history, and reads the
history of Messiah without finding in it the fulfilment of the prophecy!

To come to the study of God's plan of missions
with the merely natural eye as the organ of vision,
or the merely carnal mind as the organ of knowledge, is to see double, if at all. Either the plan
of missions, as seen in the Word, will be modified
and distorted by our defective vision, or it will
seem to be in conflict with that same plan, as unfolded and developed in history. We shall either
start with wrong conceptions and so misinterpret
history; or we shall start with correct ideas and

then, misreading history, wander in a maze of confusion and perplexity, misled by the apparent failure of history to realize the ideal.

We may therefore lay it down as an axiom that any supposed plan of God in missions which is not scriptural, cannot be really *historic;* nor can that be really historic which is not *scriptural.* In other words, the true plan of God must be read by these two guides. If we get the right focal centre, it will be seen that, like the twin pictures in the stereoscope, they harmoniously blend: if they do not, the fault is not in their disagreement, but in our seeing.

The writer may be permitted to address the reader personally and familiarly. He wishes to be honest with God, his readers, and himself. For many years he confesses that he could not bring into apparent agreement the promises and prophecies of God's Word as to missions, and the providence of God in human history. From the lofty summits of Holy Scripture there was an inspiring outlook, a prophetic prospect, which lost all its reality, if not its romance, when one descended to the lower level of actual fact, as the purple mantle and the golden veil of the mountain lose their soft enchantment as we come near enough to see and touch the bare, bleak, rugged crags of rock. There was an instinctive consciousness that the conflict was only apparent, that the difficulty lay in my own vision: either I read

Scripture wrongly or I read history wrongly, or both.

There was but one way out of the maze of perplexity: to retrace steps already taken and begin anew, to lay aside as far as possible all bias, whether of prepossession or prejudice, and, in a prayerful spirit, humbly, like a little child, seek open, unveiled eyes * wherewith to read the Word and will of God. The results are now, in brief, to be laid before the readers of these pages. Is it too much again to ask that, before pronouncing hasty judgment, the indulgent reader will undertake to get at the truth in the same spirit?

Looking first at God's Word, one book in the Bible seems entitled to a special rank as God's own commentary on missions. *The Acts of the Apostles is the Missionary Encyclopedia of the Ages.* Here, if anywhere, will be found in full, both the Divine idea and the Divine plan.

This book opens with the repetition of the Great Commission, and the prediction of the Great Anointing. It briefly outlines the whole scheme of missions, as Giotto drew a perfect circle at one stroke: *"Ye shall be witnesses unto me, both in Jerusalem and in all Judea; and in Samaria, and unto the uttermost part of the earth."* † Then it proceeds to trace the history of the witnessing Church, through the first age—the lifetime of one generation—showing how God went before to

* Ps. cxix. 18.   † Acts i. 8.

open doors of access wide and effectual, and how the Church, following His lead, gave her witness, in the *exact order* which our Lord had indicated— in Jerusalem, in all Judea, in Samaria ; then in the uttermost part of the earth, Rome, Greece, and the regions beyond.

Surely this is no accident. The New Testament opens with four Gospel narratives, all of which end with the great commission, presented in four various aspects, like a building viewed from as many sides. Then immediately follows this fifth book, in which God's leadership of His witnessing Church by His providence and grace, during one entire generation, serves this double end : first, it stands as a permanent illustration of His *purpose*, and of the duty of every successive generation of believers toward those who at the same time live on the earth ; and, secondly, it furnishes us a practical example of the general *results* which we are to expect to follow faithful witness. In one word, this book is the typical history of the first age of missions ; and a key to all future ages of Church history.

The Queen of Sheba came to King Solomon, " to prove him with hard questions, and there was not one thing hid from her which he told her not." *
Here, in this book of the Acts, is the perpetual audience-chamber of the Prince of Peace. No perplexity or difficulty has ever arisen, or will ever

* I. Kings x. 1-3.

arise, in the missionary work of the Church, for which there is not here an adequate answer and solution. We shall therefore reverently inquire, first of all, at this Holy Oracle; and, possibly, even in this closing decade of the nineteenth century, the Church may find something yet to be learned as to the true methods and principles of missions.

Seven grand features are here plainly marked in God's plan: the ruling idea and word is still, WITNESS, but this witnessing is qualified by certain definitions and limitations:

I. Its *Purpose:* the evangelization of the world.

II. Its *Result:* the out-gathering of an elect Church.

III. Its *Order:* to the Jew first and then to the Gentile.

IV. Its *Scope:* a whole Church, witnessing to a whole world.

V. Its *Method:* a division of the field, and a distribution of the force.

VI. Its *Stress:* service rendered to the existing generation.

VII. Its *Power:* essentially superhuman and supernatural.

Within these seven landmarks will be found comprised the whole duty of the Church, with all those details which serve for her complete guidance in carrying out the great commission.

These seven features it is our design, in course

of these chapters, to survey. One of them, the duty of the whole Church to witness to the whole world, has been already touched upon in the previous pages, and others will naturally be considered later on. But, just now, we may confine ourselves to one great question: What is the *purpose* which God has in view, and what are the *results* therefore which we are warranted in expecting?

This question we seek to answer in the double light of the Scripture and of history. We find it to be God's declared purpose to *have the Gospel preached throughout the world*, and thereby to *gather out from the world a believing people, the Church or Bride of Christ.* If this be so, then our true *aim* is divinely defined, and our reasonable *hope* is suggested, which need not be disappointed.

Our Lord Himself defines the *bounds* of our work: First of all, *the purpose of this world-wide witnessing is a world's evangelization.*

It behoves us carefully to notice our instructions, for they not only define our duty, but they limit our responsibility. In some matters absolute accuracy is indispensable; as, for example, in astronomical calculations. A soldier studies his orders, as an ambassador his instructions, minutely; and, in this work of missions, we who are both soldiers and ambassadors need clear conceptions of the orders and instructions of our King.

If we closely examine the entire commission entrusted to the Church by our Lord, we shall be struck by the peculiar words which he used. "Go ye," "preach the Gospel," "make disciples," "witness"; there is another word, properly translated "*teach*," but that evidently refers to an *after-training* of those who have been first evangelized and made disciples.. No unbiased reader can examine the body of instructions, given to the early Church by the Lord Himself, without observing that, first of all, He meant that there should be a *simple heralding of good tidings*, accompanied by personal witness to their truth and power, and a consequent making of disciples; and, then, that these converts should be gathered into churches, baptized, and further trained in fuller knowledge of divine truth and preparation for service.

To confound preaching and teaching, evangelization and indoctrination, is a mistake that is fundamental and initial. The didactic process is secondary and subordinate. Men are asleep—dead in sin: they must be aroused, awakened, quickened. When a house is on fire, a ship is on a rock, a pestilence is raging, or an avalanche is falling, one does not wait to give minute instructions, but peals out the trumpet note, "Escape for thy life!" So our Lord saw this world, lying in sin, and its millions going down to the death of the grave and the second death of hell with fearful rapidity; and He urged a correspondingly rapid proclamation of the Gospel. He urged on His heralds—He bade them not wait for others to come to them, but *"go"* to every creature—sweep round the globe and trumpet forth the warning and the invitation until "every creature" shall have heard.

Nor are we anywhere taught to *wait for results.* These we cannot command or control. Noah, the ancient preacher of righteousness, preached for a century—preached an illustrated sermon, in which the Ark was his grand object lesson, and every hammer's blow punctuated and emphasized his appeal; yet he made not one convert, and was compelled to see the whole world of the ungodly sink, lost in the angry flood of wrath. Isaiah, the Messianic minstrel, sung in twenty-seven chapters the epic and lyric of the suffering Saviour; yet he cried, "Lord, who hath believed our report, and to whom hath the arm of the Lord been revealed!" And the Son of God Himself, who spake as never man spake, and wrought as never man wrought, found His words of grace used as traps and snares for His feet, and His works of love attributed to the agency of the devil. The disciple is not above his Master nor the servant above his Lord; and there has not been one preacher of Christ in all the ages whose witness has not been met by more rejectors than believers. We are both to look for and pray for results, but we are not to gauge our fidelity or our success, or our Master's approval by the number of converts; nor is the herald to wait in any one field until

conversion has done its work, before he goes to
the regions beyond. The danger is common to
all; Death and Hell are mounted on their awful
steeds, and are hotly pursuing the whole host of
mankind: if those whom we warn will not hear
and heed, perhaps others *will;* and, in any case,
we owe to all the same privilege and opportunity
of hearing and heeding. With all possible haste
should the Church push her heralds on to the very
limits of the globe. Without an hour's delay, for
any cause, on any pretext, save only to receive
power from above, should we who believe urge
on this holy crusade for God until every living
soul has heard of Christ. This Gospel of the
Kingdom must first be preached among all nations
as a witness—and "then shall the end come."
Whether these words refer to the end of the Jewish
age, in the destruction of Jerusalem, or to the end
of the Gospel age, in the second advent of the Son
of Man, or to both, there is here indicated a vital
relation which the general proclamation of the
Gospel bears to the consummation of God's plan.
He is working toward an *end*, and that end is con-
ditioned upon this world-wide evangelism. God
told Lot that He could not do anything in judgment upon Sodom until he should come to Zoar.
The announcement of the Gospel, among all
nations and to every creature, is the Zoar to
which the Church of God must come, before
those grand events move to their consummation

which at once bring judgment to sinners and salvation to saints.

Notwithstanding the fact that "preaching the
Gospel as a witness" is our Lord's own chosen
definition of the work to be done, this phrase has
met vigorous and violent opposition, and been
pelted with the blows of ridicule as the sum of all
absurdities. And yet, from first to last, this is
His form of statement, alike before His death and
on the eve of His ascension.*

Is "witnessing," then, so superficial, artificial a
process, that we are to picture to ourselves some
flying courier, galloping on horseback through
village after village, announcing the good news,
and then hastening away elsewhere? To bear
testimony unto all nations is no such short, hasty,
inadequate proclamation of the Gospel message.
However important the mere work of the herald,
other forms of testimony are needful to confirm,
corroborate, establish this witness. The conversion of souls, which witnesses that this Gospel is
the power of God unto salvation ; the out-gathering
of converts from the world and their in-gathering
into the Church, which witnesses both against the
world, by separation, and unto God, by consecration ; the erection of the Christian home, which
witnesses to what Christ can do, not for man only,
but for woman and children, making the wife
man's equal companion, instead of his slave and

* Matt. xxiv. 14 ; Acts i. 8.

victim, and the mother the radiant centre of a
happy household; the setting up of Christian
school, college, printing press and medical mission
—these trees of life whose fruit is food and whose
leaves are healing; the whole array of Christian
institutions which are the peculiar product of the
faith which works by love—all these belong to
that "witness" for Christ which helps one to
judge whether indeed "He is able to save to the
uttermost all who come unto God by Him." This
is the testimony which vindicates His claim to
universal homage and world-wide dominion. We
believe the work of witnessing in all the world will
not be complete until, in every nation, the contrast
between the teaching and practice of the true
faith and of all false faiths shall thus be made to
appear, somewhat as the Kho-Thah-Byu Memorial
Hall in Burmah confronts the Schway Mote Tau
Pagoda on an opposing hill, a witness to Christ
that boldly faces and challenges that forsaken
fane of idolatry, as though to assert and maintain
the Supreme right of Jesus to worship and service.

We are not jealous for any human theory, nor
are we warring about words. But something is
wrong. Our Lord, more than eighteen and a half
centuries ago, urged an immediate and world-wide
proclamation of the Gospel to every creature;
and yet, in this closing decade of this nineteenth
century, at least one-half of the population of this
globe remain as entirely strangers even to the *fact*

that Jesus died for them, as though they were inhabitants of another planet! We have been going about this work leisurely—we have gone to nations here and there, set up the cross as a rally-ing point, sought to convert the nations and subdue whole empires for Christ. We have waited to complete this work, while the regions beyond have remained in the unbroken shadow of death. All this seems, in some respects, directly opposed to our Lord's orders.

Often as we hear in these days of the "conver-sion of nations," and the "converstion of the world," we shall in vain seek any Scriptural war-rant for such phrases or such hopes. More than this, we need not be left either to doubt or conjecture, for God has revealed His purpose concerning His kingdom. It is to grow, not by assimilation and incorporation of worldly elements, but by their separation and displacement. That was an all-comprehensive saying of our Lord to Pilate: "*My kingdom is not of this world.*" It is not to be built of earthly materials, sustained by human patronage, defended by worldly power, extended by carnal weapons. The strongholds of Satan are to be captured, not that they may be converted into the fortresses of faith, but that they may be "cast down and destroyed."

Let us understand this sublime truth: God disdains to use for His holy ends even the "high towers, that exalt themselves against the knowl-

edge of Christ." The turrets of an insolent and
blasphemous infidelity or a defiant idolatry are
never to be turned into spires for God's cathedral
of the ages. Those who imagine that this world
is to be *gradually assimilated to God,* until what is
now earthly and carnal society shall be embodied
in the Christian state, should carefully study, for
example, the second chapter of Daniel. The
image which Nebuchadnezzar beheld is the object
lesson from which we are to learn out of what
material God will build His kingdom which shall
have no end. That head of massive gold sur-
mounted arms and breast of silver, belly and thighs
of brass, and feet of iron and clay. A stone, cut
out the mountain without hands, smites the image
of world-empire upon its brittle feet; then that
stone moves and grinds like a millstone, and, with
resistless force and weight, it crumbles and crushes
that entire image into powder. Mark the emphasis
of detail: "then was the iron, the clay, the brass,
the silver, and the gold broken to pieces together
and became like the chaff of the summer threshing-
floors; and the wind carried them away, that no
place was found for them: and the stone that
smote the image became a great mountain and
filled the whole earth!"*

Words could not teach more plainly these two
truths: first, that all these world kingdoms are
alike doomed to fall; for that Kingdom "shall

* Daniel ii. 35.

break in pieces and consume all these kingdoms ";
and secondly, that God shall alike reject the clay,
the iron, the brass, and even the silver and the
gold; they are to be broken in pieces together and
swept away as worthless chaff before the wind.
From worst to best, this material offers nothing
worthy to enter into the composition of that Eternal Kingdom, just as our flesh and blood, however
comparatively fair and faultelss, cannot enter into
the structure of that resurrection body, which is
of the nature of the kingdom of heaven.

King Solomon's "drinking vessels, and all the
vessels of the House of the Forest of Lebanon,
were of pure gold—none were of silver; for silver
was nothing accounted of in the days of Solomon." * In the imperial splendor of his revenue
and riches, "he made silver to be in Jerusalem as
stones for abundance"; and he disdained to use
such common metal even for his vessels, as the
Phœnician sailors are said to have found silver in
such plenty in Spain that they made their anchors
and common implements of it. This was a type
of greater things to come, when the Prince of
Peace sets up His kingdom, and when even gold
shall be only as the paving of streets. Everything
is to be on a scale of such celestial magnificence
and munificence, that no earthly material, however
choice, shall be worthy to enter into that structure.
The New Jerusalem is not to be made out of this

* I. Kings x. 21-27.

world's best elements; but "let down out of heaven from my God"—and only colossal pearls can represent its gates, and precious stones, burning with imprisoned fire, its walls.

When God sets up His kingdom, it is "a stone cut out without hands" and growing of itself; instead of *combination* we have *comminution;* for, in comparision with the elements out of which that imperial state is to be built, the best this world can offer is but chaff.

Must we not reconstruct our conception of the kingdom which is to come? When God sets up His kingdom in a human heart, it is by no reconstruction of the old man, but by the introduction of the "new man which after God is created in righteousness and true holiness"; and the growth of the new crowds out the old, somewhat as the farmer, by the patient culture of grain, displaces weeds and thistles. "If any man be in Christ he is a new creation: old things are passed away; all things are become new." He learns the expansive, expulsive, explosive power of a new affection, that drives out every lower love or lust. So when God's kingdom fills this earth, evil will be overcome with good.

We lay stress on this, simply to maintain a Scriptural principle. So long as we labor or hope for a Christianizing and spiritualizing of the kingdoms of this world, our work is in vain and our hope is without fruition. Whatever assimilation there may be, it is external, superficial, deceptive; it will never become transformation. That very closeness of contact between the Church and the world, by which the Church seeks to penetrate and permeate the world with godliness, endangers the Church-life, while seeking to transform the world-life. The mystery of *endosmosis* and *exosmosis* reappears in the spiritual realm. Currents flow both ways: the Church does permeate the world and make it more churchly, and outwardly, perhaps, more godly; but, by the same intimate contact, the world permeates the Church, and makes it more worldly and even ungodly, till neither remains what it was and still would be in separation. Instead of what is decidedly "hot" and decidedly "cold," there is what is "neither hot nor cold, but lukewarm"—and it is *that* which God hates. "*I would thou wert cold or hot !*"

The law of SEPARATION is written, as in huge capitals, all over the Word of God, inscribed as in flaming letters upon the altars of tabernacle and temple, typified in the separation of clean and unclean in the Levitical law,* and then whispered from Calvary with a still small voice as impressively and imperatively as when thundered from Sinai's summit: "Come out from among them and be ye separate, and touch not the unclean," etc.

The stress of God's own Word upon separation impresses us as heavier, according as we ourselves

* Levit. xx. 24-26; II. Cor. vi. 17.

become more imbued with the spirit of Scripture and the mind of Christ. The Church runs no risk to-day, whether in the sphere of holy living or of mission work, so great as that found in the unscriptural notion that *the world is to be won by courting it;* that the severe standard of godliness is to be let down lower, that so worldly souls may the more easily step over into the Church. In this there has been alarming success, and the success is itself awful disaster. Our churches are largely made up of two classes, the wholly worldly and the worldly holy. The notions and maxims, treasures and pleasures, pursuits and policy—nay, the very *spirit* of the world—have found in the sanctuary of God their shrine and throne. Men who do not even confess Christ as Saviour and Lord, sit upon boards of trustees, and control the affairs of God's House. Godless musicians preside at the key-board of the instrument whose melodies and harmonies should accord with the harps and lutes of glorified saints and angels; star singers from the opera are hired to displace the praise of the people of God by a concert display of a few artists. The ministry is degraded from a divine vocation to a learned profession, whose requisite is culture, and whose perquisite is whatever price it can command. Churches rival each other in garniture and furniture, costly architecture, and often costlier debts and mortgages; the cross becomes the badge of a religious club whose exclusive, expensive privileges demand an elect, select membership. Pure, simple Gospel preaching gives way to intellectual essays, poetic effusions, moral lectures, or political harangues; while prayer-meetings languish or are turned into entertaining talks or church "conversazioni."

The result is that missionary effort either ceases, or begets missionary converts on a level with the home churches. And if, in such churches, there be no flaming zeal for evangelism, it is neither strange nor to be much lamented, since it is doubtful whether such a type of piety has much diffusive tendency, or whether it is even desirable extensively to diffuse such a type of piety, even if we could. The higher the type of piety maintained by Christian disciples, the more rapid will be its diffusion and the more will such diffusion be an extension of the Kingdom of God, and not of a secularized Christianity.

When we hear so much about "*converting nations*," the careful student of Scripture cannot but ask, Do the Scriptures warrant any such hope? What is a nation but an aggregation of individuals under one government? It has no corporate existence or personality—no mind to be convinced, no heart to be renewed, no conscience to be aroused, no will to be subjected. How any "*nation*" can be Christianized, apart from the individuals composing it, it is hard to see. But if, as such, a nation, by public official act, accepts

Christianity, acknowledges the Bible as the law of the land, the Sabbath as a sacred day of rest, protects public worship, and even establishes the Church as national, while some advantages may follow, is there not a peril involved, far greater than any danger from open opposition or malignant persecution?

How soon and how surely the *form* of godliness takes the place of the *power!* Political preferment beckons worldly men into the Church. To be a disciple comes to be in the fashion; it is the way of the majority, which is always fraught with risk. The law of self-denial gives place to the habit of self-indulgence. Piety is the best policy, and heavenly principles are weighed in the brazen scales of earthly expediency. We dare to say that, through the whole Christian era, no nation has ever, as such, become nominally Christian, without introducing into the Church marked, mani- fest, and rapid spiritual decline. And this fact is both so conspicuous and so significant that we need only to adduce a few historical examples, for the sake of the lesson which they teach us as to modern missions.

When Paul sent from Rome the salutations of the saints, "*Chiefly those of Cæsar's household,*" he did not know that, in that greeting, a shadow, no larger than a man's hand, appeared on the horizon of Church life that was soon to overspread with dense clouds the whole heaven. Three centuries passed by, and in the year 310 A.D., the *head* of Cæsar's household, himself, in camp near Mentz, claimed to see a flaming cross in the sky, with the motto : εν τουτῳ, νικα ! and thenceforth, on the shields of Roman soldiers and the banners of the Empire, that symbol shone.

To the early Church the red hand of persecution brought no calamity comparable with the so-called " Christianizing of the Roman Empire." The bloody cross of the Ten Persecutions was infinitely more a blessing than the golden cross of Royal Patronage.

The disciples of Christ found *via Crucis*, the way of self-sacrifice, changed to *via Lucis*, the way of self-indulgence; and *via Dolorosa*, where they bore the cross after Jesus, changed to *via Gloriosa*, where they wore a crown with an earthly sovereign. To confess Christ was now to bid for place and power; the millennium had come; in the person of Constantine, the King of kings had mounted the throne of the world, and in the new capital, on the shores of the Bosphorus, was the realization of the New Jerusalem ! No more the little assembly of disciples, with doors closed against the world, but with Jesus within ; no more the Church of the Catacombs, hiding from pursuing foes in the bowels of earth ; no more a band of pilgrims, strangers, sojourners, taking joyfully the spoiling of their goods for the sake of that better country with their enduring substance !

Henceforth, a court whose splendor outshone those of Oriental princes ; a hierarchy of officials which to this day remains the model of the most extravagant, elaborate, and voluptuous courts of Europe. To Constantine are traced the very *titles*, which in these modern skies of empire shine thick as stars—" excellency," " right honorable," " serenity," " duke," " count," " viscount." Enormous outlay, vast standing armies, gorgeous temples and elaborate ritual, became the features of the Christian State. To this day the Church of Christ has never recovered from that deadly blow at her very life ! A nation was converted indeed, but the Church was perverted. Petrifaction—the loss of godly sensibility, and putrifaction—the loss of godly savor, now marked the so-called " Body of Christ." The Roman Empire was transformed into a Christian state, but the true Republic of God, the Commonwealth of Christ, was deformed, and, not until a thousand years after, was it reformed.

See how history is a commentary on the Word of God. Mark how He, whose hand is behind the shifting scenery of the drama of the ages, is teaching us what peril there is in the close alliance, or even contact, between His kingdom and the kingdoms of this world. To turn the household of God into the Court of Empire, means to exchange, for the Bride of Christ, leaning on her Beloved, the Scarlet Woman, seated on the beast and from

him deriving power and authority! The conversion of a nation seems a goal of hope toward which
the passionate ardor of faith reaches; it is in fact
an illusive vision, a dream of a misguided fancy,
that draws the Church away from her simple work
of witnessing, to follow a deceptive and even
dangerous expectation.

Modern history furnishes another example of the
"conversion of a nation." On March 31, 1820,
the brig *Thaddeus* anchored off Hawaii, with the
first missionaries of the American Board. God
had gone before them, and, instead of a long, hard
fight with the bloody altars and human sacrifices
of Paganism, they found that superstition had
already struck down her own idols, and abolished
the *Tabu* and priesthood throughout the islands.*
Ten months before, Kamehameha I. had died;
and, strange to say, he forbade human sacrifices,
whether, during his illness, for his recovery, or,
after his death, in his honor; and thus, *before the
missionaries landed*, a professed idolater had dealt
the first blow at idolatry. The High Priest, resign-
ing his office, first applied the torch to the fanes
of a pagan faith. Idols came under the ban of
law and temples were reduced to ashes. For the
first time in history, a nation had flung away a false
faith without a new one to replace it, and was
without a religion. The first convert was the
king's mother, Keopuolani, and, at the close of

* Anderson. Hawaiian Is. p. 49.

1825, Kaahumanu, the Regent, and nine chiefs, became members of the Church of Christ, afterward dying in the faith. Within six years after the missionaries landed, schools covered the islands, with 400 teachers and 25,000 pupils.

As early as 1825, the Spirit of God moved powerfully on the hearts of the Hawaiians. About fifty families in Lahaina began to pray, and the number grew. Inquirers, and then converts, flocked like doves to the churches; and, in ten years more, the American Board thought the beginning of the end of its missionary work in the Hawaiian Islands had been reached.

To completely Christianize this group of islands, they here largely concentrated their working force, sending in 1836 thirty-two additional laborers. Scarcely had these new laborers come, when a tidal wave of revival swept over the islands and bore away on its crest all remaining traces of idols and their fanes. Three years more, and the Word of God was given to the people in their own tongue; another three years and the professing disciples numbered 20,000. Mr. Coan, alone, admitted 5,000 in one year, and 1,700 in one day. And in 1863, less than fifty years after these labors began in the Pacific, the Hawaiian churches took their place among self-governing, self-supporting, and self-propagating churches of Christendom. The marvels of the Apostolic age seemed to have been reproduced after a lapse of eighteen centuries.

This nation, thus Christianized within half a
century, was boldly held up before the Church as
a "glorious exemplification and proof of the power
of the Gospel in missions, for the encouragement
of the Church of God in its efforts for the conversion of the world." *

That the work here done was, and still is, one
of the most marvellous triumphs of the Gospel in
all modern times, the writer of these pages would
be the last to deny: but here stands another warning to us of the illusiveness and deceptiveness of
any hope of converting nations or converting the
world, within the bounds of this Gospel age. If
we trace the subsequent history of the Sandwich
Islands, we shall find the story of the Christianized
Empire of the Cæsars, repeated on a minor scale,
but teaching the same lesson.

Rev. James Bicknell and others have been con-
strained to publish tracts, revealing the present low
condition of religious life on the Hawaiian Group ;
and, in crossing the Atlantic in 1888, the writer
came into contact with an intelligent and prominent
Christian gentleman, residing on the islands, who
more than confirmed Mr. Bicknell's statements.
He reluctantly conceded the existence of the Hoo-
manamana idolatry. For a long time these idolatrous customs have been concealed. Kaahumanu,
herself both a convert and Christian teacher, re-
pressed them by edicts ; and the desire of the peo-

* Anderson. Hawaiian Is. p. 25.

ple to be respected by other Christian peoples, and
the fear of being ridiculed with the opprobrious
name of "pagans," acted as additional restraints.
Those addicted to practical heathenism were kept
from public avowal; but, behind this show of Christian forms, hid a fetich-worship alarmingly common. The small pebble—Kaue O Kapohakaa—
the wooden fetich, Kailaipahoa—believed to have
power to destroy life at bidding of its possessor—
and the counter-charm, Kauila, also of wood, with
many others, each of which stands for a god, may
be found worn on the person even of professed
disciples! The king himself boldly stands forth
as an idolater, and is suspected of a design to take
the headship of a fetich system. So says Mr.
Bicknell.

In a palace-room lies a copy of David Malo's
" History of Hawaii," with the legends, traditions,
and superstitions of the islands. Before reading,
seven circuits are made around the sacred table;
then the book is reverently opened, and the cred-
ulous High Priest of this royal Sanctum believes
himself in converse with the gods. This book
furnishes the basis of the present system of Hale-
naua, or the " House of Wisdom." That house
has three divisions, embracing those devoted to
astrology, chirography, etc.; and four orders of
Kahunas, who respectively practice medicine, in-
cantation, fatal imprecation, and represent divine
power. And these Kahunas preface their idola-

trous incantations with texts of Scripture! There are, of course, different classes of adherents of this system : some who are actuolly worshippers, others who have imbibed the idolatrous spirit, and others who propitiate heroes—all known by different names.

The pulpit of these islands has not hitherto publicly exposed and denounced these idolatries, says Mr. Bicknell, and many professed believers think this fetich-worship harmless. But it is another example of a people, fearing Jehovah and serving their own gods. They read their fetichism into Old Testament narratives and New Testament miracles; and even when death approaches, with its august exchange of worlds, they turn for relief to the Kahunas and their false gods. From the time of Kamehameha V. idolatry has advanced and Christianity declined.

Of course, the mission work done on these islands is not a failure, nor are its results such as should dishearten any true believer. Everywhere the preaching of the Gospel has met the same obstacles; in Christian Britain and America we have the same external lump of dough, with the same subtle leaven of worldliness and wickedness permeating and penetrating the whole three meas-ures of meal. And so it will be until He comes whose New Epiphany is to smite the Man of Sin and put the chains upon Satan.

On Christmas morning, 1814, the devoted Sam-

uel Marsden preached in New Zealand, and for
the first time told the natives the story of Christ
and His cross. After a dozen years, a religious
enthusiasm kindled its strange fires among the
people; the schools and sanctuaries were filled
and thousands asked to be admitted into the
churches; and the very life of the people seemed
to be undergoing transformation. In 1842, twenty-
eight years after Marsden first announced those
"tidings of great joy," Bishop Selwyn took charge
of his new diocese, and he enthusiastically wrote
home, "We see here a *whole nation* of pagans
converted to the faith." These words glow with
the fires of a sacred passion for the souls of men,
and we do not doubt that of the 5,000 church
members, there were hundreds who, as the good
bishop said, exhibited "signal manifestations of
the presence of the Spirit, and were living evidences
of the kingdom of Christ." But the phrase, "a
whole nation converted," then as now, became a
deceptive golden veil, hiding the truth. The vast
bulk of those 100,000 people were yet living in
sin. The last instance of cannibalism was in 1843;
the *pahs*, or fortified villages, have given place to
unguarded homes and farm-houses; barbarous
tribal wars have quite ceased, and the sea fights,
which were like ocean storms, have yielded to the
potent voice which stills even the deep. But the
bishop's enthusiastic report only prepared the way
for bitter disappointment and morbid discourage-

ment by encouraging the illusive hope that the
nation was converted. After this glowing description had kindled the fervor and ardor of his fellow-
countrymen to a confident expectation that in this
manner the whole world was about to yield before
the Gospel, it was found that this "converted
nation" had only changed the form and complex-
ion of its ungodliness; nay, to use Luther's phrase,
had scarcely "washed the dirt from its face."
European vices had taken the place of the vices
of savagery; beneath the garb of civilization hid
an unchanged nature : and two years later serious
wars again broke out, nor was peace restored until
1848. The severe earthquake which followed was
a type of volcanic fires which had only been
slumbering, but were not dead. And although,
in 1850, Canterbury province was settled on the
basis of English ecclesiastical and aristocratical
principles, with bishop, priests, lords, and baronets,
—as the province of Otago had been two years before settled by the Free-churchmen of Scotland,—
ten years later, in 1860–1, among these converted
Maoris the new religion, the *Pai Marire*, was
propagated by a body of natives called *Hau-Haus*,
who pretended to the miraculous gifts of tongues
and of prophecy; hundreds who did not resume
their old heathenism, at least renounced their
Christianity; with some the tomahawk and war-
paint again took the place of the decent dress and
pious prayer-book of the convert; and even those

who retained the externals of Christianity attempted to combine as they pleased the practices and doctrines of Christianity and heathenism. The Maoris, in their unconverted state, had a ceremony which was a sort of baptism known as *rohi*, or *iriiri;* and the consternation of the missionaries may be imagined when, within twenty years after Bishop Selwyn had pronounced this a converted nation, thousands of men who had been baptized into Christ, but had not put on Christ, were in one day baptized out of Christianity back again into heathenism ! *

Nothing can be farther from the thought of a true advocate of missions than to belittle the triumphs of the Gospel or dishearten the heart of any hopeful disciple. But, if we would avoid and avert a disappointment which is almost suicidal to Christian effort, we must hold up before ourselves and others no unscriptural expectation. In every community where the Gospel has been preached, however grand its triumphs, it still remains true, from the days of Paul at Rome until the days of that modern Paul, the saintly Duff, at Calcutta, that "some" there have been "who believed not."† If we do our work of witnessing, expecting nothing more than the Scriptures warrant, we shall not be so liable and likely to give up in despair when only the common discouragements of all Christian work confront and baffle us.

* Hodder's Conquests of the Cross, i. 35. † Acts xxviii. 24.

The warning notes which these modern examples peal out are louder and more startling, because God's trumpet sounds at our very ears, and not at the remote distance of ages. He warns us against a vain and misleading attempt *to Christianize men in masses and by the wholesale.* Our work is with individuals, even as our message is to and for every creature. One by one men are born into the family of God. In the natural world, as the scale of being ascends, there is a strange decrease in the number of offspring at a birth. Among the lowest forms of life, the fertility is overwhelming —millions in a day. But, as the grade of life rises, the number of progeny falls, until we reach the race of man, where even a twin birth is so rare as to be exceptional. Each human soul bears the stamp of a priceless worth, being coined in God's mint, one at a time. Every man may look upon himself as an individual bought by the blood of Christ, and say, " He loved *me* and gave Himself for *me.*"

The great snare of our day is the mad passion for numbers. The Diana of the modern Ephesians is the statistical table, and many are the makers and venders of these shrines of our great goddess. We have fallen upon a mathematical age. To report so many converts in one year, or boast so many accessions at one communion, is the devil's bait to catch the superficial winner of souls. We measure the prosperity of our churches, not by the

spiritual strength of the members, but by the numerical length of the roll, and some ministers lack
courage to purge the roll of unworthy and even
unknown and deceased members, lest it seem like
a mark of waning prestige and declining popularity.
Evangelists are too often caught in the same snare
of numbers, and continually tempted to parade
mere numerical results as a test of success, and so
hundreds are counted as converts who rapidly
relapse into their old life, while hundreds of others,
swept into the Church on the crest of a revival
wave, are as surely borne back when that wave
recedes. This insane clamor for " numbering the
people " is one of the main foes to missions. As
in David's case, it leads to spiritual famine, pestilence, or defeat—and sometimes to all three.
There was a year in the little church in Blantyre,
Scotland, when but one convert was welcomed to
the Lord's Table ; but that lad was David Livingstone. Converts are to be *weighed*, not *counted*.
One Cilician Saul is worth ten thousand like the Samaritan Simon. Not how many, but how much, is
the question. When he who seeks souls is content
with one at a time, and content even then only as
that one is completely transformed by the power
of the new life into a new man, we shall have a
new era of Church history and a new epoch of
missions. In *this* age, at least, God's kingdom is
to come in the individual soul, by the slow annex-
ation of the little territory won by grace within

that little world, a human heart: the kingdom of God comes not with observation.

There are some who seem more concerned about getting everybody into heaven than about making anybody fit for heaven. In God's eyes it is of far more consequence that the Heavenly City should be clean than that it should be crowded. And we must learn, in our work for souls, that salvation is measured more by the *depth* to which it penetrates than by the *surface* over which it spreads; and that it is for duty, not for results, that we are to be held accountable.

All eyes now turn to Japan, the Island Empire, in which the rapid and remarkable changes of ten years have left "nothing as it was before, save the natural scenery"; and where even missionaries have led us to hope that another decade will find the "Sunrise Kingdom" taking her place among acknowledged Christian nations. But just what, and how much, would that mean? England and the United States are leading Christian nations. Does God's sceptre sway our Congress and Britain's Parliament? What atrocious iniquities, and even idolatries, have these foremost "Christian nations" both practiced and promoted! See the great republic, holding in bonds 4,000,000 slaves, till God's hammer of War struck off their fetters! Think of such "Christian nations" flooding Africa with rivers of rum! of the land which sent Carey to the Indies, forcing opium upon China even at the cannon's mouth, and setting a premium upon lust, in Hindostan !

What does "Christianizing a nation" mean? If it be anything short of the transformation of the individuals that make up the nation, it is disaster. It is the mixing up of a profession of piety with political trickery; it is clothing abominable abuses with the sanction of religion; it is substituting popularity for purity, and the loud voice of the majority for the still small voice of the Spirit of God. The "witness" of the Church before the world implies not only separation, but antagonism, not amalgamation and assimilation. Strange to say, the way to win the worldly to Christ is not by courting them, but by making them hate us for our likeness to God and our unlikeness to themselves. To come to their broken cisterns keeps them from coming to the Living Fountains.

Conscious that, in presenting these views, the writer represents a small minority, he takes courage both from the depth of his own conviction, that this is God's truth, and from the remembrance that, historically, the truth has never yet been on the side of the majority. Both God's word and God's working, even in this, the missionary age, teach us that during the present dispensation, our watchword is *evangelization.* We are not to look for a world's conversion, which, after all these centuries, seems perhaps no nearer than at the accession of Constantine. We are to *evangelize* the world, and if the result proves to be, not the world's conversion, but the *out-gathering of the Church*, the εκκλησια, the called-out assembly, the Bride of Christ, is it not exactly the Scriptural goal of this age ? This is the only hope, warranted either by the Scripture or the history of missions, and therefore it is the only hope not possible to be disappointed. To some believers, this truth is so clear that it is a marvel that any reader of the Word or observer of history can doubt. In Acts xv. 15, the Apostle James in inspired words *outlined, at that first Church council*, the *whole plan* of the Divine Architect and Builder, and furnished a key to all evangelical history and a kind of miniature chart of the whole missionary age.

"SIMEON HATH DECLARED HOW GOD AT THE FIRST DID VISIT THE GENTILES TO TAKE OUT OF THEM A PEOPLE FOR HIS NAME. AND TO THIS AGREE THE WORDS OF THE PROPHETS, AS IT IS WRITTEN: 'AFTER THIS I WILL RETURN AND WILL BUILD AGAIN THE TABERNACLE OF DAVID WHICH IS FALLEN DOWN; AND I WILL BUILD AGAIN THE RUINS THEREOF, AND I WILL SET IT UP; THAT THE RESIDUE OF MEN MIGHT SEEK THE LORD AND ALL THE GENTILES UPON WHOM MY NAME IS CALLED, SAITH THE LORD WHO DOETH ALL THESE THINGS.'" And the apostle significantly adds, as though to assure disheartened disciples that God's plans steadily advance toward completion,—"*known unto God are all His works from the beginning of the world.*"

Here is plainly an election and out-gathering of the Church from the world. The discerning student of the Bible and Biblical history sees a manifest progress in the dispensations, but this *elective principle* is always present.

In that former age, the Jewish, an *elect nation*, was called out to guard an elect truth, the unity of God, and to forecast, in type and rite, the advent of His dear Son. During that age, the body of believers was mainly confined to one nation, and the Holy Spirit's chrism was bestowed on elect individuals, such as prophets, priests, and kings. Then came this latter age, the Christian, when an *elect Church*, gathered out of every nation, is called out from the world, to proclaim a universal Gospel for the whole world, and in the elect body of Christ to incorporate all believers. And, now that the Son of God has come, just as the altar of burnt offering in the Jewish age pointed back to the fall, and forward to the cross, so the Lord's Table witnesses backward to His advent, and forward, to His second coming. "As oft as ye eat this bread and drink this cup, ye do show the Lord's death till He come."

As, in this age, there is a widening of the elect body to embrace converts from all nations, so there is a corresponding widening of the Spirit's work. He is now bestowed on all believers of the elect Church. But, in all the New Testament, we search in vain for any promise that, *during this age, the Church will be co-extensive with the world.* There are glimpses of a *coming age,* sometimes mistakenly called the "*world* to come," when God's plan shall still broaden out—when the world-wide proclamation of the Gospel shall be followed by a world-wide knowledge of Christ; when the Holy Spirit shall again, and still more plentifully, be poured out from on high; not on elect individuals in an elect nation, nor on all believers in an elect Church gathered out of every nation, but, in a peculiar sense, "*upon all flesh*"; and so Joel's words, which found their foretaste in the Pentecost, shall have their fulfilment,—their fill-full-ment. Then, and not till then, is the family of God to become co-extensive with the family of man. And yet, even in that millennial age, the revolt at the end hints that there will still be those who persistently reject the Gospel and refuse to have this King Jesus to reign over them, and are to be dashed in pieces like a potter's vessel. It would seem that, until the very end of that millennial age, sin is not to be exterminated. The Gospel is to triumph more and more widely, but to the end there will be, as in Paul's day, some who believe not.

Each successive dispensation has thus prepared for, and has ushered in, a *greater* age to come. At first a nation, chosen out of the world; then a

Church gathered out from the nations ; and, finally, the nations of the world transformed into the Redeemer's people and subjects.   In that age to come whereof we speak, all that was in the former and latter ages shall be found, and much more. Inclusion then displaces exclusion.   And thus the three ages present three concentric circles, with ever-widening circumference.   The circle of the believing brotherhood enlarges from Jewish nation to Christian Church, and from Christian Church to a saved humanity.   The sphere of the Holy Spirit expands from elect individuals to a believing ecclesia, and then to all flesh.   And yet those who hold to such doctrine as this, scriptural as it is, are ridiculed and stigmatized as "pessimists ! "

Hundreds and thousands of the noblest missionaries have been found to hold substantially the position here taken.   David Livingstone, that "missionary general and statesman," early learned that the conversion of individuals is really a narrower and more near-sighted aim than the evangelization of the multitude.   He was the last man to undervalue the conversion of one of the least and lowest of God's creatures ; and, in the earlier part of his missionary life, bent his whole mind to work and pray for the salvation of a single soul, and with some small success.   But—though he neither grew weary of this work nor impatient at the slow fruit which was gathered, one by one, like a hand-picked harvest—his view of God's plan widened. He saw that the universal spread of the good tidings and the wide diffusion of Christian principles was the greater good, and in the end would yield a grander harvest. "To the converted " man, individually, his own conversion was of overwhelming consequence ; but with relation to the final harvest, it is more important to sow the seed broadcast over a wide field than to reap a few heads of grain on a single spot.*

We repeat the caution, that we must beware how we measure our work or our success in this world-field by the *apparent* harvest. If, by the ingathering of a large number of converts, God is pleased to set His seal on mission work, as being of a godly sort, yet this is not the infallible criterion either of fidelity or of success. Many a devoted servant of God has, like Enoch and Noah, Isaiah and Jeremiah, Ezekiel and even Jesus Himself, met with what to human eyes is not only rejection but failure. The most honest and earnest witness-bearing seems sometimes not so much to deliver man *from* as *to* the just judgment of God ; and, instead of the hearers being justified by faith, the preacher is justified in his fidelity to souls, and God is justified in their judicial abandonment. In such case is the prophet or the preacher any less faith- · ful or is God's true servant any less rewarded because the hearer is faithless ?

To measure success in missions in India, China,

* Personal Life of Livingstone, p. 157.

Africa, or even in transformed Western Polynesia, by *numerical* results, would be a fatal mistake. No: the true criterion everywhere is the *wide diffusion* of the Gospel. It is a question of extensity rather than intensity; and hence the true, divine principle of missions is not *concentration*, but *diffusion*.

The field is the world; the seed is of *two* sorts: first, the *Word of God;* secondly, the *children of the kingdom;* and both of these sorts of seed must be sown, and sown broadcast over the whole field. Depth is important, but breadth is of first consequence. It will in time be seen that God's policy of diffusion was far better than man's policy of comparative exclusion and seclusion. Ultimately it will appear that the abundance of individual conversions will be in exact proportion to the wide-spread scattering of the seed of the kingdom. The Gospel message is, as we have seen, characterized by *two* universal terms—" the *world*," which is collective; "whosoever," which is distributive; but the great collective term, *"all the world,"* precedes the distributive term, "every creature." Let us learn that our duty is to the world, and we must leave to God the "whosoever."

We have thus sought to find by searching what is God's plan or purpose concerning the Church and the world. Certain we are that He wills the largest and promptest proclamation of the Gospel, the presence of witnessing believers and a witnessing Church everywhere, even to the uttermost part of the earth. Beyond that we are sure of nothing save this, that His Word will not return to Him void, and that our labor will not be in vain in the Lord.

To all believers the divine command is, that we outgrow our babyhood—cease to be mere objects of care, and become care-takers; that we enter into that divine plan which takes in the whole Church, the whole world, and the whole age. We must be satisfied with the hope that has its anchorage in Scripture promises, do our duty, and leave results with God—undertake a world's evangelization, and not be disheartened if we find that, to the end of the age, there is only an out-gathering of the Church; and that, as in the Apostolic age, some believe the things which are spoken and some believe not. The stress of the command is on *occupation, evangelization.* A loyal servant or soldier simply obeys, implicitly, orders which are explicit. Here are our marching orders; and to follow them is to win what is better even than apparent victory, the approval of Him who will say, " WELL DONE, good and faithful servant."

Now of the things which we have spoken, this is the sum: Every saved soul is called to be a herald and a witness; and we are to aim at nothing less than this: to make every *nation,* and every *creature* in every nation, *acquainted* with the Gospel tidings. This is the first and ever-present duty

of the Church; it is the heart of the whole missionary plan. God will give us souls as our hire
and crown; large results in conversion of individuals and the transformation of whole communities will follow, as they always have followed,
a godly testimony. But we are not to *wait for
results :* we are to regard our duty as never done,
while any region beyond is without the Gospel.
Let all men have a *hearing* of the Gospel at least;
then, when *evangelization* is world-wide, we may
bend our energies to deepening the impression
which a first hearing of the Gospel has made.
But, again, let it peal out, as with a voice of
thunder, to be heard wherever there are believers!
The first need of the world is to hear the Gospel,
and the first duty of the Church is to go everywhere and tell every human being of Christ, the
world's Saviour. To stop, or linger anywhere,
even to *repeat* the rejected message, so long as
there are souls beyond that have never heard it,
is at least unjust to those who are still in absolute
darkness. Instead of creating a few centres of
intense light, God would have us scatter the lamps
until all darkness is at least relieved, if not removed.
And if to any reader it appears that this is em-
phasizing a distinction that is of little consequence,
let such an one stop a moment and consider what
would be the result if our Lord's plan were followed.

There are, we will say, about forty million mem-

bers of Protestant churches, and at least eight
hundred millions yet in *entire ignorance* of the
Gospel. Let us suppose that the whole Church,
under some mighty baptism of fire, should undertake to bear the Gospel message to every living
soul, at once. If every Protestant believer could
so be brought into active participation in this work
as to be the means of reaching *twenty of these
souls*, now without the Gospel, the work would be
done. All cannot *go*, but all can *send*. Let us
suppose again that Protestant churches should
send out *one* missionary teacher for every *four
hundred* communicants; we should have a missionary force of *one hundred thousand;* and, by
distributing this force in the entire field, each
teacher would have to reach but eight thousand
souls, in order to evangelize the world. Allowing
twenty years for that work, each laborer would
have to reach but four hundred of the unevan-
gelized each year !

We must push this work—let men call us fools,
fanatics, madmen—we can afford to bear it for the
sake of doing the will of God. When Judson had
buried himself in Burmah, and ten years' work
could show but eighteen converts, he was asked :
"What of the prospect?" His heroic answer
was : "Bright as the promises of God !" When
John Wesley proposed to go to Georgia as a missionary to the Indians, an unbeliever ridiculed him :
"What is this? Are you one of the knights

errant? How, pray, got you this Quixotism into *your* head? You want nothing, have a good provision for life, and a prospect of preferment; and must you leave all this to fight wind-mills—to convert American savages?" Wesley calmly replied: "If the Bible be not true, I am as a very fool and madman, as you can conceive. But if the Bible is of God, I am sober-minded. For He has declared, There is no man who hath left house or friend or brethren for the kingdom of God's sake, who shall not receive manifold more in this present time, and, in the world to come, life everlasting!"

With such heroic missionaries as Adoniram Judson and John Wesley, we are content to follow our Lord's leading without regard to apparent results. The command is plain: "Go ye also into the vineyard," and the promise is sufficient: "Whatsoever is right, that shall ye receive." God is a liberal rewarder, and He always exceeds His own promise. That workman is surest of blessing who does his Lord's work without the misgivings of unbelief or the exactions of a carnal spirit. The path of the missionary is the way to Calvary, but beyond the cross shines the crown.

III.

THE DIVINE WORK OF MISSIONS.

ASTOR MONOD, of Paris, beautifully suggests that all true work done by a disciple is really a part of God's own eternal, universal work, assigned to the believer. If we conceive God's work as a grand sphere, filling immensity and eternity, then every disciple's work is a part of that sphere, a small segment that lies over against him ; and, if he has spiritual eyes to discern his duty, he may read upon that work of God which belongs to him to do, his own name and the date of the present year. In other words, in God's plan each one of us is embraced, and has a definite assignment, and, for each year, month, day, and hour, a specific duty to do. What dignity and beauty and glory such a conception imparts to human life, to know that in the great mechanism of the ages, I am a part and have a place and sphere !

This thought I would now bring to the front : the work of missions is not only a toil *for* God, but a work *with* God. This is very fully and re-markably set forth in three principal passages of

Scripture, whose full force appears only as we set them side by side and carefully compare them.

" For we are *La-borers together with God:* ye are God's husbandry : ye are God's building. . . . We then as *workers together with Him,* beseech you also that ye receive not the grace of God in vain."—I. Cor. iii. 9 ; vi. 1.	" Who now rejoice in my sufferings for you, and *fill up that which is behind of the afflictions of Christ* in my flesh, for His body's sake which is the church, whereof I am made a minister." — Colos-sians, i. 24.	" When the Com-forter is come, even the Spirit of Truth, He shall bear witness of me ; and *ye also shall bear witness,* because ye have been with me from the be-ginning."—John, xv. 26, 27 ; Comp. Acts, v. 32.

Even in the New Testament no words can be found more pathetically beautiful. Here our work for souls is set forth as a co-operation with the Triune God, in three various aspects, as *co-labor, co-suffering,* and *co-witnessing.* But that which is far more remarkable and impressive in these pas-sages is, that the Father, the Son, and the Holy Spirit are individually, successively, and separately presented as personally sharing with the believer the dignity of this exalted service.

In the passage from the first Epistle to the Corinthians a careful glance shows that the word God there means the first person of the Trinity, as distinguished from the others. As to the other two quotations, no doubt can arise, because, in one the person of Christ, and in the other the per-son of the Spirit, is particularly mentioned. To compare Scripture with Scripture, to combine these fragments as in a mosaic, is to get a wonderful

picture, in which the whole conception and execution of the plan of Redemption is spread before
us in a new light, from its eternal idea and purpose
in the mind of the Father, to its execution in the
person and work of the suffering Son, and its
divine application in the witness of the Spirit to
the truth and by the blood.

There is something awe-inspiring in the fact
that, in each separate department of this work,
and with each separate person of the Trinity, the
believer is thus made a direct partaker! God the
Father is represented as beseeching men and
building up a living temple out of believing souls;
and the believer also joins with God in beseeching
men to be reconciled to Him, and in building
upon the one foundation, the temple of living
stones. God the Son is represented as vicariously
suffering for the salvation of the lost, and gathering believers into the mystical body of which He
is the head; and again, the believer is represented
as sharing with Him this vicarious sacrifice and
ministry, and as filling up somewhat, which, without the believer, would be lacking. God the
Spirit is represented as a witness-bearer, first of
all to the truth which He brings to bear upon the
mind and heart; and then to the blood whose
power he reveals in the death,·and especially in
the resurrection, of Christ; and now, once more,
the believer is presented as also witnessing with the
Holy Ghost, as though needful to complete and

confirm the testimony of the Spirit, according to the Levitical law, that in the mouth of two witnesses every word be established.

These passages, thus jointly considered, present the humblest human believer and disciple as a co-worker with God the Father, a co-sufferer with God the Son, and a co-witness with God the Spirit. Taken thus together, they suggest the highest dignity and privilege of every child of God. He is lifted to a divine level. His humble work for God is exalted to a work with God; his sacrifice and service is raised to a plane that is higher than angelic ministry. These words of the Scripture hint, if they do not affirm, that the believer is necessary to the completeness and completion of the work of redeeming a lost world. He is a part of a divine mechanism, and, until he drops into his place and co-works with other parts to produce one result, something is lacking to complete adjustment, perfect movement, and ultimate success.

I. How is this work of missions thus *a co-operation with God the Father?*

We may take the exact thought of Paul, "As though God did beseech you by us." God, like a loving father yearning over a rebellious son, or a sovereign over a revolted subject, beseeches men to be reconciled to Him. But how does He beseech, save *by us?* How is His yearning brought to the knowledge of the rebel sinner? It finds expression in the good tidings of the Gospel, but good tidings will not bear themselves; they imply *messengers*, whose feet are shod with the winged sandals of the alacrity of the Gospel, whose hands hold forth the Word of Life, and whose lips send forth words, their errant daughters. The Gospel message needs a *voice*, and John the Baptist sublimely said: "I am the Voice." Observe, a *voice*, not a mere sound, but intelligent, articulate, sympathetic, soulful utterance.

That word, "ambassador," used by Paul, holds in itself a whole body of divinity. It implies an authorized messenger, a representative of a government at a foreign court, with a definite mission and commission, and a specific body of instructions. So long as an ambassador acts within the limits of his instructions, the government which he represents speaks in his words, acts through his acts, and stands behind him with all the power, authority, and resources of a republic or an empire. An insult to such an ambassador is a blow in the face of his sovereign, an outrage upon the whole nation, which the whole government resents ; while a respectful hearing accorded to him is an audience given to the monarch whose court he represents. In the ambassador, therefore, his government is virtually present.

So far as the believer teaches God's truth and bears witness to Christ, he is God's ambassador. So long and so far as he keeps within the limits of his instructions, faithfully speaking God's Word, it is God who speaks in and through him. Behind him stand all the authority and power of the Godhead. And so Christ says to such ambassadors: "He that receiveth you, receiveth *Me*, and he that receiveth Me, receiveth Him that sent Me." He who gives us a hearing hearkens to God, and he who rejects our words turns his back upon God. Not at the last great day, only, but all through the Gospel age, the Judge is saying, "Inasmuch as ye have done it unto one of the least of these, my brethren, ye have done it unto Me." He would have us remember that, whenever we beseech men to be reconciled to God, God Himself beseeches through us.

Again Paul uses the figures of "*building*" and of "*husbandry*," to represent this co-working with God. In both these common forms of labor, architecture, and agriculture, there are the superior and the inferior workmen, and both are essential to the perfect product. In *building*, the architect and contractor furnishes plan and material; from his brain comes the idea of the structure, from his pencil, the draught in all its details, and from his quarry and shops, the material. But to the common workman are committed all the details of the actual work; he receives the building material, as brought to the ground, he studies and minutely follows the plan, and according thereto puts in place stone and timber. The architect may furnish only instructions and material, and may himself never appear in person on the site.

So in *husbandry*. The owner of the estate projects the improvements, furnishes the implements, and supplies material. His are the soil and seed, the field and crop. But he works the farm through his servants, and may himself never tread the field, plough the furrows, sow the seed, or reap the harvest.

The veil of parable does not hide the truth. God is building up a temple of believers. The plan and work are His; He designs the working plan, He provides the building material, and, when brought to the temple platform, no tool needs to be lifted upon it to fit it to its foreordained place in the great structure. But who are His *builders?* Paul and other apostles, as wise master-builders, laid the foundation, in Jesus Christ, and you and I are to carry on and carry up the Temple of the Ages.

The centuries go by; God buries workman after workman, but the *work* never ceases. The world itself is but the scaffolding about the Church of God, made to aid in its erection, but to be torn down and burned up when the cap-stone of God's cathedral is laid.

The whole work is therefore *one*. Every disciple who faithfully witnesses to God, is one of God's builders. It matters not how prominent or obscure, however great or small in human eyes,

He may be working down in the quarry, where the crude material is hewn and shaped for the building, or in the shops, where the timbers of immortal cedar are gotten ready for the frame-work, or the beaten gold for the furnishing and garnishing; or he may stand on the platform where the living stones are lifted to their place, builded together for an habitation of God through the Spirit, and where the whole building, fitly framed together, groweth into an Holy Temple in the Lord; but, wherever his place and whatever his work, he is building for God and working with God. God has chosen to work by him, and cannot, without abandoning His eternal plan, do without him; and when, in all its final glory, the building stands complete, each workman shall, in beholding its perfection, trace the living stones which his hands have shaped for it and placed in it; and—how could it be otherwise?—he shall share in the glory, as he has shared in the toil! The Divine Architect of the Ages condescends to choose human beings to carry out His thought and plan, according to the pattern shewed in the Mount; and so, reverently, let it be said, God waits for man's co-operation in His temple-building!

We turn to consider, a little more in detail, the *agricultural* figure: "Ye are God's husbandry," *i.e.*, the product of God's tillage. But Paul says just before, "I have planted, Apollos watered, but God gave the increase." All our labor of ploughing, sowing, reaping, would yield no crop if He did not give soil and seed, sunshine, dew, and rain. Equally true is it, that all these gifts of God could produce no harvest, without human hands to till the soil and sow the seed, to put in the sickle and gather in the sheaves. God's harvest hangs on your toil and mine: it is the union of the divine and human husbandmen that gives the crop!

Yes, the field is the world, and the "good seed" is not only "the Word of God," but it is also "*the children of the Kingdom.*" And for a double reason. If the good seed of the Word of God is sown and scattered at all, the children of the Kingdom must be the sowers; and if the blessed harvest of souls is ever to be reaped, the children of the Kingdom must sow not only the Word, but themselves, in the soil of society! And so they of whom the world is not worthy, and of whom it contemptuously says that they "bury themselves out of sight among the heathen," do indeed "*bury* themselves," because seed never sprouts until it is buried in the soil! Like their Master, they dread most of all to abide alone, and, like Him, shrink not from Gethsemane and Golgotha, so that, dying, they may no longer abide alone, but dying, live, and, living, bring forth much fruit. And, because there are some who, as God's good seed, are buried for His sake, this missionary age has its harvest-fields which give both seed for the sower and bread for the eater. THE FIELD

IS THE WORLD ! * That, only, bounds missionary activity; and who dares remove the ancient land-marks which the Lord Himself hath set up ! The field is world-wide; we must not narrow it down within a smaller circumference, nor select any portion of it as the exclusive or favorite spot for our tillage.

Our Lord's figures of speech never veil the sense. His illustrations illustrate. They are windows that let in the light upon the inmost recesses of His doctrine, and we may walk safely so that our feet do not stumble. We have seen windows whose elaborate carved frame-work and stained glass patch-work seemed ingeniously devised to shut out light. But, when our Lord sets a window in the structure of His discourse, light pours through it unhindered, as through transparent panes.

This metaphor needs no explanation. "The field is the world." What object more common and familiar to the eye of His hearers than a field at some stage of tillage ! And, when He would point disciples to the sphere of their work for God and for souls, He stretches His hands toward the cardinal points of the compass and says, "*the world.*" Wherever on this globe man is, there is the soil for our sowing; and so long as man is found on earth, so long is this holy husbandry to go on, until no part is left desert, or unchanged

* Matt. xiii. 38.

into the garden of the Lord. What a conception of work for and with God! A field that has no limits of territory but the space of the habitable earth, and a labor that has no limits of duration but the Gospel age itself! Wherever there is a human creature, and so long as the race survives, the work goes on.

The field is the world. *Vast* indeed is this field. Probably two-thirds of the entire area of the solid surface of the globe is inhabited, and in some parts densely; the aggregate population of the earth is close to 1,500,000,000, a number too large to be easily comprehended. A pendulum whose arc measures a second would take *fifty years*, day and night, to mark so many seconds; in other words, it would take half a century, day and night, for this immense multitude to pass by a given point at the rate of one every second. And, in that august procession, we should find but *one in fifty* a member of any Protestant communion, and but *one in two hundred and fifty thousand* a missionary from Protestant churches to heathen lands; and so the field lies yet waiting for the workmen: the larger part of it has yet to be broken up with plough and harrow and sown with the good seed.

The field is not only vast, but it is one of *ever-recurring need.* We cannot till any field for all time to come. Every spring brings the sowing-time and every autumn the reaping-time, so that

every new season presents a new field for the
plough and the sickle. And it is so with the field
of the world. Three times in a century, the population of our globe gives place to a new generation; so that if to-day the whole world were
evangelized, within thirty years a new generation
would present a new need of the Gospel message.
And hence the greater demand for constant, persistent, and world-wide missions: the more this
work is neglected, and the longer, the more it gets
beyond us: the thicker and ranker the vile growths
become which must be uprooted to make room
for the Gospel. Whereas, if the Church of Christ
should once overtake the wants of one generation,
it would be comparatively easy to *keep* the ground
clear and occupy the entire field in the generations
to come. We thus owe a double debt, first to a
world lying in sin, to sow it in every part with
the seed of the kingdom; and secondly, to the
Church of the generations to come, to prepare the
way for the successful work of those who are to
follow after us.

Every nobler motive combines to inspire prompt
and energetic world-husbandry. Delay compli-
cates the problem and duplicates the task. Once
let the Gospel message be proclaimed to every
living creature, and henceforth there has been one
complete sowing of the whole field; everywhere
harvests begin to appear, and their yield supplies
additional seed for another sowing. Once to meet

the needs of the race is to render comparatively
easy the supply of recurring need.

But again, every field has its *crises*. When the
sowing time comes, the seed must be put in the
furrows—it is *now* or *never*. When the harvest
ripens, the sickle must be immediately put at work ;
again it is now or never—ripeness borders on rot-
tenness, and the crop which is not reaped is soon
not worth reaping. So the world-field presents its
crises. When the soil lies fallow and waits for the
sower, if he goes not forth with his seed, he loses
his chance; and, when the fields are white with
harvest, to wait is to forfeit both his chance and
his crop. And, in some part of the wide field, it
is *always* a crisis : either the sower or the reaper
is in demand, and sometimes both, for sometimes
God's harvests come so fast that the ploughman
overtakes the reaper, and the treader of grapes him
that soweth the seed.

Our Lord, whose apt metaphor thus teaches us
so many lessons about the *field*, is not less instructive as to the *seed*. It is a curious fact that, as
already intimated, in the great chapter of the kingdom, Matthew xiii., two parables out of the seven,
and these the first two, present the same *field*, the
world, but not the same *seed*. In the former
parable the " seed is the *Word of God* " *—in the
latter, " the good seed are the *children of the Kingdom*." † In this difference lies a sublime lesson.

* Luke viii. 11.   † Matt. xiii. 38.

God sows His field with two kinds of seed: His *Word* and His *disciples.* It is the Bible with the believer behind it—the Gospel of salvation, with a gospeller, a saved soul, to proclaim it; the message of life, borne by the living messenger, the Word of God with the witness of God. Both the truth as it is in Jesus and the renewed soul as he is in Jesus are necessary in this seed-sowing of the kingdom.

But, more than this, there is a *connection* between these two parables and these two sorts of seed. At the first sowing, the Son of man Himself was the sower, and the seed was the Word of God; but, when that Word sprang up and yielded fruit, that fruit was not a new message or word from God, but a *believer.* And thus we sow the Gospel, and the crop is a crop of *souls;* we get from that first sowing of the Word of God a harvest of the children of the kingdom, who, in turn, become seed for a new crop of believers. Here is the great hope of missions, and the real secret of God's plan. Were we to bear the seed of the Gospel at once into all the world, and faithfully sow it, there would be a crop of *converts* throughout the world, who, in their turn, would become God's good seed, to sow the regions beyond. It is a very remarkable fact that the *native converts,* in every land where missions have been established, have within one generation furnished, on the average, five times as many evangelists, teachers, and native helpers as the original missionary force. To-day, out of somewhat more than 40,000, that represent the total force of the workers in mission lands, over *thirty-five thousand* have been raised on the spot, as the crop of missionary labor. In China, India, Africa, the South Seas, by far the bulk of all evangelists are converted natives. And, if the Church could be aroused to such holy effort as would once insure the sowing of the whole world-field, within fifty years the number of native converts that would take up the work of missions among their own countrymen might make unnecessary all foreign missions in the Church. Christian nations might speedily be left free to turn their attention to developing the life and power of the Church within their own borders, and to evangelize their own territory.

Hence again appear the crime and folly of this long delay. Not only is the field left without the seed of God; not only does the crisis of opportunity pass, and generation after generation perish without God; but we are losing crop after crop that would furnish seed for the sower—nay, would *sow itself*, and soon make our further work almost needless. A land like Japan or China or India, thoroughly occupied for Christ, *once sown in all its extent with the Gospel*, would be changed from barrenness to fertility, and be turned into a field of supply, like some vast stretch of waste land which has been overgrown with tangled thickets, prolific thistles, rankest weeds, and poisonous creepers, transformed not only into a fruitful meadow, but into a gigantic *seed-farm*, from which all the supplies for future sowers might be drawn !

It would be a mistake not to call attention to yet another of those marvellous analogies suggested by this figure, used by our Lord.   No crop is perfectly developed or ripe until its "seed is in itself after its kind."   Compare again these twin. parables.   The former presents four kinds of soil; in the first, the seed gets no *hold*, but is borne away by birds of the air.   In the second, the seed gets no *root*, and soon withers away.   In the third, it gets hold and root, but no *room ;* the soil is preoccupied with germs, and they crowd the good seed: the consequence is that, while it lives and grows, it never attains perfection.   A long thin blade shoots up, but it has no ear, and so no full-grown corn in the ear.   It has in itself no *seed of propagation* and no power of reproduction : there may be straw, but not grain—there is root and blade, but no ear or kernel.

What is that but the professed disciple who does not believe, or takes no part in missions !   It would perhaps be harsh and uncharitable to say that such are not believers ; but, if so, they are so choked with cares of this world, deceitfulness of riches and lust of other things, that they bring no fruit to perfection.   Life everywhere, in plant and animal, shows its maturity and perfection by the

power to beget other life like itself. And hence
the disciple that does not *make* disciples, the
Christian that has no passion for souls and no
power to win souls, who has no work for Christ,
who is not himself a seed of God to drop into the
soil and yield a crop of other holy lives, should
candidly ask whether indeed he is himself a child
of God? The new life of God in man is never
fully developed until it becomes life-producing,
life-begetting. Where there is no seed, there is
probably no genuine divine plant.

No more alarming sign exists in the Church of
to-day than this, that so small a part of our church-
members ever convert a soul to God! With all
our so-called refinement, education, culture, social
influence, the Church has but few who are at
work for souls, and who will at last bring in arm-
fuls of sheaves.

It is a curious fact in botany, that we may
cultivate a plant until we destroy the ovaries or
seed-vessels, so that the plant can no longer prop-
agate itself. The wild rose, for example, has a
fully developed ovary, but the beautiful double
rose, full of leaves and beauty, the crown of horti-
culture, reveals no seed-vessel. We find an an-
alogous fact in the world of mankind. There is
a sort of culture which is fatal to service. It
develops a fine mind, a ready tongue, graceful
manners, a beautiful person, but there is no love
of souls, no power to win them—no holy self-

propagating seed of new lives. And, while the Church perhaps never stood so high as now in wealth, in culture, in commanding worldly influence, it is only here and there one blade in God's harvest-field that bears the ear swelling with the full, ripe corn that God can use to sow His field, and bring thirty, sixty, an hundred fold returns!

We seem more solicitous about large crops and thick crops, than about *heavy* crops. To have a great church-roll of cultured, distinguished people, to boast of numbers, social standing, riches, intellect, is our snare. The beloved Moravians that lead the van of the missionary host have no pride of numbers, and care only for fruitfulness in service; and the genius of Herrnhut finds utterance in their Litany: *"From the unhappy desire of becoming great*, gracious Lord and God, PRESERVE US!"

The attentive student of the Word of God will observe a progress of doctrine—an unfolding of the Divine purpose as to missions. The Old Testament type of piety emphasizes the *preservation and conservation* of truth and goodness. The New Testament lays stress rather upon the *promulgation and propagation* of the Gospel. To the prophets of old, the body of believers was a *flock* to be shepherded, and the sacred courts, a *fold* for their in-gathering. But, when Christ begins to reveal to His disciples the genius of the NEW AGE,

He says, " Follow me and I will make you *fishers
of men*." In this one phrase, "fishers of men,"
there lies a little world of suggestion. While a fold
suggests the Church, and the sheep, the disciples,
and the shepherd, the pastor and teacher ; the lake
or sea suggests the world ; the fish, the unevangel-
ized and unsaved ; and the net, the means of grace
by which they are to be surrounded, and, in a
blessed sense, ensnared, or taken captive ; and the
fisher stands for the *evangelist* who goes to tell the
Gospel story to those who know it not. Sheep
are not to be *caught*, but *fed :* fish are not to be
fed, but, first of all, caught. In the New Dispensation, whatever prophetic office the minister
of Christ is to fulfil in shepherding the lambs and
feeding the sheep, he is never to forget that the
more important office, certainly the more emphatic
function, is that of the *evangelist*. He is to look
for his *field*, therefore, not in the church, alone, or
mainly : the *"field is the world"*; and—as we shall
have occasion often to repeat—believers, far from
being merely plants in the Lord's garden, to be
tended by Him, absorbing His thought and care,
are themselves the "seed of the Kingdom," to be
sown in that broad field of the world, as the germs
of a new harvest for God. How many intelligent
disciples there are, who have not yet gotten from
the Old Testament into the New ! They still think
of themselves simply as the *objects* of pastoral care.
They are the Lord's frail plants, and not a few of

them are very frail and need a great deal of tend-
ing. The pastor must move constantly about
among them, digging about their roots, gathering
out the stones, pulling up the weeds, watering
them, shielding them from too much sunshine,
plucking away their dead leaves, pruning away
their dead twigs, tying up their drooping stems
against a support, to prevent them from falling
altogether prostrate. There are thousands of these
sickly plants, that never grow healthy and strong
—in fact, the very means taken to remedy their
feebleness keeps them sickly and dependent. And
what is the result? Our pastors cannot be evangelists: it takes so much time and thought to care
for the insiders that they have neither time nor
strength to care for outsiders. The minister of
Christ is resolved—we had almost said *dissolved*—
into the mere *shepherd*, and ceases to be in any
large sense a *fisher of men*.

Beneath the very shadow of our church-spires in
our great cities, the " great majority " lies, almost
utterly neglected. The " bitter cry of outcast
London " arises unheard and unheeded in the ears
of hundreds of church members, who imagine that
they have done their duty when they have built
churches, hired ministers, and then themselves
helped to fill the churches and claim the ministers
as their own hired servants! And if, in addition
to this, they ring a church-bell and announce public
worship, and provide preaching, they are not to

blame if the great unwashed majority stay away and perish in dirt and sin !

The evil we are exposing and rebuking is a radical one—so deep-seated that to uproot it would overturn the very soil of society. Church members selfishly claim the minister, and even the evangelist. It has long been with the maturest disciples a question whether, in our Church economy, the place of the evangelist has not been perverted. Here, in our great cities, from one-half to two-thirds of the poorer workmen live in neglect of the Gospel. If there be any class of home heathen that has a claim on the evangelist's labors, it is those who, in "highways and hedges," do not yet "come in." It is to them that our Lord says, *"Go ye."* And yet, when evangelists come into our centres of population, instead of going down among these lost souls for whom nobody seems to care, they labor for the most part in our churches, where the people are often overfed and overfat on their fare. Nay, to assure the more éclat and enthusiasm of numbers, from three to twenty churches will unite, and call an evangelist to labor among them ; and then Christians will crowd the places of assembly so that those who are not habitual hearers would find but little room if they came.

That much good is done by these devoted men, who even in this fashion labor as evangelists, we are not disposed to deny. But whether this is the normal sphere for evangelistic work, we more than doubt. During thirty years of pulpit and pastoral labor, my own mind has been more and more impressed with the conviction that, instead of the Church's needing the labor of an evangelist to supplement that of the faithful pastor among his own membership, the pastor needs to reach beyond his own flock and be more than a shepherd, a "fisher of men," casting his net into the wider sea of the world; and that, instead of encouraging his people to think of themselves as plants to be tilled, he is to instruct them, in God's name, that they are themselves to be fellow-helpers with him in sowing the whole world with the Gospel, and planting this wide field with believers. Nothing needs to be emphasized more, in this Laodicean age, than this, that the Church is not the "*field*," but the "*force*"; not the object of the labors of God's husbandmen, but itself the body of laborers who are to be thrust forth into the field, which is the world. Until this is understood and felt, and practiced upon—until, from the sphere of dim and distant idealization, it passes into prompt and practical realization, we shall have no new era of world-wide missions!

The whole Church of God should be a great body of evangelists; and, instead of first absorbing pastor after pastor, and then, like insatiate sponges, demanding the ministrations of evangelists besides, church-members should say to their minister: "Let us alone, and go after the lost; when we need you, we will send for you or come to you; but we leave you free to seek the unsaved, and whatever we can do to help you, we are ready to do. Be our leader and we will follow—lead us out into the world-field and set us at work—lead us out into the battle-field and set us fighting." What a new epoch will dawn on the Church and on the world when disciples are ready, as soon as they have found Jesus, to leave even His immediate presence and go, like Andrew and Philip, to find a Peter and a Nathanael and bring them to Jesus !

We have not touched the depths of this great truth, even yet. Every witness for God who goes forth to sow the seed, and himself *become* seed for this harvest, prepares for not one crop alone, but many successive crops. And remember our Lord's singular words : " Thirty, sixty, an hundred fold." It is of the nature of crops that they are *cumulative* —successive harvests advance, not by arithmetical, only, but by geometrical, progression. Each crop yields seed for the next, and every seed brings forth an ear, with seed in the ear. A single seed thus yields a blade, whose ear furnishes thirty fold ; and so the second crop is nine hundred fold, the third crop nearly thirty thousand fold, and the fourth crop nearly a *million* fold, upon the seed first sown.

Let the seed and its harvest become to us God's own parable of missions. To measure the fruit of one life, or even of one witnessing word or godly

deed, we must stand at the end of all things, when
the sheaves of the last harvest are garnered.   The
immediate results of a life of labor for God often
seem small; but results which are effects, become
in their turn new causes for new effects, and so the
harvest multiplies, with a rapidity so marvellous,
that the ultimate outcome of a single life staggers
not only faith, but imagination itself!   Saul the
persecutor voluntarily turned from a tempting
worldly career to become Paul, the disciple of the
Nazarene and the apostle of the Gentiles.   Not
to speak of the glory of his attainments, who
became more and more radiant with godlikeness
"as he neared the perihelion point," look at his
service as a preacher, a winner of souls, an organ-
izer of churches, a writer of epistles ; and remember
that the influence of his character, life, and writings is growing with every new year of Christian
history !

An example may help us to form some slight
conception of the possible fruit of one godly missionary life.   In darkest Africa, in Chitambo's village in Ilala, beneath a moula tree, lies buried the
heart of that great missionary explorer, of whom
Dr. Blaikie aptly says, that the Romans would
have surnamed him Livingstone *Africanus*.   In
his rude grass hut he was found, at four o'clock
in the morning, not in bed, but kneeling at the
bedside, his head buried in his hands, and both
buried in the pillow.   Without attendant or com-

panion, on this furthest journey, he had, like
Enoch, been translated while walking with God
along the pathway of prayer. But, long before his
pulseless heart had been deposited beneath that
moula tree, that heart had been *buried in Africa*
for Africa's redemption. And, for all time to
come, it will be the germ and seed of other holy
lives, both among the sable sons of that dark
continent and among those who dwell in other
climes.

To-day there is one who walks among princes,
on whose breast flash the shining medals of high
honor, whose praise is in every mouth, and whose
well-earned rewards fall about him like a rain of
gems—one whom History already crowns as
Africa's great explorer—whom we hope History
may on her future scroll record as Africa's greater
emancipator.

Henry M. Stanley is himself but one fruit of '
that buried heart at Ilala. It was, according to
his own confession, those four months and four
days, spent in the same tent or boat with David
Livingstone, which made of that intrepid explorer
a new man. Mr. E. D. Young had already said
of that lowly spinner of Blantyre, " He was the
best man I ever knew." But, when Stanley sought
to pay *his* tribute to that humble missionary, he
could find no words adequate, except Pilate's confession as to his divine Master, "*I find no fault
in this man !*" Reviewing these months of com-

panionship with Livingstone, he says: "My days seem to have been spent in an Elysian field;" and, when the parting hour came, and he sought by one long, last look to fix those blessed features upon his memory, Stanley found that he could see but dimly. The hero of a hundred battles, with nerves of steel, was not a stranger to tears when he turned away from the man who was the greatest blessing and benefactor of his life. Already had his sceptical habits of mind found their overwhelming refuting argument in that saintly life whose every lineament was vocal with godliness.

Two scenes in England's famous Abbey have already become historic. One was April 18, 1874, when, in the centre of the nave, the dust of Africa's great hero was laid to rest; and when Stanley lifted his hand from the pall of his great friend, to lay it upon his unfinished work, and that same year start from Zanzibar to explore Equatoria. And the other scene was July 12, 1890, when, as he led his bride to the altar, the marriage procession halted to lay one more tribute on Livingstone's grave in token of the debt which could never be paid! And yet Henry M. Stanley is but one fruit of that buried heart. Who shall say what harvests, world-wide and enduring as eternity, shall yet wave, as the product of the seed that was sown by David Livingstone in the soil of Africa, when he "buried himself" in the Dark Continent!

II. We are also represented as being brought, in the work of missions, into close *fellowship with Christ.*

The language used by Paul, and already quoted, is extraordinary. Let us hear again his words : " Who now rejoice in my sufferings for you and fill up that which is behind of the afflictions of Christ in my flesh for His body's sake, which is the Church, whereof I am made a minister."

Such language is startling : it suggests a sort of incompleteness in the sufferings of Christ, a lack which only the disciple can fill. To understand this, we must remember that the redemptive work advances to completeness by *successive stages.* When our Saviour, on the cross, said, " It is finished," " *atoning death* " was complete. When He rose from the dead, *justifying* work was complete. When He sent the Holy Spirit, the *applying* agency was complete.

But one more step must be taken. The cross, the rent tomb, the coming Spirit, needed a proclaiming *voice,* to tell of Him who was delivered for our offences and rose for our justification ; and to be the mouth of the inspiring Spirit. Three links there were in this golden chain by which man and God are to be reunited. There was the link which the cross supplied in the place of a broken link of *Law;* there was the link that the Resurrection supplied, in place of a broken link of *Life;* there was the link which the Holy Spirit supplied in place of a broken link of *Love;* but still the chain did not reach to man. It was one link short. How was the work of Christ on the cross and in His rising—how was the power of the Spirit in His coming, to lay hold on men! Hear this same Paul: "Whosoever shall call on the name of the Lord shall be saved. How, then, shall they call on Him in whom they have not believed? And how shall they believe in Him of whom they have not heard? And how shall they hear without a preacher? And how shall they preach except they be sent?"* Give us the Church, moved by passion for souls, sending forth the herald and witness—give us the herald and witness, proclaiming everywhere the good news; then we have men hearing, hearers believing, believers calling, and being saved.

Will any one tell us how, without this last link, the other three are to reach mankind with saving power? Is the blood-stained cross to plant itself on every hill and in every valley, and then the dumb Tree of Curse to speak to men of Him who on that cross bore their sins? Is the sepulchre in the garden to transport itself into the regions beyond, and there repeat the awful scene that made angels rejoice and demons turn pale and soldier guards become as dead men? How is the Holy Spirit to find utterance for these great truths of salvation, *except through believers?*

* Rom. x. 14, 15.

Paul was neither extravagant nor irreverent; yes, something remains, after Christ's finished atoning passion and justifying work,—after even the Spirit's descent,—to *"fill up that which is behind."* A preacher, a witness, who is cleansed by the blood, justified by the life of Christ, renewed by the Spirit, is needful, is necessary, if all this stupendous display of grace is to reach the unsaved soul. The believer is the missing link—add this, and God the Father, Son, Holy Ghost, brought into close contact with the lost, can apply the blood, the Word, the regenerating power. But, while this last link is lacking, what is to secure the needful contact and connection?

There is something awful and overpowering about this truth. Yet it is not too high to be apprehended. I have been wont as a pastor, like many of my brethren, to seek, in every case of conversion, to trace the human link by which the new soul was united to God. I have never yet found *one case* where some human agency had not been used by God. Some godly father or mother, sister or brother, Sunday-school teacher, pastor, evangelist; perhaps a stray word dropped by the way, a simple invitation to a church service or a prayer-meeting, a tract or book slipped into the hand—in some cases, nothing more than a *tear* that told of deep fountains of feeling, or an earnest *look* in which the soul found a voice; but always a *human soul* somehow coming between God and

another soul and filling up that which would otherwise be lacking.

We are not prepared to say that this rule is so
universal as to be without an exception. Missionaries tell strange tales of souls prepared, like Cornelius, for the visit of the preacher, before he
came ; or led by some stray copy of a fragment of
the New Testament, to call on the unknown God.
But, even here, who can tell what human agency,
that can no longer be *traced*, has left its footsteps
on heathen soil—may this not be the springing up
of seed, sown in darkness, by some hand now
again turned to dust in the grave ? And is not
the very Bible itself the work of man, though it be
the Word of God ? However many exceptions
there may be, even exceptions prove the rule, and
the rule is that, without the agency of believers,
unbelievers are not made believers. A saved soul
always comes in to be the means by which sinners
are turned to saints.

It is the old story of rescue repeated on a more
august scale of application. God's ladder will not
reach the lost in this House of Doom unless *you
add your own length to the ladder!* And so, as we
are co-workers with the Father, we are co-sufferers
with the Son. His cross is dumb, His tomb is
dumb, until we give to them a voice. We are to
tell men how He died, and rose. Even the Word
of God needs a human witness. If we ask the
Ethiopian eunuch who is intently reading the

Messianic poem of Isaiah, " Understandest thou
what thou readest ? " he answers : " How can I,
except some man should guide me ? Of whom
speaketh the prophet this, of himself or of some
other man ? " And thus, even to those who have
the Word of God, there is needed one who has
learned, by experience, to interpret that Word to
others.

Paul uses a phrase which is itself an interpreta-
tion of his meaning : " For His *body's sake,* which
is the Church." In a body, all is mutual dependence and interdependence. " The eye cannot say
unto the hand, I have no need of thee ; nor again
the head to the feet, I have no need of you ;"
" nay, much more, those members of the body
which seem to be more feeble are necessary." *
Here is the Divine parable of the Body of Christ.
That body is one with many members, and all,
however feeble, uncomely, less honorable, are
necessary, if not to vitality, at least to vigor. The
hand depends on the feet, and both, on the eyes
and ears. Nay, even the *head* depends on the
activity of the members over which it presides.
If the head wills to go—how can it unless the legs
and feet bear it elsewhere—or, if it would have
some work done which the brain devises, how,
unless the hands produce what we call handi-
work ? We have an exalted " Head "—He might
have been divinely independent of us ; but, when

* I. Cor. xii. 22.

He chose to be *Head* and take the Church for His *body*, He chose also to depend on the co-operation of the humblest member. Henceforth, even the *Head* cannot say to the feet—the highest to the lowest—"I have no need of you!"

Now, whenever believers neglect souls, and, for the sake of their own indolence and indulgence, leave the lost to die unsaved and unwarned, there is *schism in the body*—σχισμα,—rent, division. The head yearns to reach out and save, but the great nerves no longer act. It is as though a sharp blade had cut through the spinal cord, and motion, if not sensation, is gone; the muscles and sinews no longer respond to the will, and, in sight of the lost, the body stands inactive.

This universal evangelism is thus necessary alike to accomplish the will of God, overtake the wants of the world, and energize and exercise the life of the Church. It is the one thing needful from any and every point of view. If missions languish, in so far God and man part company, the human race sinks lower in vice, crime, and sin, and the Church runs the risk, not of apathy only, but of *apostasy*.

Everything else depends on the health, strength, growth of the Body of Christ. As soon as missions fall into neglect, that body becomes enfeebled; and when any part of the body is inactive the whole body is more or less crippled, if not paralyzed. No truth is more enforced in the Word than the *unity* of the Body of Christ.* We are taught that both development and activity depend on the whole body's working together. Both edification and evangelization demand that "the whole body, fitly joined together and compacted by that which every joint supplieth, according to the effectual working in the measure of every part, maketh increase of the body unto the edifying of itself in love." †

As Mr. Hudson Taylor well says, one may stand near a burning house or sinking ship and yearn to save those who are in danger of death; but by no possibility can the outstretched arms reach one that is a yard and a half away, unless the legs and feet carry the whole body forward to the scene of action. It is comparatively in vain that a few members of the Church, which is Christ's Body, seek to be heroic in self-sacrifice for the lost, and to uplift and redeem heathen and pagan peoples, while the Church as a whole is idle and indifferent. The best effort is both restrained and restricted, and there can be no large outreach, no strong uplift; the most consecrated missionary band finds, in an apathetic Church at home, a hindrance more fatal to success than the most violent opposition where Satan's strongholds stand.

Never yet—certainly not since the apostolic age—has the whole body moved together in the

* Rom. xii. ; I. Cor. xii. ; Eph. iv.
† Ephesians iv. 16.

direction of missions. Whatever reaching out
there may have been on the part of some of the
more active and vigorous members, the body, as
such, moves very slowly, if indeed it is not standing still. The Christian Church has volume of
voice enough to make the whole earth hear the
Gospel message, if the whole capacity of that voice
were but used; and if the whole energy of that
body were once put forth the results would be
astounding.

Wherever there is a true passion for souls and
a will to co-operate with God, no believer can be
kept idle by any felt incapacity, or by the iron
bonds of "circumstances." Tabitha may have
been a bed-ridden cripple, to whom nothing was
left as a means of serving but her *hands.* But she
could hold a needle, and that needle was the angel
of God to the poor orphans and widows of Joppa,
and has been the suggestion of Dorcas societies
ever since.

There is in Matthew x. 41 a remarkable word
of promise: "He that receiveth a prophet in the
name of a prophet shall receive a prophet's reward." To the Jew the prophet outranked both
priest and king—because, while *they* represented
man before God, *he*, the prophet, represented God
to man, the medium of divine communication.
Hence a prophet's reward was regarded as highest.
And it is noticeable that the only two human
beings ever translated without death were Enoch

and Elijah, two prophets. Our Lord says that to *receive* a prophet for his office' sake is to receive a *prophet's reward*, *i.e.*, to rank as a prophet, and share his recompense. This is a wonderful unfolding of God's method of administering rewards. But there is a divine philosophy in it. A prophet, however charged with a divine message and the Divine Spirit, is but a man—compassed about with human infirmities and limitations. He has but the voice, the strength, the power, the life, of one man. You are not a prophet, but suppose you do, and can do, no more than *make that prophet a greater power.* You can welcome him to your home with a generous hospitality; your board feeds his hunger and quenches his thirst; your bed rests him when weary, your sympathy cheers him when despondent; your love and kindly ministry put new vigor in his frame, new light in his eye, new force in his voice, new courage in his heart. He feels stronger and lives longer because you have been to him a source of help and hope. Have you not really shared his work, and is it not meet that you share his reward?

We may borrow from the two Testaments favorite forms of figure, given to illustrate God's thought; the trumpet in the Old, the lamp-stand in the New. What is a trumpet but a mere means of adding volume to the voice, so that he who, otherwise, could reach but a few hundreds, may now speak with power to hundreds of thousands?

What is a lamp-stand but an arrangement for raising a burning lamp so that its ray may pierce the
darkness more effectually, by being lifted above
obstructions ?

The body of believers constitutes a trumpet, to
give to the voice of the preacher penetrating power
—a lamp-stand, to lift the light of testimony so
that it may shine farther.   And, as every atom of
the trumpet or lamp-stand contributes to the result,
so every true believer helps to make the Gospel
message and the Gospel witness sound louder and
reach the farther.   The dumb man may thus help
the speech of others to be heard, and the most
obscure disciple help to lift others to a higher level
of service.   And so, " if there be first a willing
mind it is accepted according to that a man hath,
and not according to that he hath not."   Nothing
can prevent you from being, if you will, a missionary, a prophet, a burning and shining light—
in God's eyes, you are what, with all your heart,
you *will to be;* and the work you will to do, but
cannot, is the work which to Him you do and for
which you are rewarded.

An example from history may help to make this
plain.   While Livingstone was in Africa, a Mrs.
McRobert of Scotland, unable in person to share
his toils, sought prayerfully to help his labors
to greater effectiveness.   She had saved twelve
pounds, and gave her consecrated offering to him
that he might hire a native African as a body-

servant. This good woman received God's prophet in the name of a prophet. She sought to promote his comfort, spare him needless toil and the exhaustion and exposure that might bring a fatal strain to mind and body amid African wilds. Livingstone used the gift to hire the faithful Mebalwe; and, when at Mabotsa, a lion seized Livingstone by the shoulder, tore his flesh and crushed his bone, there seemed no hope for his life except God should work a miracle. While that beast's paw was on his head, Mebalwe, that native teacher, diverted the lion's attention from his master to himself and risked, as he nearly lost, his own life, to save that of Livingstone. How little did that humble Scotch woman foresee that her twelve pounds would indirectly be blessed to the prolonging of that priceless life for the toils and triumphs of thirty more years! And who shall dare to say that Mrs. McRobert was not, in God's eyes, a sharer in the wonderful work which he was spared to do in opening Equatoria? Who shall presume to say that she who received a prophet for his office's sake, and after her manner and means helped him in his work after a godly sort, is not a sharer also in his reward? That twelve pounds made Mrs. McRobert joint owner in those thirty years, with all their glorious fruit. Through David Livingstone she lived and wrought among Africa's sable children.

Ah, ye who live at home and sigh for larger

service—ye whose are the silver and the gold,
and the rich jewels of the cradle—what if you,
who cannot yourselves *go*, would *send!*   What if
the fruit of your grounds, and brains, and the
more sacred fruit of your bodies, were given to
God!   How many large gifts would fill missionary
treasuries to overflowing and make missionary
hearts swell with even fuller hope and joy!   How
many small gifts, bestowed out of the abundance
of poverty, with self-sacrifice and prayer, like seed
steeped in tears, God would use as He knows
how, as the germs of a great harvest!   How
many children, begotten in prayer, filled with the
Holy Ghost even from the womb, would be sent
forth from homes that had nothing else to give,
and make parents partakers in the prophet's work
and reward, by the giving of Samuels and Johns
and Timothys to the work!

God invites us all to join Him in the work of
missions.   And once again, with solemn intensity
of emphatic conviction, I record the growing, life-
long conviction, that the supreme charm of missions is that it represents God's own march through
history; and that, therefore, he who is most enamored and engrossed of this work of giving the
Gospel to the destitute millions of the race, is most
closely in link with God and in line with His
march.   There are modern Enochs and Elijahs
whose close walk with God invites translation : they
are the Careys, the Morrisons, the Livingstones,

the Hanningtons, the Judsons, the Williamses, the Hunts, the Pattesons, whose absorbing passion is Christ and He alone—and who in the sublime work of world-wide witness join the Triune God in winning the world for Immanuel.

This explains the promise of Christ's personal presence with the witnessing host. The last command, " Go ye into all the world," is very emphatic, but not less marked are the preface and the conclusion between which it stands. Before it is the declaration: "All power is given unto me in heaven and in earth ;" after it, the prophecy and promise : " Lo I am with you alway, even unto the end of the age." By no accident is it that the perpetual command, " Go ye—make disciples of all nations," is placed between this declaration and this promise : they are the buttresses of adamant by which that commission is supported. In that word, " Therefore," all the logic of missions is centred. Our Lord says, " Because the All-Power is mine, and my All-Presence is yours, all the days, even to the end of the age, THERE-FORE go ye into all the world," etc. And, so far and so fast as the Church obeys, and goes everywhere and to every creature with the Gospel message, the All-Power will be manifested and the All-Presence enjoyed !

We need then to think of Christian missions as pre-eminently God's work—and ours, because it is God's and we are His and workers together

with Him, permitted to share this supreme privilege. The power and energy are not therefore
human, but divine, and in any and every exigency
we have but to appeal to Him, get new courage
and confidence in the secret place of prayer; and,
because His trumpet never sounds retreat, we
shall never take a step backward, but always forward; and even those steps which seem backward,
if we are following Him, are really advances, as
waves recede only to rise to a higher flood-mark.

III. Our survey would be very incomplete
without at least a glance at the believer's *co-operation with the Holy Spirit.* The Spirit was especially
promised as Christ's witness. " He shall *testify* of
me," and will " guide you into all truth "; for " He
shall not speak of Himself, but whatsoever He shall
hear that shall He speak "; and " He will shew
you things to come." " He shall glorify me; for
He shall receive of mine and shall shew it unto
you." This language is explicit.* The peculiar
office of the Holy Ghost is *testimony to Christ ;*
and, like any other true witness, He does not
speak of Himself, testify to Himself, or glorify
Himself. He brings Christ forward into prominence—His person and character, His obedient
life and vicarious death, His resurrection, ascension, and second coming. He testifies to Him,
before He comes, by the prophets He inspired;
then He testifies to Him, when He comes, by the

* John xiv., xv., xvi.

evangelists whom He guided and whose memories
He quickened; and so to each new believer He
continues to open the word and unveil Christ's
blessed person, and in the heart disclose His power
to save and sanctify, and so to witness to Christ
still.

Our Lord says: "And ye also shall bear witness* "; it is in the Greek, the same word as that
applied to the Spirit. In what sense is this *co-
witness* true ?

Of course there was a special sense in which
those early apostles and disciples witnessed to
Christ, because they had from the beginning been
with Him, and could testify to His words and
works, His life and death and resurrection and
ascension. But we have now to do with the wider
question—of the co-witnessing in which all true
believers share; and in its way it is fully as important as the other. First of all, the believer testifies
with the Holy Ghost to the power of Christ, as a
personal and present Saviour. And it is no
irreverence to say that believers can bear witness
to some truths which even the Spirit of God cannot so effectually attest. He can hold up the
Christ of prophecy and the Christ of history—
present Him on the cross and on the throne; and
keep Him before our eyes as the object of admir-
ing, adoring Love. But the Holy Spirit knows
nothing of sin and salvation from sin; and, unlike

* John xv. 25–27 ; Acts v. 32.

Christ, having never taken upon him our nature, knows nothing of our infirmities and temptations as one who has suffered in the flesh. The Holy Spirit, therefore, needs and requires the believer to witness, from personal knowledge, to *the actual work* of Christ *in* the soul, as He Himself witnesses to His work *for* the soul.

We may pass this obvious thought, in order to develop another, far less obvious, but perhaps more important. The Holy Spirit needs believing witnesses as the *channels of His utterances* and the *vehicles of His Power and grace* to unbelieving souls.

When our Lord first brings out clearly the work of the Spirit, He expressly says, " I will pray the Father and He shall give you another Comforter that He may abide with you forever; even the Spirit of Truth, *whom the world cannot receive*, because it seeth Him not, neither knoweth Him; but ye know Him, for He dwelleth with you and shall be in you." *   Paul reminds the Corinthians that the natural man does not receive, and cannot discern, the things of the Spirit of God ;† and that even to the princely intellects of this world the wisdom of God is foolishness.

The remarkable and emphatic testimony of these and kindred passages is that the Holy Spirit, who is perceived and recognized by disciples; who dwells with and abides in them, and is by them

* John xiv. 16, 17.   † I. Cor. ii. 12.

received and known, is not in unbelievers, and is
not by them either perceived or received, and
cannot be. And, yet, we are taught with equal
explicitness that, unless by the Spirit of God men
are convinced of the sin of unbelief, are renewed
in mind and heart and will, are born again from
above, and made new creatures in Christ Jesus,
they cannot enter, or even see, the kingdom of
God. At this paradox many have stumbled. The
Spirit of God must work a saving and radical
change in the natural and carnal man, and yet
such a man is incapable of either receiving the
Spirit or even knowing His nature.

There is but one way to explain this enigma or
resolve this paradox—the Holy Ghost *reaches
ungodly souls through the godly.* He dwells in,
and works through, *believers.* He cannot abide
in a sinful and unbelieving heart, but He can
dwell with him who is of a humble and contrite
spirit and trembleth at the Word of God; and
can use *his* faith and utterance and experience
and witness, to lead unsaved souls to repentance
and faith. Christ said to the woman at the well,
" Whoso drinketh of the water that I shall give
him, it shall be in him a well of water, springing
up into everlasting life." Mark the rapid progress
of thought : first a *draught* of living water received
—then a *well* or spring of water opened and
gushing up within—then a *stream* of water flowing
out. The believer first *drinks*—then becomes a

spring, and then a *channel* for the outflow. And so that woman no sooner drank, than the new spring of life sent out its waters even to the thirsty souls of Sychar. Again, at the Feast of Tabernacles, as the water from Siloam was poured out on the morning sacrifice, Christ cried aloud, "He that believeth on me, out of his belly shall flow rivers of living water—this spake He of the Spirit which they that believe on Him should receive."

Now to what purpose does the spring send forth streams, but to quench the thirst of the needy? Why does the Holy Spirit make the believer a fountain of life, but to flow *through him* to the souls of the dying? Here is the grand mystery of this fellowship with the Holy Ghost: He chooses to employ human vessels and channels for conveying His own power and grace.

If the New Testament be carefully examined, it will be found, in almost if not quite every instance of conversion, that the Holy Spirit *used a believer as His instrument.* Andrew was used to reach Peter; Philip, to reach Nathanael; Philip the Evangelist, to teach the eunuch; even Saul probably got his first impressions from the dying Stephen. Peter became the channel of the Holy Ghost to Cornelius and his kinsmen and friends. Paul and Silas were the vehicles of communication with the Philippian jailer; and, in brief, in the whole work of the Spirit upon unbelieving souls, He appears to have been *dependent upon believers* as media of impression and communication. So far as we know, in all His ordinary workings, human agency is indispensable to the completeness of His operations.

While we carelessly say that the " Spirit of God strives with ungodly men, moves in their hearts, is influencing their conscience and conduct," have we any warrant for affirming that the Holy Ghost in any case dispenses absolutely with this agency of the disciple? or if He ever does, is it not, as we have said, so rare as to constitute an exception?

In the inception of the work in Japan, it is said that the first six converts to the Christian faith were the consequence of picking up a stray copy of a Testament that was found floating in the Bay of Yeddo, and of the inquiry thus aroused; and that, before the first missionary had landed on those shores, the Holy Spirit had led these natives to the knowledge of Christ. But even here, exceptional as was this case, the Gospel narratives which were thus blessed to the conversion of souls were the work of human pens, witnessing to Christ.

The bearing of these thoughts on missions is vitally important. We pray for the Holy Spirit to "descend upon all people," even upon those among whom no laborers have yet gone. How much warrant have we for such prayer? What if no blessing can come to the souls in inland China or interior Africa, in the Soudan and in Thibet, until *believers are there as channels of blessing!* What if this be

our Lord's meaning, that the Gospel must be first
preached as a witness, by a witnessing Church
among all nations, before the end comes! What
if the one condition of the Spirit's descent "on all
flesh" be that God's witnesses must be wherever
"all flesh" is found, to become the medium for
such descending blessing—to call it down, and to
receive, recognize, and convey it when it comes!

Let this very remarkable fact be duly emphasized that, in the whole course of missionary history,
no people have ever been brought to salvation;
and, so far as we know, no individuals have received the Spirit of God, until some one or more
of God's messengers have *been among them*, either
in person or through the products of their pen.
Some wandering evangelist, colporteur, tract dis-
tributor—it may be some simple unlettered disciple—has passed that way; a Bible, a tract, a word
of counsel, a prayer, a testimony has been left behind; and, years after it may be, blessing has come.
But the records of missionary biography and history may be searched in vain, to find a modern
Pentecost without some Peter or Paul, some
Dorcas or Lydia, some Philip or Priscilla, or at
least some obscure human instrumentality, to become a receiving and distributing reservoir for the
water of life!

It is this deep conviction that the Spirit of God
will not accomplish His sacred travail for souls,
until believers are everywhere present as His

human agents, that leads me to press, with persistent exhortation and entreaty, the immediate and world-wide scattering of missionaries. While we concentrate our forces in a few fields we may indeed insure blessing *to those fields*—but we are rendering blessing impossible where there are no laborers. If the Church would but obey her Lord, and take whatever men and means are at her disposal and distribute them over the whole world-field, the most important condition would be supplied for an out-pouring of the Spirit *on all flesh*, because in every part of the habitable earth some of Christ's witnesses would be found!

Such thoughts may well absorb and entrance us. They set the ministry of missions in a new light. Round about the lowliest sphere of work for God, a rainbow bends, like that which curves its sacred bow about His throne. It gilds and glorifies the darkest cloud of trial, and turns even tears of anguish into radiant prisms of promise. In remotest regions beyond,—in inland China or darkest Africa, there may be those who, unknown and unobserved of men, toil hard to teach the ignorant and to save the lost; but there is not one of them all who is not intimately sharing the work of the Blessed Trinity, actually supplying some lacking instrumentality or agency, necessary to fill up to completeness, and carry to success, that divine work. How important even the most obscure worker is, only eternity can show.

The work of witnessing derives its principal
charm from its close *association* with God. When,
in that eleventh chapter of Hebrews—that " West-
minster Abbey of Old Testament Saints,"—Paul
gives examples of the witness-bearers of past ages,
next to Abel, the first martyr, comes *Enoch*, whose
brief record was : "And Enoch walked with God."
All witnessing to God is walking with Him ; and
to bear witness to Him is to have Him bear witness to us, as He did to Enoch, who, before his
translation, "had this testimony that he pleased
God." This is, of itself, the all-sufficient reward
and recompense of our work *for* Him : it is also
work *with* Him, and brings us into close and
conscious fellowship with Him. When we undertake this world-wide witness to Christ, He comes
and walks beside us, and His personal presence
becomes our heaven. And, like Thomas of
Aquino, when offered our choice of a reward for
service, we could answer, *"Non alium nisi Te,
Domine."*

IV.

THE DIVINE SPIRIT OF MISSIONS.

ORD LYTTON called color, "visible music." To study missions and become absorbed in this work, is to find in it the fullest visible expression of the invisible Spirit of God, the incarnation of godliness.

Some motives and impulses belong to a low level, such as those which spring from appetite, avarice, and ambition, the lust of the flesh, the lust of the eyes, and the pride of life. One needs to be scarce more than an animal, at most an intellectual animal, to feel the sway of such aims as belong to our grosser nature.

Rising a little in the scale of motives, we reach a class that belong to a higher level, such as spring from man as a member of the household, of society, of the state, of the human brotherhood. We call these impulses domestic, patriotic, philanthropic. Self-love, if not selfishness, is largely mixed up with these three measures of meal, and leavens the whole lump. No human being who guards self-interest can be indifferent to the purity and harmony of the family, the unity and prosperity of the state, or the progress and welfare of man as man. We are not independent of each other, but dependent members of one body.

To a yet higher level of motive, which few reach, it is now my privilege to point—may I not also say?—lead, my readers. But let us understand, beforehand, that this is an altitude in which the worldly and the carnal nature can no longer breathe freely. Such a height has an atmosphere of its own, too pure, too rare, for sensual, sordid, selfish souls to inspire. And, of those who have climbed to those lofty heights, and there abide, there is but one possible explanation: it is because God hath given them of His Spirit. The spirit of missions is not only *akin* to the Spirit of Christ: it *is* the Spirit of Christ. And we shall now try to find what it is which, in the missionary spirit, constitutes the divine and Christlike element, to which so few really attain.

Our inquiry touches the work of missions at its root: "As a man thinketh in his heart, so is he": out of the heart flow the issues of life. Whatever lack there is in missions as an enterprise is to be traced to something wrong or wanting in the spirit of disciples. And here all new beginnings must themselves begin. Like Elisha, we need to follow the bitter and brackish stream back to its fountains, and cast in the salt at the spring; then all that flows from it will give evidence of new conditions at the fountain head. Let us carefully search, then, the real source of our lack.

The great practical problem, whose solution demands the prayerful and prompt attention of every believer, is this: How may the Church of Christ carry the good tidings round the world, during the lifetime of this generation? For the present generation of the saved to reach the present generation of the unsaved, is the one question of the hour that leaves all others far in the distance. To the solution of that problem in God's own way, the Church, and every member of it, should bring all the brains, heart, conscience, will, money, intelligence, and enterprise at command. To aid, so far as we can, in the accomplishment of this work, it behoves each of us solemnly to give ourselves and our substance, our tongues and our pens, for whatever time may be left us. To this work let me once more earnestly invoke others.

The solving of this problem is not a matter of method, or means; but primarily of a mind and heart and will, that is according to Christ. All machinery, however complete, depends for effectiveness upon its motive-power. Here force is generated. Wheels and levers are but the channels through which power has play; and, however intricate and complicate the mechanical adjustments, there cannot even be motion, much less efficient action, unless and until force is created or applied. The gigantic ordnance-gun, ball, charge, all wait for the spark. And all our best, wisest, most complete methods of mission work

will stand like a motionless machine, until the
Spirit of God becomes in disciples a spirit of missions, and generates spiritual force adequate to
move and to keep moving the wheels of Christian
enterprise.

1. Of course, the *Spirit of Faith* is the secret of
all other Christian attainment. This we assume
as beyond the need of argument. What the root
is to the plant, what the spring is to the stream,
that faith is, to all the beauty and growth and
power of a child of God. Not only in prayer,
but in all our work, "without faith it is impossible
to please Him." We must first of all receive
Christ by believing, and in believing He must
receive us, so that we are His and He is ours, by
the mystic bond of unity. When we are in Him
by faith, and He in us by love, all else becomes
possible; and without Him we can do nothing,
and are nothing.

Taking this as granted, we proceed to ask what
are the real *fruits* of faith, which the true spirit of
missions reveals and ripens in us?

2. We answer, first of all, the *Spirit of Obedience.*
There is no justification for missions that is
either possible or needful, except the plain, explicit
repeated command of Christ. We have our
"marching orders ": that is enough. "Go ye into
all the world, and preach the Gospel to every
creature." That settles the matter, and leaves no
argument or vindication to be added or needed.

The question, " Do missions *pay ?*" is both irrele-
vant and irreverent. It *always* pays to obey
authority, especially when authority is supreme.
And so clear is our Lord's command, that the
process, by which that command can be made of
none effect, would make void the whole Word of
God. Eyes that are so dim as to see no such
duty enjoined on the Church must be blind. And
only in the dark ages, when the very candlestick
of God almost ceased to shine, was the debt of a
Christian to a lost world even *doubted.* Nothing,
to-day, is to the Church its shame and its crime,
as is this, that, since Christ gave this last command, nineteen centuries have struck on the clock
of the ages ; and more than sixty generations have
lived, sinned, suffered, and died, with an aggregate
population from ten to twenty times the present
number of the human race. And yet, with this
positive command standing before us like Christ
Himself, and pointing to the great world-field ;
and with the facts of awful spiritual destitution
staring us in the face, the great bulk of the human
family has perished, and will, in this century, continue to perish, not unsaved only, but unwarned !
For such a state of things, no adequate apology
or excuse is possible.

Our obedience to our Lord's will should be *immediate.* It has been long enough delayed, and
the time is short. We firmly believe, and the conviction enters into the very marrow of our being,

that the disciples of Christ should at once organize efforts and occupy the whole world; that the whole field should be mapped out, and the whole force be massed together; that we should then proceed carefully to divide the field, so that no part should be overlooked; and then to distribute the force so that no part should be unprovided for. This lesson is taught in the miracle of the loaves; the first command of Christ was, "Make the multitude to sit down in companies of fifty and a hundred." That showed the disciples just how many people there were to be fed, and helped them to make sure that each company and each person should have attention, and provision for their needs.

In apostolic days we have this miracle of the loaves translated into action. What were perhaps a thousand disciples, in all, among so many as the world's population? And yet they undertook to "preach the Gospel to every creature." Peter and James went to the "circumcision": James became bishop of the Church in Jerusalem, and looked after Judean Jews. Peter went to the far East, among the Jews of the "elect dispersion," and the peoples among whom they dwelt. John went to Ephesus, the centre of the Diana worship, and the gathering-place of vast multitudes. Paul went westward and travelled over most, if not all, of the countries of Europe, between the Golden Horn and the Straits of Gibraltar. Philip

went down to Samaria, and, if tradition be trustworthy, the eunuch whom he led to Jesus went
further down into Ethiopia and founded the Alex-
andrian Church. And, on this principle of division
of the field and distribution of the force, the
Church, when fewest in numbers and feeblest in
strength,—when there were no steamships or steam
carriages, no printing-presses, or even New Testaments, actually accomplished more nearly the
evangelization of the world than the Church, in
the pride of her prosperity and power, with every
door open before her, and every facility that even
modern progress has supplied, has ever done since !
The prompt and universal obedience, in the apostolic age, to Christ's last command, made the very
priests of pagan fanes tremble lest the altars of
their false gods should be forsaken !

Our obedience should be *implicit* as well as immediate. We should mark even the minutiæ of
our Lord's command, and follow exactly as He
leads. For example: He indicated an *order*, " to
the *Jew* first, and then to the *Gentile*." " Beginning at Jerusalem " is a phrase constantly perverted
to mean that home-work is to take precedence ;
and we forget that its true meaning is that, first of
all, *God's chosen people* were to be sought and
taught. Those early disciples everywhere began
with the *Jews;* whether at Jerusalem, Antioch,
Rome, Alexandria, or Constantinople. Wherever
Paul went, from Antioch in Syria, to Antioch in

Pisidia, to Salamis, Iconium, Lystra, Derbe, Philippi, Thessalonica, Athens, Corinth, Ephesus, Troas, Miletus, Rome, he first went into the synagogue of the Jews, or, if there was no synagogue, sought out and spake unto the Jews, wherever they resorted and he could get a hearing; and only after they rejected his message did he turn to the Gentiles. Has it nothing to do with our comparative failure in modern missions, that the despised Jew has been perhaps more shamefully neglected than any of the worst heathen, lowest pagan, or most bigoted Moslem peoples? Missions among the ancient Israel of God, as an organized movement, are but of recent date, and even now the eight millions of God's chosen nation are scarce approached by us. Here and there a few scattered laborers have been all that God's people have sent to open the blinded eyes of those who see the Messianic prophecies as yet through a veil. The grandest epoch of missions will not begin until God's Church undertakes to do as Christ bade her, beginning at Jerusalem.

The way of exact obedience is the way of constant blessing and of sure success. God has "not cast away His people whom He foreknew," and He will have the Gospel proclaimed to them first of all, not last of all. It is a noticeable fact that the missionary enterprises which to-day are reaping largest harvest in other fields are those which embrace missions to Israel among their forms of labor. To pass by the Jew in the effort to reach the Gentile, is a plain violation of the declared plan of God, and the slightest neglect of His plain command or revealed mind imperils all our other work. The blindness which is upon the mind of the Hebrew people, is no excuse for our neglect —for only when they turn to the Lord can that blindness be taken away; and how can any man be expected to turn to the Lord unless the truth is preached to him?

The Prussian army is the terror of Europe, because every citizen is a soldier, and, when the order goes forth, the army can be mobilized in a day. And it is only such faith and such obedience of faith that begets heroic courage. Confidence in God takes no account of obstacles. When Martin Luther, at Augsburg, was asked, " What will you do now, with kings and priests, cardinals, and even the pope himself arrayed against you? " " Put myself under the shield of Him who hath said, ' I will never leave thee nor forsake thee'! " True missionaries are always heroes ; they have as their helmet, breastplate, and shield, the Divine promise, " Lo, I am with you alway," and that Presence is vanguard and rereward. To know that one is in the exact path of duty is to know that all things work together for good, in a divine harmony.

Nothing will be so *irresistible* as the Church of God when her obedience to her Lord is *absolute.*

In the 277th year of the Hegira, and, in the vicinity of Cufa, that famous Arabian preacher, Carmath, assumed the imposing titles of Guide, Director, Demonstration, Camel, Representative of Mohammed, John Baptist, Gabriel, Herald of Messiah, the Word, the Holy Ghost. After his death his name was even more revered by his fanatical followers. His twelve apostles spread themselves among the Bedawins, "a race of men equally devoid of reason and of religion"; and so successful was their preaching that all Arabia was threatened with a new revolution.

The Carmathians were ripe for rebellion, and the secret of their power was a vow of blind and absolute submission to their Imam; a secret and inviolable oath was their bond of brotherhood. Leaving tracks of blood, they moved along the Persian Gulf, and the province of Bahrein bowed before them; far and wide the desert tribes lowered their standards before the sword of Abu Said and Abu Taher, his son, until they could muster on the field a force of over 100,000 fanatics. Their approach was like that of an avalanche—they neither asked nor accepted quarter, and bore everything before them.

Even the Caliph trembled as they advanced. They crossed the Tigris, and, with desperate daring, with only five hundred horse, knocked at the gates of the capital. By special order the bridges were broken down, and the lieutenant, in behalf of the Caliph, told Abu Taher that he and his force were in danger of annihilation. "Your master," replied the fierce commander, "has thirty thousand soldiers, but, in all his host, not *three* such as these." Then, turning to three of his followers, he bade one plunge a dagger into his breast, a second leap into the Tigris, and a third fling himself from a precipice. Without a moment's waiting or a murmur of discontent, each one obeyed. "Go," said he, "and tell what you have seen; and before the night falls, your general shall be chained among my dogs." It was so; before the sunset, the camp was surprised and the threat executed ! *

What could not our Lord do, against the most defiant strongholds of Satan, if He had even a little band of followers who, without hesitation, questioning, or reasoning, simply *obeyed?* Nothing can stand before a Church whose only law is the Will of God, and the motto of whose crusade is "*Deus vult.*"

3. It is almost superfluous to say that the spirit of missions is a spirit of *Love*, for in Love it finds both its corner-stone and cap-stone.

But Love itself is a virtue and grace which few possess, or even understand. There are *two* kinds of love: one is that of complacence, finding pleasure in its object and evoked by the discovery of admirable and attractive traits. The other is the

* Gibbon, v. 323-4.

love of benevolence, which depends upon an inward impulse rather than an outward attraction.
It is this latter sort of love which was not found
in Greek philosophy. It was conceived as Jesus
was, of the Holy Ghost, although, like Him, born
of a regenerate humanity. It is not a personal
affection, founded and grounded on moral esteem;
for such love in the nature of things reaches only
to those whom we personally know, and to comparatively few of them. The love to which we
refer now, is *charity*, good will expressed in good
deeds, whether to friend or foe, and extending
even to those personally unknown. While complacent love is exclusive and intensive, this love
is inclusive and extensive; it is universal and impartial; and is not so much an affection as it is a
principle, and so James calls it " The Royal *Law*,"
or rule of life.

Only as we understand such love can we know
the spirit of missions. God loved us when we
were enemies, and in this commends His love
both to our gratitude and our imitation. We are
to love as He loved, without respect to the
character of the object, or any recompense even
in kind. Nay, the more unlovely and unlovable
the object, the more will such love be drawn into
exercise, for the greater is the debasement and
need of the object, and therefore the more benevolence is evoked.

Such love embraces, of course, *all being.* It is

absolutely a stranger to caste and all invidious distinction. To such love, no human being is remote. Selfishness counts all who are not neighbors and friends, as barbarians, as Thales, though wisest and best of Greeks, looked on all outside of Greece; and even those who are geographically near are often sympathetically remote, as the Samaritans were to the Jews; for selfishness will have no dealings with those who give no promise of a return in temporal advantage or reciprocal favors.

No barrier between man and man has ever been so formidable as *caste;* and whether based on blood and birth, brute force or brain force, money or culture, social position or religious pride, it still remains the most persistent foe to human brotherhood. Against its walls of adamant, Love arrays her mightiest artillery, and, could Love but sway all our hearts, these walls would fall like those of Jericho. In the brotherhood of faith, the Church of Christ, God meant that, for once, the world should find a true democracy, with no barbarian, Scythian, bond or free, male or female —all, in Christ Jesus, one. And He meant that this Brotherhood of Christ should, in the whole world without, recognize one brotherhood of *man*, among whom no discrimination should be made, save in favor of the most distant, destitute, and degraded. And, where Love's law rules, the least and lowest, the worst and most worthless, actually take precedence in her holy ministry. All lines of color, race, blood, birth, clime; all differences of intellectual development, emotional life, or even moral purity, are to fade away before the charity that, like the mantle of snow, falls from heaven to fill up all inequalities and cover over all defects. The caste spirit, wherever it prevails, is the fatal foe of Christian missions and of Christian brotherhood. It is vain to abolish slavery and serfdom if this survives. It is possible to hold men in slavery by fetters of prejudice as well as of iron. There may be "uttermost parts of the earth" not a stone's throw from our churches and homes, because their inmates are absolutely strangers both to our acquaintance and sympathy.

All this is impossible where Love sways her golden sceptre. She makes all mankind one brotherhood and all the world one neighborhood; and every human soul that needs help becomes on that account our neighbor and brother. The negro is "God's image carved in ebony." Judea, which is at our doors, will not hide Samaria, which is near by but with an alien population, nor will either or both cause us to forget the regions beyond, even to the uttermost part of the earth.

Nay, let it be repeated, if Love lays stress upon any class among the objects of her divine ministry, she will turn, first of all, to those most remote, because their darkness is deepest, their need the sorest, their degradation the most extreme : in this case distance is the measure of destitution and of the demand for help.

That anonymous proverb, "Charity begins at home," if not invented by the devil, is appropriated by him to serve his ends. Love counts every needy soul a neighbor, and counts no cost in relieving with heart and hand every want or woe. If Love begins at home, it is only a beginning, a starting-point for the farthest goal of service. But selfishness begins at home, and stays there. To her a neighbor is one who will return favors by favors, and who pays in some form for every gift bestowed.

It takes but little experience of worldly society to see how hollow and shallow it is. Even its courtesies and attentions, its generosity and cordiality, have selfishness at the root. Parties are given, where every invited guest is one who has acted, or is expected to act, as host to those inviting; presents are given to those who have laid the givers under obligation by their previous gifts. One call is a return for another, and if the friend is out and the card can take the place of the call, just so much time is saved. Courtesies are returned for courtesies, just as slights are returned for slights; and how often, could the veil of decent form be removed, would it be found that the gift was grudgingly bestowed, the invitation reluctantly given, but a dire necessity compelled both, simply because it never would do to be under uncomfortable obligations. What is all this but a commercial system of exchange? Hear our blessed Lord: "When thou makest a supper call not thy friends, nor thy brethren, neither thy kinsmen nor thy rich neighbors; lest they also bid thee again and a recompense be made thee. But when thou makest a feast call the poor, the maimed, the lame, the blind; for they cannot recompense thee, for thou shalt be recompensed at the resurrection of the just!" * "Love ye your enemies, and do good and lend, hoping for nothing again, and your reward shall be great and ye shall be the children of the Highest, for He is kind unto the unthankful and the evil." † Matthew adds, "Be ye therefore *perfect* even as your Father which is in heaven is perfect," but in the corresponding and parallel passage, Luke says, "Be ye therefore *merciful* even as your Father in heaven is merciful." The perfection we are to aspire to is the perfection of love, of unselfish benevolence. Ah, yes, that is the perfection of the missionary spirit. It asks only, who has *need of me*, my money, my witness, my ministry? No bargaining for returns in kind or otherwise, no thought of personal gains, now or by-and-by; no calculating policy or worldly expediency. The seed is cast upon all waters to float, it may be, to most distant shores, where the harvest never will be seen until eternity reveals it. And in nothing do we need more a new spirit in missions than in the utter and final abandonment

* Luke xiv. 12–14.   † Luke vi. 35.

of that selfish policy which bestows money and
labor most lavishly only where the returns in some
form are likely to be most abundant and rapid.
In God's eyes many a gift, so called, is but an investment made on a commercial basis for the sake
of the profits it is expected to yield to the giver.

Paul wrote to the Galatians of the *"Offence of
the Cross."* Wherein consists that offence? Not
only in this, that it demands the renunciation of
self-righteousness as merit, of the world as an idol,
of worldly wisdom as my pride, of personal achieve-
ment as my glory—no, the cross is to the natural
and carnal heart most of all an offence, because it
teaches me that *self must be crucified*, that I am to
give without hoping to get, and lose my life to
save life; to love where I am hated and to serve
where I am met, even in serving, with the scourge
and the thorns, the wagging head and the scoffing
tongue, the mocking and the spitting—in a word,
the cross instead of the crown!

How utterly the Crucified lost sight of self!
He emptied Himself of all that heaven held to
come to earth, and then emptied Himself of all
that earth had left Him, for the sake of Love's
divine mission. Who was ever so poor as He!
He had nothing but a stable to be born in, nothing but a manger to be laid in. He had not so
much as a place where to rest his head; even His
cross was not His own, and His grave belonged
to another. It is pathetically written that, to the

traitor He left His purse; to the soldiers, His robe; to the beloved disciple, His mother; to the dying thief, His promise of paradise; to the penitent Peter, His pardon; to His Father, His last breath and departing spirit, and to His followers, His peace. Naked He came into this world; while here He got nothing, though He gave everything; and naked He went the way to the tomb. Do you wish to follow Him? Count the cost; for along that way self must be left behind to walk with Him. This is bearing the cross, to accept self-abnegation as the badge of discipleship, and consent to lose ourselves to save the lost.

The spirit of missions we need, for it measures our likeness to our Master and the value of our service. To cherish and cultivate that spirit is to grow in the image of our Lord. It will fill the heart to overflowing, and out of the abundance of the heart the mouth will speak and the hand will give; then, witnessing and working will react upon the heart which inspired them, and so the very love which compels utterance and endeavor is relieved, refreshed, and reinvigorated by the words and works of love. See how God ordains that duty shall bring delight! The spring makes the stream, but the outlet helps the inlet. Choke up the spring and it ceases to be a spring. When water stops flowing it stops running. Only a rill, locked up in ice-bonds, becomes motionless. Action reacts on the actor.

And as surely as we grow God-like by cultivating the spirit of missions, we shall rapidly decline
and decay, in all that is most vital to our soul's
life, when we quench that spirit. While some are
asking, especially as to the weaker churches, how
can they do mission work or give to the mission
cause? I would ask, how can they live without
it? Of the Church, as of the individual, it is true
that to save life by such means is to lose it. The
Church that leaves the lost to die without the
Gospel, risks its own destruction. It is therefore
a question how, if we do not undertake to save
the world, we can save ourselves. During the
ages when missions to the heathen comparatively
ceased, the Church scarcely survived ; and Bishop
Thoburn has said that God would sweep away the
Church from the earth if missions were deliberately
abandoned.

Dr. Burns Thompson calls attention to the fact,
in botany, that the light, heat, moisture, and nutri-
tion which are so helpful to growth where life exists,
actually promote and hasten decay where life is
not. It is a corresponding fact in spiritual experience, that the most abundant blessings become
only curses where they are not used for the ends
which God designed, and the peril of our souls
and of our churches lies in the very conditions
which, if we are faithful, insure prosperity.

It is not a question, therefore, merely of evangelizing the world and fulfilling our mission : it is

a more vital question of preventing heresy in doctrine and iniquity in practice from petrifying or putrifying the very life of the Church. Paralysis in missions is the sign of death to piety.

In Retzsch's illustrations of Faust, there is a representation which is not easily forgotten. The demons are contending for the soul of Faust and trying to drag him down into the abyss of ruin. The angels from above watch, with intent eyes and absorbed attention, the desperate struggle; and, plucking the roses from the bowers of Paradise, fling them down, as though they were hailstones with which to pelt the heads of the fiends. And as those celestial roses fall, and pass into the sulphurous atmosphere of the pit, they are suddenly transformed into burning coals, which, as they touch those demon forms, burn and blister and torture. A parable lies in that etching. All blessings, though they leave heaven as the very blooms of Eden, when they touch the disobedient and ungrateful soul turn to withering curses. The Church that leaves a dying world to die, a lost race to wander in the dark, feeling after the God whom the Gospel would reveal as not far from every one of us; the Church that turns the very privileges which God gives her into a silken hammock of selfish ease, and the very means of a world's evangelization into the provision for worldly indulgence; the Church that, with large numbers, great wealth, high social standing and culture, perverts the golden sceptre God gave her for universal conquest, into the weapon of self-enthronement, sitting as a queen and revelling in luxury, making the courts of God her court of empire, and leaving a world in destitution, while she furnishes and garnishes her palaces,—such a Church would do well to read that Epistle to Laodicea which contains perhaps the most terrible rebuke which God has ever administered to His professed.people.

We need this warning note to sound all around the horizon like a thunder-peal: the Church that does not take up her work for a world of lost souls is already a dying Church. To keep out Jezebel and the Nicolaitanes, to prevent the sanctuary of God being turned into the synagogue and seat of Satan, and the ardor and fervor of a first love with its first works from giving place to the disgusting, nauseating lukewarmness of a formalism that is neither one thing or the other,—for all this disaster God's great antidote is this, to be all, always, and altogether engaged in bringing unsaved souls to the knowledge of the truth. This is the tonic, the stimulant, the preventive and preservative medicine.

There is now-a-days a Laodicean tendency to undue self-gratulation. We talk of our world-wide organizations for missionary work, of our millions of money given for Gospel triumphs, of our great army of 6,000 men and women, and 35,000 native evangelists and helpers. But how little do we think of the disgraceful disproportion between our opportunity and our endeavor, the laborers we send to the field and the immense multitude of disciples that remain at home; the millions we give to missions and the billions of wealth we keep in selfish coffers or spend in selfish luxury. Think of some thirty or forty million of Protestant church-members, sending one man or woman out of every 5,000 or 6,000 to the foreign field—where one out of 500 would give us at least 60,000 missionaries! Think of giving ten or twelve millions of dollars a year to represent all these millions of Protestant disciples—a paltry pittance of forty cents a year as the average contribution, less than two mills a day! Behold that awfully accusing pyramid of comparative expenditure, that reveals a diminutive apex of $12,000,000 for missions, while as we descend, we find twenty times as much spent on public education; forty times as much on boots and shoes, and as much more on cotton fabrics; fifty times as much on woolen goods; sixty times as much on meat; one hundred times as much on bread; one hundred and fifty times as much on tobacco; and from one hundred and eighty to two hundred times as much on strong drink! One hundredth part of the annual income of professed disciples in Protestant congregations would yield to missions annually at least 200,000,000 dollars!

We congratulate ourselves that we are now

completing a full century of organized missions; but do we remember that it is but the *first* century of modern missions ? that, after apostolic days, there were a thousand years when missionary effort so far ceased that we call that millennium the Dark Ages ! that, after the trumpet tongue of Luther sounded the clarion peal of the Reformation, the awakened Church waited three hundred years longer before even the *debt* to a dying world was commonly acknowledged; and that, even now, not *one-third* of the church-membership are actually either working, giving, or praying for a world's evangelization ? If looked at from a true point of view, we shall see that all that is yet done or attempted is an insignificant fraction of what is both possible and practicable.

Never, even in the joy of missionary conquests, can the thoughtful disciple forget this shame and reproach of the Church, that, since our Lord, ascending to His throne, said, " Go ye into all the world and preach the Gospel to every creature," sixty generations of men have lived and died, embracing an aggregate multitude estimated at no less than twenty times the present population of the globe; that is, from twenty thousand to thirty thousand millions of our fellow-men ! a number so vast that if they could march, one by one, past a given point, one a second, it would consume from seven to ten centuries, day and night ! And yet—again we put it on record—with the command

of Christ in her ears and the word of life in her
hands, the Church has permitted this immense
multitude to go down to death, without even the
knowledge that a Saviour has died, reaching the
great masses of them !

4. The spirit of missions is the spring of *tireless
and ceaseless endeavor.* May we not call it, *Passion for Souls*, and for Christ's conquest of the
world ?

The Moravians lead the whole missionary host
in their devotion to a world's redemption. Their
leader, Count von Zinzendorf, like John the Baptist, seems to have fallen heir to a legacy of grace,
and his whole life bore the seal of a peculiar consecration. When but four years old, he covenanted
with Christ : " Be Thou mine dear Saviour, and I
will be Thine," and from the window of his grand-
mother's castle used in his childish simplicity to
toss out letters to the Lord in which he told Him
all that was in his heart. When at ten he was
Franké's pupil at Halle, he formed little prayer
circles, and instituted the " Order of the Grain of
Mustard-seed," whose members were bound by
sacred pledge to seek the souls of others. Tho-
luck's famous motto became his own : " Ich hab'
eine Passion und die est Er, nur Er." Parisian
seductions and social cups of enchantment vainly
sought to draw him from Christ. When he wedded
a countess, it was still only in the Lord, and they
two cast away all rank and riches, and girded

themselves like pilgrims, ready to start for any field if God should show them His will. The world became his parish; and his property, the Lord's offering.

The seal of the *Unitas Fratrum* was a lamb, bearing the cross of resurrection, from which depends a triumphal banner with the device: "*Vicit Agnus Noster: Eum Sequamur.*" No wonder that Dober and Nitschmann, at St. Thomas, were ready to sell themselves as slaves to reach slaves; that Stach and Boemish were ready to go to the ice-bound pole, Schmidt to the Bushmen and Hottentots at the Southern Cape, and that Pagell and Hyde and Jäschke laid siege to the stronghold of the Grand Lama on the frowning heights of Thibet. Pagell and his wife spent at Poo a quarter century of toil, and then in death were not divided. For five months their colleague at Kyelang could not visit them, for the impassable snows of the Himalayas block the roads for three-fourths of the year. Pathetic as is the tale of their self-denial, sickness and death, the brethren at the Nicobar Islands, in the Bay of Bengal, perished after sufferings that were even more extreme, and with not even a native catechist or solitary convert to close their eyes. Such are the men and women of whom the world was not worthy; of whom even a worldly Church is not worthy.

Where this enamoring passion for Christ and for souls is found, consecration of self and substance is as natural and necessary as breathing.

On Henry Clay's sarcophagus Fred Graeff has chiselled this, Clay's noblest utterance: " I can with unshaken confidence appeal to the Divine Arbiter for the truth of the declaration that I have been influenced by no impure purpose, no personal motive—have sought no personal aggrandizement; but in all my public acts I have had a sole and single eye, and a warm, devoted heart, directed and dedicated to what, in my best judgment, I believed to be the true interests of my country." That is the voice of patriotism; and shall the disciple not be able to say as much for the sake of his Redeemer and His Kingdom? Shall a statesman's devotion to his country outrank our absorption in God?

Besser tells the story of a redeemed slave— bought in a slave-market by a rich and generous Englishman for twenty pieces of gold, and then presented with a purse of sovereigns with which to buy a home and begin a freeman's honest life. " Am I free, to go where I will and do as I will? Then let me be your slave, I owe all to you—I have been by you redeemed.* "

The same spirit breathes in the birthday resolve of Miss Frances E. Willard, to give herself wholly to her Redeemer and Lord, " for the fulfilment in the highest possible degree in body, soul, and

* Lange. Commentary, I. Pet. p. 25.

spirit, of the declaration, 'A habitation of God through the Spirit.'" When Elizabeth Fry, the "female Howard," died at sixty-five, after such a life of Christlike philanthropy as few women have ever known—for half a century she had been able to affirm that she had never awakened from her sleep in sickness or in health, by day or by night, without her first waking thought being, "How best may I serve my Lord?"* When not more than eighteen years of age she established a school for eighty poor children in her father's house. Fifteen years later the deplorable plight of the women in Newgate prison drew her to their side, and alone, unguarded, she entered the inner prison, where one hundred and sixty of the worst were immured, and won them by her mingled dignity and courtesy, her holiness and humility. Many of them then for the first time heard at her lips the word of grace. Before three years more had passed she was a systematic visitor. Newgate's dark cells began to be lit up with the gospel of love, order, sobriety, neatness; intelligence began to displace riot, lust, filth, ignorance, and indolence. She established schools within prison walls, found work for women and Christian instruction; studied how to abolish slavery, advance education, and improve the condition of British seamen; and dispensed her charities with an unbounded liberality. And, like many a saint whose name is not in man's

* "Christian Womanhood," p. 241.

calendar, she could say, "Nothing is too precious for my Lord Jesus Christ."

Not until we can measure the value of the blood paid for our redemption can we measure the extent of our infinite debt to the Redeemer. There is but one way to pay that debt even in part—we are "put in trust with the Gospel." Debtors to Christ and, for His sake, to a dying world; and trustees of the Gospel of His grace that, with the boundless riches committed to us as trustees, we may discharge the obligation we owe as debtors!

No form of selfishness is more subtle and fatal to spiritual life than the polite form of fashionable *greed.* The worship of the golden calf is carried on in our very sanctuaries. Avarice is insatiate; it cries give, give, and lives to get and keep and hoard, and feast the evil eye and lust of gain on the sight of its gold.

In a British manufactory, a merchant comes in at 9 o'clock in the morning, and goes out at 5 o'clock in the afternoon, having done nothing else but count his sovereigns, and arrange them in piles of ten; and this he has done every day but Sunday for twenty years. Gold is his master, and he is an abject slave—the sovereign is indeed his Sovereign. He himself has been electroplated—changed into a coin—has a metallic ring, and will "drop into his coffin with a chink."

Passion for Christ and for souls checks such greed and makes all giving of our substance a

free-will offering. Redemption includes not only
me, but *mine.* A great German defines socialism
as decreeing, " What is thine is mine," and Christianity as teaching us to say rather, " What is
mine is thine." But Dr. R. W. Dale finely says
that the epigram needs further correction. Christianity teaches us to say, "What seems thine is
not thine ; what seems mine is not mine : whatsoever thou hast or I have belongs to God ; you
and I must use it according to His will."

The revival of the Scriptural doctrine of stew-
ardship is the only hope of the Church in the
direction of a larger and an adequate *giving.* So
long as we think of our money as our own, we
shall hold it as our own ; but when in our eyes it
is God's, we shall learn to give Him back what is
His own.

The spirit of missions is the spirit of *absorption*
in God. And, strange to say, we are never so
strong and puissant in our own individuality and
personality as when we are lost to ourselves because absorbed in Him. We find our lives in
losing them, and find ourselves in losing ourselves.
One of our current cant phrases is " losing our
will in His will," and too often this condition of
complete consecration carries with it the idea of
a sacrifice of positive manhood, manliness, character, power. We all feel that the will is the focal
centre of all being ; in the will all other elements
of power converge, and thence diverge again or

radiate into action. To have no will of our own suggests, to many, a body without a backbone—like a flabby jelly-fish—with no real energy even in resistance to evil, not to say in aggressive movement.

To be absorbed in God is the loss of nothing, but the gain of everything. It is the paradox of life, that you are never so fully and mightily yourself as when you lose yourself in God.

Here is a man whose mill is moved by a waterwheel. That wheel depends on a small stream which at times runs low and almost dry, and at such seasons the wheel moves slowly and feebly, if at all. But near by flows a mighty river, fed by exhaustless mountain springs and melting snows. He taps that river: he digs a channel from its banks to his own little rill; he turns into that narrow sluice-way the mighty, steady momentum of those everflowing waters, and now he has not lost his rill—he has only gained a river.

Even so, when we surrender our will to God, there is no loss of human will-power, but only the gain of divine will-power. Through the narrow channels of our uncertain, unsteady choice, He pours the mighty flood of His resistless resolution—the will of God energizes, quickens our will; and the wheels of action move with a firmness, fulness, force, and fervor to which we were before strangers. In our weakness we are strong; in our folly, wise. We can do all things and bear

all things through Christ, who strengthens us.
The youths faint and grow weary and the young
men utterly fall, but we wait on the Lord and
renew our strength ; mount upon wings as eagles,
run and are not weary, walk and do not faint.
Our Lord began His active career while yet a boy
of twelve years, with a significant motto : " Wist
ye not that I must be about my Father's business ? " His identification with the Father was
such that it was natural, necessary, involuntary, to
be engaged always in His Father's work. And
this makes all work easy, that I am doing it for
God, with God, in God. He abides in me and
I in Him ; I work for Him, and He works in and
through me. There is no hurry or worry or flurry
about a true work for God. Why should I be
anxious and disturbed and careful if I am simply
bearing His yoke—the yoke which He shares,
and in fact bears. Will He not take care of the
burden and see that the load is borne or is drawn ?
From the moment that you take God as your sole
Master and Lord, remember this—you are henceforth to take no anxious thought for the morrow
—to be careful for nothing, but trust and not be
afraid, trust and be kept in perfect peace. If there
be anything you are doing in which you find it
needful to worry, be assured *that* is not God's
work, but *your* work—something you have taken
upon yourself to do at the beck of pride, ambition,
greed, or some worldly impulse. For if it is only

God's work you are about, He is at the head and will not suffer it to come to naught. This lesson of perfect peace is the first and last lesson taught and learned in His school: if it were sooner learned, all life would be vested with heaven's charms. Take up your work as His commitment, do it for Him and unto Him, and in dependence on His Providence and Spirit; nothing will so banish all undue anxiety and carefulness.

There is no higher seal and sanction put by God on missions than this, that those who work in this great field manifest His spirit in a marked degree. Here is the apostolic succession because here is the apostolic mission and spirit. Faith begets implicit obedience, self-sacrifice, consecration, absorption in God, the marks of the highest heroism and loftiest unworldliness. Robert M. Cust, Esq., has pronounced the true missionary the highest type of human excellence, and his calling, the noblest; missionaries, he says, are the salt of the earth.

May we not say even more, that they seem to be identified with the goodly fellowship of the prophets, the holy company of the apostles and the noble army of martyrs? They have been the pioneers in all lands, like Carey in India, Perkins in Persia, Morrison in China, Judson in Burmah, Allen in Korea, Hepburn in Japan, Williams in the South Seas, Livingstone in Africa. They have gone nowhere without leaving the traces of

God. They have compelled recognition, respect,
and even homage; as Mrs. Grant compelled Nes-
torian bishops to think of her body as the temple
of God, as Mrs. Judson won the Burmese so that
they kissed her passing shadow, and Eliza Agnew
at Oodooville led a thousand daughters of Ceylon
to bow at the feet of her Saviour. To-day if even
ungodly men seek the grandest types of manhood
and womanhood they turn to Paul, to Eliot, to
Brainerd, to Gutzlaff, to Schwartz, to Moffat, to
Hunt, to Patteson, to Zinzendorf, to Mackay,
to Scudder, to Taylor, to Thoburn, to Harriet
Newell, Fidelia Fisk, Rosine Kraff, Melinda
Rankin—in fact, their name is legion, and it is
vain to discriminate by individual mention, among
such a host.

In 1818, the Colonial Government, fearing the
spread of leprosy, erected a temporary asylum in
the romantic valley of *Hemel en Aarde* (Heaven
and Earth), so called because, far from human
habitations, it was walled in by rocks, with only a
strip of sky above. In course of time a larger
hospital was built, and Lord Somerset, the governor, wrote to the directing board of the Mora-
vian Church, asking for a missionary to manage
the institution and teach the inmates the faith of
Christ.

In January, 1822, Rev. Mr. Leitner and wife
became voluntary exiles for Christ and entered
upon their repulsive and self-denying work. They

were in constant contact with those who were
crippled and deformed by this loathsome disease,
though they supposed such contact to be contagious and fatal.   Love transfigured their toil with
celestial charms.   For more than seven years they
sought to heal and save the souls of those whose
bodies were wasting away.   And when Mr. Leitner died, in 1829, in the same devoted spirit his
successors wrought for ten years more.   In 1846,
the hospital was removed to Robben Island, near
Cape Town, and Missionary Lehman and wife
followed the lepers to their new home amid the
dangerous rocks of Table Bay, and were met by
the joy of those poor lepers, who broke forth in
praise to God.   They began to teach ; and in 1860
John Taylor left all to bury himself among these
lepers and lunatics, where he likewise toiled till
death.   For forty-five years, and until the appoint-
ment of an English chaplain dispensed with their
services, these Christlike Moravians clung to this
leper home.

Such absorption in God is the soul and secret
of heroism.   What has nerved timid men, and
even delicate and shrinking women, to face death
with every attendant torture, firm and fearless, but
this—that they were lost in God ?

When Jerome of Prague was led to the stake,
he embraced it with smiles of gladness.   As
around him the wood and fagots were piled he
sang, " Hail, happy day ! " and then broke forth

again into chanting the Creed, which, as he said to the throng about him, was the song of his Faith. When the executioner went behind him to light the pile, he said to him, " Come hither and kindle the fagots before my eyes ; for, had I feared, I had not come here, having had so many opportunities of escape." And when the flames leaped high and the wood crackled in the fire, high above rose the calm clear notes of the martyr's voice, while his body was consuming as a whole burnt-offering on the altar : " This soul of mine, in flame I offer up, O Christ, to Thee ! " And to this day few spots on the continent are more sacred to Christian pilgrims than the place where those last words proved that death had lost its sting.

As I stood in April, 1890, on the highest tier of seats in the Coliseum at Rome, one scene of past ages stood most vividly, almost visibly, before my imagination. Beneath the canvas canopy a vast throng is gathered, of 80,000 spectators. Yonder on his raised marble throne sits the Emperor Trajan, and near him the proud senators, and vestal virgins with their lamps. Amid the surge and swell of this sea of human voices, impatient for the sport, an old man comes, trembling with age, into the arena, his long white hair falling to his waist and mingling with his beard. It is Ignatius, the disciple of John ; and if tradition be true, the " little child " of Mark xi. 36. He bears the second surname, Theophoros, or the Christ-bearer; and in his interview with Trajan showed himself so utterly unworldly that the emperor gave him the opprobrious name (Κακοδαιμων), one possessed of a demon, and condemned him to be led a prisoner from Antioch to Rome, and there fed to the wild beasts for the delectation of the people.

As the fierce lions are let loose upon him, the old saint falls on his knees and is heard to say: " O ye Romans, know ye that not for any crime am I brought here, but that by this means I may attain to the fruition of the glory of God, for love of whom I am made prisoner. *I am as grain of God's field, and must be ground by the teeth of lions that I may become bread for His people, fit for His table."*

How long, think you, the world would wait for the knowledge of this salvation, did the spirit of that martyr burn in Christian bosoms! Such a flame of holy zeal consumes all greed, all pride, all ambition, all selfishness, while it burns and glows and shines with celestial fires, and makes life itself a reflection of shekinah glory! When God's people would rather be ground between lions' teeth than that the hungry souls should go without bread, the world will soon find spread from pole to pole the banquet board of Redemption.

The spirit of missions not only brings its own reward; it *is* itself a heavenly gift and its own compensation. Walter Scott puts into the mouth of Jeanie Deans, when pleading for her sister's life with the Queen, those memorable words :

" It is not when we sleep soft and wake merrily ourselves that we think on other people's sufferings. Our hearts are waxed light within us then, and we are for righting our ain wrangs and fighting our ain battles. But when the hour of trouble comes to the mind or the body, and when the hour of death comes that comes to high and low,—lang and late may it be yours! O, my leddy, then it is na *what we hae dune for oursells, but what hae dune for others,* that we think on maist pleasantly."

Yes, but long this side of that august hour when life passes before us as in procession, for review, the true child of God who hath partaken of His Spirit has learned the higher compensation of fellowship with Jesus. His yoke is easy and His burden is light, and even His cross is no longer heavy.

Somewhere I have met a fable, that when God first made the birds He made them without wings. With gorgeous plumage and sweet voices endowed they could shine and sing, but could not soar. Then He made wings and bade the birds go take up these burdens and bear them. At first they seemed a heavy load, but as they bore them upon their shoulders and folded them over their heart, lo ! they grew fast—the burdens became pinions, and that which once they bore now bore them up toward heaven. The fable is fact. We are the wingless birds, and our duties are the pinions. When at the beck of God we first assume them, they may seem but burdens. But if we cheerfully and patiently bear them, they cease to be a load. The burdens change to wings—they bear us up and on toward the cloudless heaven of His presence. As the beloved Samuel Rutherford says, "The cross of Christ is the sweetest burden that ever I bore: it is such a burden as are wings to a bird or sails to a ship, to carry me forward to my desired haven.

"Schola crucis est schola lucis."

Fellow-disciples, let us cheerfully take up our duties, and the wingless birds shall find those duties turned to delights, and the burdens borne for Christ transformed to pinions to bear aloft the burden-bearer to the cloudless realm of the divine presence!

V.

THE DIVINE FORCE OF MISSIONS.

ROM man's creation until now, one great question has occupied human research, viz: *What is Power?*

Whence comes, in any sphere, the faculty or *ability to do*—to accomplish a work, to achieve a result? Back of effects lie causes, but many causes are also effects, and it is power which makes a cause efficient and sufficient to produce an effect. The question we now suggest concerns the origin of force and the primal secret of efficacy.

What men have sought in the sphere of natural philosophy, we are now to seek in the sphere of the moral and spiritual. In the prosecution of Christian missions what is the secret of success, the source of power? In discussing this question we are getting further toward the heart of our great theme. We have seen what constitutes the spirit of a true missionary; but this inquiry is even more radical.

The secret of power is not human, but divine, and even so far as it is found in humanity has an element of divinity. The Word of God, which proves in all things such an adequate guide, teaches us the whole truth that we need to know upon this subject.

We select two representative passages, which again we put side by side for comparison and completeness of view.

"And Jesus came and spake unto them saying : "All POWER is given unto me in Heaven and in Earth.
"Go ye therefore and teach all nations. . . .
"And lo I am with you alway even unto the end of the age.   Amen."
Matt. xxviii. 18–20.

"And behold I send the promise of my Father upon you ;
"But tarry ye in the city of Jerusalem until ye be endued with POWER from on High."   Luke xxiv. 49.
"But ye shall receive POWER after that the Holy Ghost is come upon you."
Acts i. 8.

It will be noticed that here *three times* we have this word "power," and the repetition is significant. In the first case, it is associated with the *Son*, who here claims for Himself omnipotence, both in heaven and in earth.   In the second case, it is associated with the *Father*, as proceeding forth from Him, and as His gift in connection with the mission of believers ; and in the third case, it is associated with the *Holy Spirit*, as His enduement and endowment.

Again, it is noticeable that in one case the power is linked with Christ's promised presence ; and in the other it is distinctly termed "the promise of the Father."   Where such manifest care is taken in the discrimination of language, it would be trifling to suppose that there is intended to be no corresponding discrimination in the thoughts.

Long and close study of this theme satisfies me that the line of distinction here drawn is not only clear, but very important. The power, vested in the Son and exercised by Him, and the power, bestowed by the Father and realized by the Holy Ghost, resident in and exercised by believers, is not and cannot be the same. The subject touches all missionary work at points so vital that it is well to give careful attention to the exact language used in each case. The inspired Word of God is written with divine care and discrimination. It reminds us of a master-painting, in which not only the bolder and more prominent outlines and strongly contrasted objects repay close study; but where the most delicate shades of color and lines of drawing have a significance, like the most minute features of the Parthenon where, as Penrose has shown, every line was the sign and fruit of artistic genius.

Our Lord says, "All power is given unto me in heaven and in earth; and lo, I am with you alway, even unto the end," etc. The word here used is not power ($\delta\nu\nu\alpha\mu\iota\varsigma$), but ($\varepsilon\xi o\nu\sigma\iota\alpha$), *authority*, rule, dominion, jurisdiction. Christ is head over all to the Church, and governor among the na-tions. His is *administrative power*, on the throne of universal empire and on the field of battle and conquest. This truth is further beautifully and

impressively set forth in two conspicuous passages
of Scripture, one of which is a didactic psalm and
poem, the other a historic narrative which hides
an undoubted allegorical meaning behind the
historical fact.   Comparing spiritual things with
spiritual, we may draw from these Scriptures some
grand and instructive and inspiring lessons; and
because they are representative passages, we may
well examine them minutely.

1. The first of them is the second Psalm.   Here
the Psalmist has a far-sighted vision of Messiah,
as set by Jehovah, upon the throne of dominion;
and it clearly pertains, not to the *triumphant*, but
to the *militant* period.   All are not subdued under
his sway, but in a state of rebellion and revolt.   It
is not a converted world over which Messiah holds
the reins of empire, but over a godless and faithless host of rebels.   "The heathen rage," as in a
tumultuous assembly, and the peoples of many
lands meditate and cogitate in anger and malice,
how they may overthrow the kingdom of Immanuel.   "The kings of the earth set themselves" in
a posture of defiance, as did Goliath against the
army of Israel and Israel's God, in resistance both
to Jehovah and to His anointed Theocratic King;
while the rulers, like a great sanhedrin of Satan,
meet in council to conspire against them, and, like
yoked oxen that chafe under restraint, seek to
break asunder their "bands" and cast off their
"cords."   There is no mistaking such a figure,

We seem to see the enemies of God rising up against the Father and the Son with frantic tumult; at first like the wild surge of a stormy sea, a disorganized mob of rebels, raging heathen, and angry peoples. Then the opposition takes form —is organized under leaders; their kings take a stand against God, and their rulers meet in council to conspire and combine in a league of hatred. Already they feel the bands of Messiah's yoke tightening about them and the cords of His rule holding them fast, and they toss and plunge like a mad bull to get rid of His restraint. The whole sound and movement of the original, by a rhythm that is as majestic as iambics and as musical as rhyme, conveys the fury and rage of these plotting foes, who rashly rush against the bosses of Jehovah's buckler.

But Jehovah, seated unapproachable in the highest heaven, laughs, scoffs, at their vain resistance, as the stars scoff in derision at those who would quench their eternal fires or shoot them down from their place in the heavens. God sees their plannings and kickings against Him to be vain ; they only hurt themselves on His goads !

In the midst of their vain boasting, and as they are gathering for organized assault, Jehovah in holy wrath speaks and acts. Herder and others compare the rhythm of the original and the choice of terms to words rolling like thunder, followed in the second clause by a deadly scattering of lightning-bolts. While they mutter helplessly on earth, God thunders from heaven and hurls down the bolts of His displeasure.

"Yet"—notwithstanding all this impotent rage— "Yet upon my holy mount, as for me, I have set my King." The reference is to *David*, who, as type of Messiah, was *thrice* anointed and was God's acknowledged king on Zion, while as yet seven years of hostility were to intervene before all the tribes submitted to his rule. And now Messiah takes up the word of Jehovah and declares the Divine decree. He says, "I will tell of a decree eternal, unchangeable by virtue of which I reign. Jehovah said unto me, Thou art my Son, and as Son, heir to my empire." "This day have I, even I, begotten Thee." As Messiah is represented as uncreated and eternally begotten, this cannot refer to existence, as then begun, but to a new existence, or career, a re-begetting by virtue of which Messiah now takes the throne of the world, and of all that it involves. What that day is, other Scriptures leave us in no doubt—it was the day of Christ's *Resurrection.** Hebrew scholars tell us that the word here translated "begotten" may refer to either parent, but more strictly belongs to the *mother*. The earth, from her womb, His grave, on that day brought forth God's first born from the dead, henceforth to have in all things the pre-eminence; and to reign over the earth

* Acts xiii. 33; Rom. i. 4; Col. i. 18.

that, in this new birth out of death, brought Him
forth, declaring Him to be "the Son of God with
power by the resurrection from among the dead."
The examination of this psalm has been thus
tediously explicit, because, upon our right understanding of the circumstances in which these
words are spoken, all else depends. Jesus, rising
from the dead, claims the throne of the world,
which the first Adam forfeited by sin. The world
is not ready for His rule, though He is ready to
rule the world. His sceptre is in His hand and
the decree has gone forth ; from that Resurrection
Day when He rose for our justification and broke
the power of death and the devil, the throne of
the world was His. But the heathen and the
peoples at large were yet in revolt both against
Jehovah and against His Messianic King. Amid
this confusion of tumult and riot, God again says :
"Ask of me and I will give thee the heathen
for thine inheritance and the uttermost parts of
the earth for thy possession." That is to say, like
an irresistible monarch, even the *revolted* subjects
are part of His "inheritance," and the uttermost
parts of the earth that have neither yielded to His
rule nor heard of His resurrection belong to His
"possession." This verse has, in countless cases,
been made the text for missionary sermons ; and
from it have been drawn prophecies of Christ's
. gracious conquests in converting all mankind.
But does this verse or this psalm bear any such

construction? Read the next verse: "Thou shalt
break them with a rod of iron: thou shalt dash
them in pieces like a potter's vessel." Remember
the nations and their kings are in *revolt*, and they
are broken with an iron sceptre, dashed into fragments like a potter's vessel that cannot be mended.
(Jer. xix. 11; Matt. xxiv. 51; Rev. ii. 27; xii. 5;
xix. 15.) And what is the conclusion? The
Psalmist counsels immediate and universal submission; seeing the resistless power of Jehovah and
of His anointed, and the impotency of human
rage, He appeals to rebels to lay down their
weapons, and, instead of kicking against the rule
of Messiah, kiss Him in homage and serve Him
with holy trembling and trust.

This psalm may be regarded as the key to a
large part of both New and Old Testament truth,
and we have followed it, verse by verse, that this
key might be in our hands with which to unlock
the prophecies and open the real inner meaning
of the promises. Christ, when He rose from the
dead, ascended to the throne, and assumed the
sceptre. He had already been secretly anointed
for kingship far back in the ages of eternity.
Now a second time anointed by the Holy Ghost,
He took the throne with the concurrence of His
chosen *Church*. The time is coming when, by the
consent of a converted humanity, He will be once
more anointed universal King, and reign over a
regenerate earth. Meanwhile the sevenfold period

of resistance must pass, and in that period we are now. When Christ, risen from the dead and about to take another step upward to the throne, said, "All power is given unto me in heaven and in earth. Go ye therefore and disciple all nations, and lo, I am with you alway," He knew that hundreds and thousands of years lay before Him and His Church, during which that rule was to be disputed and antagonized; He was sending disciples forth as sheep among wolves; they would be persecuted, imprisoned, slain; His witnesses would be martyrs—death would be the end of their service and suffering—instead of seeming victory, apparent defeat. And so He held out no false hopes—no assurance that the time had come to restore again the kingdom to Israel, or to begin His millennial reign. He knew that, while two tribes might acknowledge Him, ten would be in revolt. Century after century would pass and still the world would not have Him to reign over them; and even the Church would fall into apostasy and a form of godliness take the place of its power. But He says, "I go to my Father and yours, my God and yours," "I go to take my sceptre," "All power is mine in heaven and in earth. Go ye therefore—make disciples from all nations—everywhere preach—bear witness. You shall be hated of all men for my name's sake; you shall be scourged, put in prison, put to death, but all this shall turn to you for a testimony—a part of your witness-bearing. You will find the heathen raging, the peoples plotting, kings and rulers conspiring; let them try to demolish my throne and break the bands of my rule! Their efforts shall be met with derisive scorn." The wrath of man shall praise Him, and the remainder of wrath will He restrain. When crises come which can in no other way be met, and violence reaches its height of daring and defiance, the Messianic King vindicates Himself and His servants; He stretches out His hand and with His iron sceptre breaks into pieces His foes.

Here is the hope of missions in the darkest days —this Psalm, so often applied to the Church Triumphant, was meant for the Church Militant; and never was it needed more than now, when, in so many parts of the field of missions, we seem met, as among the Brahmans of India and the Mohammedans of Persia, by persistent resistance. Christ has all power and is on the throne, "Go ye," missionaries—He is "with you alway," even to the end of this age of organized and violent opposition. When you find yourselves driven to the wall and the cause seems hopeless, appeal to Him, and He will appear for you: it may be in the conquest of grace, it may be in the awful conquest of wrath, but rejoice, He is King!

An example or two of this interposition should be put on permanent record. The year 1839 was the great pivotal year of Turkish missions. Per-

secution bared her red right arm. The bitter
hostility of the Armenian Church broke out in a
storm. The despotic head of the Turkish government, Sultan Mahmoud, united his civil power
with their ecclesiastical, to extirpate the Christian
heretics. The work, begun in 1831 by William
Goodell, seemed likely, after twenty years, to fall
in a crash into ruins. Mr. Sahakian, an evangelical Armenian and teacher, was thrown into prison
without trial, or even knowledge of the charges
made against him. He and Boghos Fizika, another of like character, were sent four hundred
miles into exile. Der Kevork, a pious priest, was
put in a cell. The Greek patriarch thundered out
a bull of excommunication, and nothing less than
the banishment of all the missionaries was determined upon. The persecution waxed hotter and
fiercer, and the missionaries were formally accused
before the Sublime Porte, and Messrs. Hamlin
and Goodell, who were the only ones at that time
in the country, expected summary orders to leave.
An order was obtained from Mahmûd for their
expulsion, and that of all missionaries. Commo-
dore Porter could not interpose, as the treaty with
the United States was only commercial, and there
seemed no human hope. In that darkest hour of
Turkish missions, the pioneer Goodell, in his
peculiar way, said: "The Great Sultan of the
Universe can change all this." The missionaries,
sorely beset, took refuge in the 91st Psalm. They

besought the Lord to come down as in the days
of old, and make the mountains flow down at His
presence. While their hands were yet lifted in
prayer, on July 1, 1839, *Sultan Mahmûd died.*
Not only did God interpose, but by a series of the
most striking providences on record in history,
the power of their foes was broken. Six days
before, the Turkish forces had been routed near
Aleppo ; an exhausted treasury absorbed governmental attention; a fearful conflagration visited
Constantinople, August 9th, and from 3,000 to
4,000 houses were reduced to ashes. God's hand
was laid heavily on the Armenians who led in the
persecution. And so marked was the evidence
of a divine interposition that it was a common
saying that God was taking the side of the persecuted and vindicating their cause. In fact, a
council was called and the exiles were recalled,
and all rigorous measures suspended. The leaders
were unchanged in spirit, but they were not un-
awed. They saw an Almighty Hand uplifted to
arrest the arm of intolerance, and they *dared* not
go forward.

Abdul Medjid, at sixteen, succeeded his father.
God's work took a fresh start, and four months
later, before a grand imperial Diet, he caused to
be read to the august assemblage the first formal
Bill of Rights, the Magna Charta of Turkey, the
Hatti Sherif of Gûl Hané, the primary charter of
liberty which was the first of a series of constitu-

tional guarantees culminating in the Hatti Huma-youn of 1856. When it is remembered that the Sultan's throne represents one of the most despotic governments ever known, nothing can account for such concessions except the power of Him in whose hands are the hearts of kings, and who turneth them whithersoever He will.

Siam furnishes another marked illustration. From the time, in 1819, when the first Christian book, a catechism from the hand of Mrs. Ann Hasseltine Judson, was printed in Siamese, and the first step was thus taken toward the evangelization of that Oriental Eden, down to 1851, but little progress was made. Dr. Gutzlaff and Rev. Mr. Tomlin, who arrived in 1828, appear to have been the first Protestant missionaries to set foot on Siamese soil. They undertook labor among the Chinese residents in Bangkok, began to heal the sick, and distribute books. The Jesuits sought their expulsion; the suspicious natives charged them with being spies and seeking to incite the Chinese to rebellion. Mr. Tomlin was taken ill and went back to Singapore; Dr. Gutzlaff himself, after less than two years' stay, sailed for China, leaving behind him the whole Bible translated into Siamese, and one baptized convert. Then, twelve days later, came David Abeel, the first American missionary to Siam. Dr. D. B. Bradley, of the A. B. C. F. M.; and Dr. Wm. Dean, of the American Baptists, came in 1835; and the merit-making

Buddhists became jealous, and complained to the government. Various events conspired to excite the people and disturb the king, and it was rumored that a plot was on foot to burn down the houses of the mission. Five days were given the little band to leave the premises, and they were scattered in different directions, finding shelter as best they could. In 1840, the Board of Missions of the Presbyterian Church of the United States assumed the entire work of evangelizing the Siamese. Rev. W. P. Buell and wife, who came that year, had to leave in 1844. Three years elapsed and Rev. Stephen Mattoon and Samuel R. House, M.D., came in their stead. They undertook the work bravely, studied, preached, printed books, and practiced medicine. But the suspicious king, jealous of their growing influence and the "merit-making" of the physicians, actively though secretly opposed them. This malignant despot threw all his influence against the missionaries. He so controlled his slavish subjects that none of them would sell or rent a house for the use of the missionaries, or even a site on which to build. Their native teachers were thrown into prison, their servants fled, and the people would not so much as sell them food. Opposition, carried to the point of starvation, seemed to leave room for no choice: they must leave Bangkok by the next steamer. To make things worse, Sir James Brooks, who came to treat with the Siamese king in behalf of Great

Britian, was so insulted that he left in anger, threatening to invoke the aid of force in opening the country. Humanly speaking, the missionary labors begun thirty-two years before were about to come to a disastrous conclusion. There was but one hope; it lay in an appeal to the throne of Grace. The missionaries looked, for deliverance, to God. The kings of the earth again took counsel to break His bands asunder and cast away His cords. But at this critical juncture, when all these complications were culminating, He who sits on the throne stretched forth His rod of iron and broke in pieces, like a potter's vessel, this treacherous king. April 3, 1851, he died. And,—what is far more wonderful,—upon that death hung a change in the whole state of affairs, and all succeeding history was to be cast in a new mould. We write it in large characters, that he who runs may read, even at a cursory glance. There was one man in the kingdom, MAHA MONG KUT, in the cell of a Buddhist monastery, who had been taught in language and science by Rev. J. Caswell, a missionary of the American Board. His heart was full of friendliness toward the missionaries and of the liberal and catholic policy imbibed through familiar contact with his Christian teacher. Upon him the choice of the assembly of nobles fell, and the priest left his cell to mount the throne of the "Sacred Prabahts." For seventeen years he reigned, a scholar and a gentleman who appreciated civilization, and inaugurated the most enlightened and progressive policy ever known among Asiatic sovereigns! Every condition was changed. Missionaries found permanent homes—and even a welcome at court. And that very year the women of the mission were admitted as teachers into the royal harem. The work begun by the deft and delicate hand of the seraphic Mrs. Judson was, after a generation had passed away, carried on by her sisterhood. And from that time to this, during forty years, the world has looked with astonishment upon the attitude of the Siamese nation, that in one day was changed from hostility to friendship in answer to believing prayer. Maha Mong Kut proclaimed religious liberty throughout the land, in 1870, and his son has followed his example in all liberal policy.

Chulalangkorn, who succeeded Maha Mong Kut, has been called the "wisest and best ruler" the kingdom has ever known, and with his wife has been the friend of Christian missions. Born in 1853, he is now but thirty-eight years old, and has reigned since November 11, 1868.

These two instances, out of hundreds, are chosen as striking illustrations of Christ's divine administration of missions. Here rulers conspired against God's anointed; everything to human eyes threatened the wreck of years of work for His kingdom. And, when the crisis came, He sent forth His word, and His invisible messenger brought death to impious monarchs. Like a potter's vessel, they were shivered in pieces, beyond repair or remedy. And of such interpositions of Providence missionary history is full.

2. The other passage which throws light upon our Lord's promised presence and power, is the story of the *Capture of Jericho*. No one can study that narrative without saying within himself, " Which things are an allegory." The book of Joshua is the book of a militant Church, the wars of the Canaanites; it is the book of entrance and conquest, possession and dispossession ; even in the promised land God's people found long, hard fighting, and every inch of advance disputed. The capture of Jericho is the first great step, the typical conflict ; and notice how it was conducted. A strange personage appears on the scene and announces himself to Joshua as " the Captain of the Lord's host." Joshua perceives his divine character, and humbly and adoringly gives into his hands the sceptre of leadership.

His directions were explicit, and were implicitly followed. The city was to be compassed about once a day for six days, and seven times on the seventh day. The Ark of the Testimony was borne—the priests blew the trumpets, and at a given signal the whole host shouted with a great shout of anticipative victory. Then, without one blow being struck, or one carnal weapon being used, the walls fell flat, and it remained only for the host to march over the ruins and take the city

captive.   What an object lesson on missions !   A
militant Church undertakes to take possession of
the earth promised to her as her joint inheritance
with her Lord and Head.   At every step her
advance has met with deadly opposition.   But the
Invisible Captain of the Lord's host is on the
battle-field, and his orders are explicit.   We are
to surround every stronghold, we are to bear the
sacred treasure, our testimony for God, in the very
van, and blow the trumpet of the Gospel herald.
We are not to meet violence with violence, or hate
with hate ; we are to use no carnal weapons, rely on
no worldly alliances of power or patronage, wisdom
or wealth.   It is not by power nor might; the
weapons of our warfare are not carnal, but mighty
through God to the pulling down of strongholds,
casting down imaginations and every high thing
that exalteth itself against the knowledge of God,
and bringing every thought into captivity to the
obedience of Christ.   This is the way to fulfil our
obedience, and so revenge the disobedience of
men.   Let men deride our methods ; as we scorn
worldly policy and simply blow the Gospel trumpet,
God is pleased by the foolishness of preaching to
save them that believe—that the excellency of the
power may be of God, and not of us.

    This, then, is the dual power of Christ's promised
presence.   He is on the throne, watching over the
affairs of His Militant Church.   He scorns the
impotent malice of His foes and, when they persist

in rage, breaks them in pieces. The same sceptre that to His Church is golden—the sceptre of defence and protection and blessing—is to implacable enemies an iron rod of destruction and wrath and cursing. And He, who from the throne sends forth law and judgment, from the battle-field directs the fray and leads on the host; and, if we but cultivate the clear-seeing eye, we may behold His white plume and white horse as He rides forth conquering and to conquer.

This story of Jericho is full of inspiration in the work of missions. It shows us the Invisible Captain of our salvation, standing sword in hand on the very field of battle, our General-in-Chief. He is not only *our* captain but, " Captain of the Lord's Host," *i.e.*, the *angelic* host, for the armed men of Israel are never once called the host of the Lord—though once, in Exod. xii. 41, referred to by a kindred title. And here again we observe the curious correspondence between the scene at Jericho and the words of that last commission. "All power is given unto Me in heaven and on earth " —on earth, for He is Leader of a militant Church; in heaven, for He is Captain of the angelic host. While we go on sounding the cornets of Jubilee and proclaiming the Gospel, surrounding the strongholds of Satan, He is with us, and commands an innumerable company of angels; the powers of heaven are arrayed on our side, and, were our eyes open, we might see the horses and chariots of fire—they that be for us are more and mightier than all they that be against us. The angels of God encamp round about us and fight for us in the dark day of battle. Here, then, is the first and foremost hope and faith of the Church in her mission work. The Lord Jesus is on the throne holding the reins of empire, and on the field of conflict directing the campaign. No defeat is possible, for all the heavenly host are our allies. In the midst of the dust and smoke of battle, when victory seems to perch like a bird of evil omen on the banners of the foe, and when we know not which way the tide of battle is turn-ing, we are to stand, like the famous gunner of Waterloo, by our guns and our flag, and lift the eyes of faith upward.

And now, it may be asked, what more is needed? Let it be observed that, thus far, we have power, exerted on behalf of the Church, guid-ing, guarding, and governing disciples, and assuring final triumph over all foes of the kingdom. This is administrative power.

But there is another field for the display of power. The work of missions is primarily *con-structive*, not *destructive*. It aims to save, not to slay, and seeks to destroy foes by making them friends. We want another sort of power, working upon the minds and hearts of men and converting the sinner into the saint, and the unbeliever and disbeliever into the believer. We need a power

that shall induce men voluntarily to yield to Christ
—not simply compel them involuntarily to sub-
mit; to take His yoke upon them of choice, not
of dire necessity, like vanquished foes. And just
this is the *Power of the Holy Ghost*, promised of
the Father, and which our Lord counted of such
importance that He bade disciples tarry until they
were endued with this power from on high. Here
the word is not authority, εξουσια, but power,
δυναμις. A new *dynamic force* was to be communi-
cated. The Son of man came to seek and to
save that which was lost—not to destroy men's
lives, but to save them. And therefore, while He
holds the rod of iron, and when necessary will
use it, He would have all men to be saved and
come to the full knowledge of the truth. And so
He holds this rod of iron in reserve, while He
extends the golden sceptre of His grace and love
and pardon. His holy anger tarries until the enduement from on high has done its work on disciples and wrought its sweet persuasion on unbelievers; then, when only obstinate and obdurate
and reprobate rejectors of grace remain, He turns
about His gracious sceptre and uses the iron end
of it for destruction.

The promise of the Father, then, is the bestow-
ment of the Spirit of all power and grace. Pentecost was the beginning of the fulfilment of that
promise, and Pentecost was typical. We see how
this power is to be manifested all through this Gos-

pel age, from the manifestation of it then. First it *came upon* disciples, an enduement and endowment. It was a baptism, a chrism—a clothing with heavenly energy, an anointing with celestial unction. This imparted to the whole man a new, pervasive, persuasive charm, which wrought wonders—convincing the mind, persuading the heart, converting the will. Three thousand under one simple sermon yielded immediately to God. Here is power *in the disciple*, fitting him to witness, and working *on the unbeliever*, moving him to repentance, faith, conversion, and confession. And now nothing more can be required. The full secret of success is absolutely found. The Church of God, tarrying at Jerusalem for the Divine anointing, now goes forth to work and to war. Her witness is convincing and persuading, and all because a heavenly and indescribable charm invests her messengers. Wherever they go, taught what to say, and how to speak, they win a hearing. Men tremble even on the throne; peasant and prince alike bow before a divine message borne by a messenger who is manifestly clothed with the livery and insignia of heaven.

Then, when. grace has done its work and persistent foes who will not yield to love would conspire to ruin and wreck a believing Church, the power that Christ holds in reserve for the crises of His kingdom is brought into awful exercise.

3. Moreover, it seems plainly taught us that there

are times when this protective and destructive
power acts *co-ordinately* with the grace that converts and saves, both by way of preparation and
co-operation. Judgment sometimes paves the way
for mercy, so that mercy rejoices in judgment.
The judgments of our King are abroad in the
earth, and the inhabitants of the world learn righteousness. The penalties with which He visits
evil-doers operate as a check upon ungodliness
and turn the less obdurate transgressors unto God.
_ Who has not been struck with certain phrases
in the Old Testament, as when God calls the
swarms of locusts, Joel ii. 25, *"My great army
which I sent among you!"* And any one who
has ever lived in tropical climes and witnessed the
terrible devastation they leave behind, will understand such a phrase. These swarms come like a
living deluge; they cover the entire face of the
firmament. In Southern Asia and Northern Africa they frequently appear in clouds that hide
the sun and sky; the noise they make in their
marching and feeding is like that of a heavy rain
or hail falling on a forest. And the fields where
they forage are swept clean of every green thing,
and a thousand miles is not an extraordinary
stretch for them to cover with desolation. A great
army indeed, both in their countless hosts and
awful power.

There is something awe-inspiring in the thought
of the whole creation constituting God's obedient

host of armed warriors, the winds His messengers, flames of fire His ministers, the sea moving at His bidding, and the lightning-flash acting as His vassal. Caterpillars and canker-worms, flies and locusts, floods and droughts, snow-flakes and summer heats, all obey and fulfil His Word. But let us consider that they not only avenge His broken law, but prepare the way for His Gospel! How many doors has the skeleton key of Famine unlocked in India, in China, in Persia, in Syria! The floods recently prevalent in the Middle Kingdom were God's evangelizing agencies. The inhabitants see the impotency of their false gods to avert calamity, and the indifference of their own people to their extremity, while the "foreign devils" deal bread to the hungry and clothing to the naked, and give shelter to the homeless; and thus famine, pestilence, plague, drought, and a thousand forms of evil are God's preachers, that with loud voice proclaim the powerlessness of all idolatry to save or help, and point to the living God and the cross of Christ, as the hope of the world.

We need to get new conceptions of Christian missions and the Power behind the mission band. We are waging warfare against iniquity and idolatry; the campaign is world-wide and age-long, the foes are daring, desperate, diabolical; the strongholds crown every hill-top, and are seemingly impregnable; but the Leader is Divine; His strategy, His methods, His weapons, insure victory. His hosts are not earthly and human only, but heavenly, and the Church has only to be obedient, cultivate unity within and loyalty to her Lord, and in faith blow the cornets of Jubilee and use the mighty rod of prayer, and His banner is over the whole host. Every Roman soldier saw in the outspread pinions of Rome's silver eagles a signal of two things: first, a triumphal flight in wars of conquest, and secondly, a sheltering wing for every Roman citizen in the hour of peril. So to us must the banner of the Cross mean victory and safety, conquest for Christ, defeat of all foes, defence for all believers. God is the guard of His people. "The nation and kingdom that will not serve Thee shall perish." Has our Lord given His Spirit to save and sanctify? He has also "created the Waster to destroy"; He used Babylon as a hammer wherewith to smite the nations on the anvil of judgment; and then broke the proud hammer itself in pieces. And, when the kings and rulers conspire to wreck His Church and break His rule, His holy wrath, like angry waves on the seashore, shall sweep over them, and as with the sand-hills and forts which children build on the strand, leave not a trace behind!

4. Before bringing this discussion to a close, the power of the Holy Ghost should be considered in its relation to *our fitness to proclaim the good tidings.* The authority of Christ in government and warfare touches our security and final success. But this

touches our *duty* and *responsibility*, and the extent
to which His power is exerted in our behalf may
depend upon the measure of our conformity to
His will. Let us now therefore look, for a little,
at the effect of the enduement of power in making
the missionary mighty in his work for God.

In all work in which man co-operates with God,
the power is in part human and in part superhuman and divine; or, to speak more exactly, the
power is to be viewed from both its human and
divine side, in order to be fully apprehended.

Bearing in mind that great word, "witness,"
which is the key to our whole work, it is manifest
that we can never separate from a complete conception of power in mission work, the character
and qualification of the witness-bearer. Buffon
said of "Style, it is the man"; and the manner of
man the missionary is will limit even the exercise
of the power of God. Power depends for effectiveness upon the appliances and instruments
through which it finds play. Friction is resistance
to motion, and practically, reduction of motive-
power. Even God's power may be hindered in
action.

The element of *naturalness* in testimony is one
of the first conditions of power. Constraint and
restraint, if they do not tie the tongue, put fetters
upon speech and limit its freedom. And besides,
they are contagious and infectious. What embar-
rasses the witness, hinders the hearer from a ready

reception and a frank response. But, when we speak out of the fulness of our heart, the speech is easy, fluent, natural, necessary; we win a hearing by our earnestness and absorption in our theme. He who "cannot but *speak*," will find others who cannot but *hear*. There is a strange eloquence, convincing, persuading, in any man who has a message which he must deliver; there is about any speaker who is thoroughly enamored of his theme, a fascination which even an unlettered and stammering utterance cannot altogether destroy.

The *efficiency* of a true witness, set on fire of a deep heart experience, is next to omnipotence: it carries before it all opposition like a flame fed with oxygen and fanned by high winds. Again we affirm it: the power to convince and persuade is the power of being convinced and persuaded. A doubt on our part begets a doubt in others; confidence that knows no hesitation draws others after us as a mighty ocean steamer draws in its wake smaller craft. Hence it was that Theremin defined "eloquence, a *virtue*." An uncertain utterance moves nobody: the whole man must be behind his message, the *vir* behind the *vis*. A positive man may be wrong, but like God's anointed king he melts or welds other wills into his own, by the white heat of his own conviction. And hence the simplest believer may attain a power as a witness which none of the princes of this world knew. It is not the rhetoric or the logic of the schools which charm and sway, fascinate and captivate the souls of men. They listen as to musical sounds, or curious echoes, or the deep swell of the sea, but they are not moved. The Latins heard Cicero's enchanting speech, and they said, " How beautifully he declaims ! " The Greeks heard Demosthenes' energetic, impassioned utterance, and they clenched their fists and said, " Let us go and fight Philip ! "

Sir William Hamilton one day said to Dr. McCosh, " Your friend, Dr. Guthrie, is the best preacher I ever heard." He answered that he did not wonder at the opinion, but was surprised to hear it expressed, by so great a logician, of one not specially possessed of large logical power. Sir William replied with great emphasis, " Sir, he has the best of all logic ; there is but one step between his premise and conclusion." We are not sure that the great Scotch metaphysician ever uttered a profounder saying.* On the other hand, how we instinctively detect, through the glamour of fine oratory, the features of the disingenuous and dishonest man ! " Surely," said Dr. Guthrie himself to Dr. James Hamilton, " there must be something great about *that* man "—referring to a demagogue who for some years had been drawing the people after him. " Well," said Dr. Hamilton, in his quaint, quiet way, " no doubt ; he is a *great imposition !* "

* Life of Guthrie, 1, 322.

Paul uses the significant phrase, " Demonstration of the Spirit." There is no process of logic
that is equal to His, for convincing of sin, of
righteousness, and of judgment. The most elaborate human argument often fails to demonstrate;
the Spirit of God opens the blind eye and flashes
conviction instantaneously upon the soul.

The pilgrim to Scotland reverently stands in the
graveyard of old Greyfriar's Church in Edinburgh.
Here, on the 25th of February, 1638, the National
Covenant was signed, the old Earl of Sutherland
setting the example. A moved and mighty multitude surrounded a raised horizontal gravestone in
the open air of heaven. And they were not content to sign that Covenant in ink. Ah, there were
men in those days; they were seen to open a vein
in their arms and fill their pens with their blood,
to mark how they would shed that blood when
the battle-day came; and nobly did they redeem
their pledges."* That tombstone is vocal, and,
when men want to be heroic, they go to that
churchyard and stand mute before the martyrs'
tablet and the sacred slab, and breathe and drink
in the spirit that makes hearts brave and wills
strong.

Paul's logic was this of the new life: "We also
believe and therefore speak"; and so, though they
ridiculed his bodily presence as weak, and his speech
as contemptible, wherever he went he got a hear-

* Life of Guthrie, I, 363.

ing, for there was that in him which compelled it. "Father Vassar," in Boston, had a marvellous fascination, which gave him access to those who seemed to repel all ordinary approach. One day he accosted a worldly and fashionable woman, and, although an entire stranger, asked her plainly whether she had ever believed in Jesus to her soul's salvation. When her husband, as worldly as she, came home to his dinner, she told him of the strange man who had met her and at once engaged her in conversation about her soul. "Had I been there," said her spouse, "I would have told him to go about his own business." "But, husband," said she, "if you had been there you would have thought that he *was about his own business.*"

"He that winneth souls is wise," but the wisdom is not learned in human schools. Experience of God's grace, a rich schooling in God's university, is the only adequate qualification: this power to witness is the power of the Holy Spirit indwelling, and inworking, and then outworking though the lips and the tongue, and the grander utterance of the life. When God dwells in us and gives us a true, deep knowledge of Himself, He lays the foundation for power in testimony. It is the baptism of the Spirit that made such a mighty witness even of Peter, turning cowardice into courage, and the traitor into the leader, so that he, who once could not face an accusing maid, stood and faced the great Jewish Council, daringly defying the august Sanhedrin! If we are to have new power in missions, we must have a higher standard of living. The believer who is transformed into the likeness of Christ is himself the apologetic for Christianity; for in him even the unbelieving, gainsaying world must see 'and read the "many infallible proofs" of a God, a Christ, a Holy Spirit, a regenerate character.

And therefore do we steadfastly maintain that no great power can attend Christian missions, while in the Church Christian life sinks to a low level. Such a life can beget no life of a higher sort, and our missionaries will, in their work, represent our uncertain convictions and our divided affections, and their unbelief and worldliness will make God's many mighty works impossible on the foreign field.

It was October 7, 1805, thirteen years almost to a day from the day when that mission compact was signed at Kettering, that Carey, Marshman, and Ward, at Serampore, drew up their famous spiritual "Covenant." It covered twelve printed pages octavo, and was read publicly at every station at least once a year.

If any one would see what sort of men God chose to lead the van of His modern missionary post, let him study that "Form of agreement respecting the great principles upon which the brethren of the mission thought it their duty to act in the work of instructing the heathen." Dr. George Smith calls it a *Preparatio Evangelica*, and well adds that it "embodies the divine principles of all Protestant scriptural missions, and is still a manual to be daily pondered by every missionary, and every church and society which may send a missionary forth." *

We give here its most important parts, for personal reflection :

"IT IS ABSOLUTELY NECESSARY :

1. "That we set an infinite *value upon immortal souls.*

2. "That we gain all *information of the snares and delusions* in which these heathen are held.

3. "That we *abstain from all those things* which would increase their prejudices against the Gospel.

4. "That we *watch all opportunities* for doing good.

5. "That we keep to the *example of Paul*, and make the great subject of our preaching, Christ the Crucified.

6. "That the natives should have an *entire confidence in us* and feel quite at home in our company.

7. "That we build up and *watch over the souls* that may be gathered.

8. "That we form our *native brethren to usefulness*, fostering every kind of genius and cherishing every gift and grace in them,

* Short History of Missions, p. 165.

especially advising the native churches to choose their own pastors and deacons from amongst their own countrymen.

9. "That we labor with all our might in forwarding *translations of the Sacred Scriptures* in the languages of India.

10. "That we establish *native free-schools* and recommend these establishments to other Europeans.

11. "That we be *constant in prayer and the cultivation of personal religion*, to fit us for the discharge of these laborious and unutterably important labors. Let us often look at Brainerd in the woods of America, pouring out his very soul before God for the perishing heathen, without whose salvation nothing could make him happy.

12. "That we *give ourselves unreservedly* to this glorious cause. Let us never think that our time, our gifts, our strength, our families, or even the clothes we wear, are our own. Let us sanctify them all to God and His cause. O, that He may sanctify us for His work! No private family ever enjoyed a greater portion of happiness than we have done since we resolved to have all things in common. If we are enabled to persevere, we may hope that multitudes of converted souls will have reason to bless God to all eternity for sending His Gospel into this country."

In this solemn compact, which sounds like an apostolic document, twelve cardinal principles are carefully set forth.

1. Valuing human souls at an infinite worth.
2. Informing themselves as to their actual needs.
3. Avoiding all putting of stumbling blocks in their way.
4. Watching opportunity to do good unto all.
5. Preaching Christ Crucified as their one theme.
6. Inspiring confidence by a Christlike life.
7. Establishing schools for Christian education.
8. Watching over and training native converts.
9. Raising up a native ministry for service.
10. Translating the Holy Scriptures into the vernacular.
11. Cultivating prayer and self-culture in piety.
12. Surrendering self unreservedly to God and service.

To this nothing-remains to be added to give completeness and symmetry. It reads like an inspired paper. The marks of the Holy Ghost are upon it. And we commend it to all friends of missions, and especially to all who have in view or in thought the field of missions. It need be no matter of wonder that, although the first Hindu convert, Krishna Chundra Pal, was not baptized as a Protestant believer until 1800, fifty years after Carey's death, the native Protestant community, in 1884, numbered half a million, with

ordained native pastors outnumbering the missionaries, and every decade witnessing an increase at
the rate of eighty-six per cent. !

Let this covenant be to the Church of Christ,
as we start on a new century of missions, a trumpet
peal of God for a new advance. A higher type
of piety is the great demand of our day. Spiritual
power depends upon spiritual *life.* Never will the
Holy Spirit set a premium upon low spiritual attainment by resting, in Shekinah glory, upon a
Church in whose courts are the idols of this world.
While the Word of God is neglected, prayer de-
generates into a form, and worship into ritual;
while the line of separation is obliterated between
the Church and the world, and the whole life of
the Church is on the lowest level, we shall look in
vain for the anointing from above.

How preaching and witnessing may be made
more attractive and effective is a question whose
vital importance transcends almost any other. The
great need of the modern pulpit is spiritual *power.*
With all the learning and culture of the ministry,
a nameless deficiency exists; and the lack, to
whatever traceable, is a lack of *power.* Even
where preaching attracts, how seldom it effects
that great end, the salvation of souls ! Why is it
that even those sermons which gratify, do not
satisfy, and many preachers who draw the crowd
do not win men to Christ? There seem to be
scholarship, intellectuality, and sometimes spirit-

uality, and yet but little of that seal and sanction which the Spirit sets on the most successful preaching by using it to convict and convert.

The lack of power may exist where there is no lack of *truth.* Without God's truth there will not be God's power; but there is not always power even where there is truth, for these two are not synonymous in this wicked world—would they were! We have carelessly adopted that pagan maxim : "*Magna est veritas et prævalebit,*" though all human history shows its fallacy and falsity. Men have always *known* more truth than they have *practised.* God Himself preached the truth in Eden, yet even there Satan's lie proved mightier. Noah preached truth for a century in the antediluvian world, and made not a convert. Greece and Rome and France knew truth enough to have saved them, but these, the most refined and martial and cultured of nations, have crowned falsehood and vice with the diadems of truth and virtue.

Truth, spoken in a sinful world, finds wrong and error mighty enough to keep the mastery : the Gospel itself, the very truth of God, needs something added to make it the *power* of God; and, what that is, the promise of the Father, fulfilled in part at Pentecost, reveals. We are now studying the science of spiritual dynamics, and may learn what makes our witness a dynamic force : "Ye shall receive the power of the Holy Ghost coming upon you." Unction, as it is called

by John, the Chrism (κρισμα), is that anointing
for service which helps men to reach, touch, move,
and mould the mind, heart, will, of the hearer.
Our mistake is fatal if we conceive of power in
missions as human. Even the most convincing
argument, the most captivating rhetoric, the most
exalted eloquence, do not imply this power.
Unction has a logic, rhetoric, eloquence of its
own.

The power to move men Godward is a power,
purely of God, and must be carefully distinguished
from all channels through which it flows, or means
by which it works, as the lightning is distinct from
the cloud it charges, or the wind from the wave
it heaves and rolls. This enduement of power
defies all *analysis.* The secret seems to lie now
in the glow of ardor and fervor, and then in tears
of tenderness; now in the logic of reason on fire with
conviction, and then in the logic of love warning
and inviting. So also does it defy *description*, like
savor, flavor, fragrance. But one may be pro-
foundly sensible of its presence or absence. A
sermon may be full of learning, empty of life—the
mummy of the Gospel, the form without the soul
—dead orthodoxy, wrapt in the cerements of the
grave and having the odor of decay.

But, while we may not describe, define, analyze
Unction, we may know its evidences and effects.
First, when the power of the Holy Ghost comes
upon us our *eyes are anointed* as with eye-salve,

and we *see.* We have a new apprehension of divine truth. Light takes color from the media through which it passes. Our minds and hearts and tempers and temperament give color to our notions of God. A tyrannical temper makes His will seem arbitrary and unreasonable; a vindictive spirit gives His wrath a lurid glare; a morbid heart makes even His promises seem gloomy, and a forceless, nerveless amiability makes even His mercy seem lax and His love insipid.

No man is fit to teach God's truth until he is taught of God, and, to be taught, he must come into vital contact and sympathy with God. And so the power to witness implies a power to *think rightly* of God. Then we vividly see the real lost state of souls, and their awful need, and the wonders of grace and the possibility of salvation. This sense of reality of divine things no man has until the Spirit of God unveils his eyes and anoints them with His own eye-salve.

Then we need power to *present* what is thus conceived. The modes of the preacher have as much to do with the effectiveness of his message as have the moods of the hearer. If he is clothed with power from on high, whether he thunders forth the peal of the law or with still small voice whispers the grace of God, Sinai and Calvary will be alike subduing.

God's preachers and witnesses are the *interpreters* of His truth. Like a musician, who gets beyond the

mechanical performance or the originating genius,
and enters into the secret life of the composer,
the preacher must interpret to the hearer God's
idea or thought. Many a humble man, who has
no fluency of speech, or grace of gesture, no power
to flash auroras or rain meteors, has power to
make God's truth clear and cogent, and move
minds far superior to his own in culture and power.
This we must understand and feel as we never
have felt it. As Dr. T. H. Skinner used to say,
God may give to a church and its pastor every
type of piety but that which is found in a *sense of
the powers of the world to come*, and men will remain
unconverted, but he who is to save souls must
have *this* sense. This gives logic both of argument and feeling—this makes words now like
drawn swords, keen at the edge and keener at the
point; now like a hammer, that breaks even the
rock; and now like fire, that burns and melts.
The hearer feels a spiritual force grappling with
his convictions, conscience, will; and, if he is not
compelled to yield to Christ, he is at least compelled to consider and make a decision.

This power of the Holy Ghost is probably the
one gift and grace that cannot be *feigned.* An
unconverted man may build a symmetrical discourse, faultless both in matter and style; a hypo-
crite may assume, like an actor, what he neither
feels nor believes; but to wield the sword of the
Spirit so as to pierce to joints and marrow,—that

requires Holy Ghost power, holding, nerving, guiding the arm.

This promised "anointing" gives quality to the *witness-bearer* as well as to his message. The ancients thought purest virtue aromatic to the sense, and it is true that this divine chrism makes the whole man fragrant, investing even his person and presence with a nameless charm, so that, like Lord Chatham, "there is something in the man finer than he ever said." The anointed witness is like Aaron; even to the fringes of his garments the holy oil runs down, and all his robes smell of the myrrh and aloes and cassia out of the ivory palaces of the Heavenly King. He becomes like some instrument, long played upon by some master musician, whose very fibre loses its harshness and coarseness and takes on a new quality.

This power clothed Peter at Pentecost, made Stephen irresistible even before his stoners, and made Wesley and Whitefield the mightiest preachers of the last century; this power made Edwards at Enfield, and Nettleton, in the simplest repetition of a text, mighty to move and sway a whole audience.

Be assured, the greatest lack of missions, both at home and abroad, is the want of this anointing. Tarry before God till you get it. No waiting for this is wasting time. Better one day, with power from on high, than a hundred or a thousand in its absence. God would not have us neglect the natural basis of studious and systematic preparation, for grace sets no premium on sloth, and a mind and heart fitted by devout study of the Word of God is most likely to be endued.

Nor would God have us neglect the *spiritual* basis, in general purity and piety of character. The anointing implies previous cleansing, as the Levites were washed with water before they were anointed with oil. But, beside and beyond this, God would have us feel our deep need of the promise of the Father. May the Spirit of God be to us all a Socrates, to bring us from ignorance and impotence unconscious to ignorance and impotence conscious. Then let our need *drive* us to God. Let the securing of this unction be our supreme aim and absorbing prayer. Putting away the ambition to originate brilliant and startling thoughts, or weave the golden and silver tissues of ornate speech—we must get so near to the heart of God that we shall care more for the groan of one wounded soul than for the shouts of thousands that praise the beauty of the bow or the grace of the archer. " Tarry until you are endued with power from on high." What is needed is a heart that can hurl hot shot at the citadels of Satan ; not the iron tongue of passionate denunciation, or the silver tongue of flashing rhetoric, or the golden tongue of persuasive oratory, but the tongue of fire set aflame by a coal from heavenly altars.

Here—reverently let it be recorded—here lies
the basis and bottom of all power in subduing this
world for Christ. After the whole armor of God
is endued, there must still be vigor and vitality to
wear it and wield it. Our weapons are mighty
only when we ourselves are first strong in the
Lord and in the power of His might. The pan-
oplied soldier needs still the nameless charm and
investment of a divine baptism and chrism.

This, then, is the complex yet simple power of
missions—Christ on the throne ruling the Church,
restraining the powers of darkness, and extending
His shield over His own; Christ on the battle-
field riding His white horse and leading His
Church to conflict and conquest; marshalling His
heavenly host and the great armies of an obedient
creation to bring His plans to consummation;
then the Holy Spirit, enduing His witnesses and
making them the power of God to win souls.
When our ministers and missionaries recognize and
realize this need, cherish this aim, and breathe
this prayer on every field of missions, a new force
will be felt and a new power manifested. Then
we shall see results on the whole field. Doors will
open, until not a hermit nation remains or one
shut gate confronts us.   ·

Gigantic barriers will be removed and walls of
adamant will crumble. Converts will be multiplied till they spring up like grass along water-
courses. Congregations will gather, churches will

be organized, schools will be established—everywhere, even in the deserts, streams will burst forth and flow God-ward, turning the wilderness into Eden ; native evangelists will press into the regions beyond, opposition will only make disciples strong, and martyr fires only kindle flames of love to God and man. Before a Church that enthrones Christ in the heart and follows Him everywhere, before a Church baptized with the fire of the Holy Ghost, nothing can stand. Francis Xavier stood before China and saw its vastness loom up like a mountain that shut out the very sky, and he cried, " O rock, rock, when wilt thou open to my Master ? " And that rock still stands, the Gibraltar of heathenism. God waits to be *asked*, and wills to give us all this power simply for the asking. A dying world is about us—nay, a dead world—but the Word of Life is in our hands. O for the Spirit of Life ! Let Him endue us, and our speech is no more with enticing words of man's wisdom, but with demonstration of the Holy Ghost. In the Valley of Indecision the wind of Heaven breathes, signs of life appear—the dry bones move—bone cleaves to bone: the skeleton of creed is clad with the flesh of faith, and, where the slain of Satan lay, the hosts of God encamp. For such power from on high let us so earnestly seek, that every breath of spiritual life shall become a prayer !

THE DIVINE FRUIT OF MISSIONS.

HE fruit of missions constitutes a seal from God upon the work and the workmen.

When Mark brings his Gospel narrative to a conclusion, he significantly says, " And they went forth and preached everywhere, the Lord working with (them) and confirming the word with signs following." The Lord co-operated with His appointed and anointed workmen, and confirmed their work and His own word by appropriate signs.

In the book of the Acts of the Apostles, at least one representative instance is given of the various signs promised. Take Paul's experience alone. At Philippi, he cast out the demon from the divining damsel; at Ephesus, he laid his hands on disciples and they spake with new tongues; at Melita, he shook off the deadly viper that fastened on his hand and felt no harm; and at Ephesus likewise special miracles were wrought by his hands, so that from his body were brought unto the sick handkerchiefs or aprons,* etc.

* Acts xix. 11, 12.

There are those who affirm that, *at no time* in subsequent Christian history, have supernatural signs ever been absolutely lacking, as evidences of the presence and power of Him who promised, saying, " Lo, I am with you alway." It is quite noticeable that, while this promise of the Lord's *presence* extends " to the end of the age," no such language is used about the *signs;* the difference in terms is very remarkable: " And these signs shall follow them that believe." Here it is not said that those particular signs shall continue to be wrought, alway, even to the end of the age ; but only that they " shall follow," as they did, for an indefinite time. Had our Lord meant to assure us that such signs should be as perpetual as His presence, it was easy for Him to add one word, " alway," to make that plain. But He did not, and we infer that there was and is a deep reason. He foresaw that, while some signs would always follow faithful preaching and true believing, *these* were not to be perpetually wrought ; and that, while *some* signs would always be needful to accredit the work as His own, these particular signs might not always be necessary, or even expedient. As a structure rises from base to cap-stone, we find it best to change the form, face, and even nature, of the material. The huge unhewn blocks which are laid as the foundation would be awkward, ungraceful, and unduly massive, in the superstructure ; and so stones of lighter weight, chiselled into beauty and polished into lustre, wrought often into delicate forms, slender columnar shapes with capitals of exquisite tracery, airy arches and lance-like pinnacles, rise toward heaven. There is not more difference between the rough, bulky bulb of a hyacinth and the tender, slender petals, than between the rude and massive basal stones and the white blossoms which burst into stony flowers above them. But all are equally parts of one building. And so the primitive signs, wrought in the apostolic age, had their special design and served their special purpose. They laid the base of apostolic work and testimony; but, when foundations were thus laid, it was perhaps better that, as the structure rose upon this base, the supernatural character of the work should be attested in different ways, and the form of such attestation change with the demand of each new age; so that, while supernatural signs should never cease, they should acquire new force from their very variety. And, with Professor Christlieb, we firmly hold that, in the history of modern missions particularly, we find numerous occurrences which unmistakably remind us of the apostolic age; * and, he adds, " We cannot, therefore, fully admit the proposition that no more miracles are performed in our day."

In fact, it is not rash to assert that there are still, in this remote day, supernatural signs curiously corresponding to the miracles of the first

* " Modern Doubt and Christian Belief," 332.

century.* Perhaps we need not hesitate to call
them " modern miracles," since a miracle is simply
a *wonder* and a *sign* combined, *i.e.*, something
transcending the power of man, to which God appeals as a sign of His power. " The blind receive
their sight," when eyes, long blinded to sin and
holiness, are opened to see the deformity of the
one and the beauty of the other. " The lame
walk," when moral impotency and inability are
divinely displaced by power to resist even the
most mighty temptations and to break the bonds
of the most enslaving vices. " The lepers are
cleansed," whenever the very blood becomes rid
of the vile virus of lust, and the unclean beast becomes virtuous, humane, holy. " The deaf hear,"
when ears, hopelessly insensible alike to the warn-
ings of justice and the invitations of mercy, and
which even the thunders of Sinai could not pierce,
now catch the whispers from Calvary and the still
small voice of that Spirit that comes not in earthquake, storm, or roaring conflagration. " The
dead are raised up," when those who have been
destitute of all the energy, the sensibility, the
vitality, and the activity of spiritual life, waken
like Lazarus to cast off the death-damps and
grave-clothes, and walk with God and work for
God, and war against sin and Satan ; when that
upper story of our triple being, the true observatory of the spirit, which sin turned into a death-

* " Modern Miracles," by Lelia Thomson.

chamber, again becomes the shrine and throne of the Holy Ghost. It is by no means certain that these moral miracles are not in their way more convincing signs of divine power than any others wrought in a lower sphere.

That great Messianic prophecy and poem, in Isaiah,* more than hints that earlier signs may give way to later ones, not less convincing and conclusive in their way. "Instead of the thorn shall come up the fir-tree; and, instead of the brier, shall come up the myrtle-tree; and it shall be to the Lord for a name, for an everlasting sign that shall not be cut off."

The exact language here used must not escape us. In Genesis iii. 17, 18, we read: "And unto Adam he said, Because thou hast . . . . eaten of the tree of which I commanded thee, saying thou shalt not eat of it; cursed is the ground for thy sake; in sorrow shalt thou eat of it all the days of thy life. Thorns also and thistles shall it bring forth unto thee." A tree was the occasion of sin, and so the very soil which bore the tree was cursed, and thorns and thistles borne by the ground became signs of curse.

When Jesus, the second Adam, bore up to the cross the sin that cursed the first Adam and the Adamic race, He bore on His royal head a "*crown of thorns.*" Little did those soldiers know that in their mockery they were unconsciously prophesy-

* Isaiah lv. 13.

ing ; for He who lifted up the thorns on His own bleeding brow was to remove the curse even from the ground. The whole creation has a redemption, and in His crucifixion that redemption was signified and symbolized. As a tree brought the curse, so a tree bore the curse away. He who hung on the cursed tree has transformed the tree of the knowledge of good and evil into a tree of life, and He wore as His crown the thorns that were the signs of curse. And now hear the prophetic promise of what is to be the *ultimate* result: " God's word that goeth forth out of His mouth " shall be like " the rain that cometh down and the snow from heaven," pure, celestial condensations and distillations, and it shall not return to Him void, but shall accomplish His gracious pleasure, and shall prosper in its holy mission. Under the distillations of that life-giving Gospel, the earth, which caused to bud * thorns and briers, shall cause to bud a harvest of heavenly fruits which give " seed to the sower and bread to the eater." And the sign of this accomplished redemption shall be that, "instead of the thorn shall come up the fir-tree, and instead of the brier shall come up the myrtle-tree."

Can any figurative expression be plainer ? Instead of the vile, accursed, vexatious, and vicious products of the soil, shall be trees and plants, the most beautiful, useful, fragrant, and fruitful. And

* Gen. iii. 18, Margin.

this shall prove a divine husbandry. All the toil and skill of man has not been able, in six thousand years, to expel thorns and thistles. They are found everywhere, they spring up spontaneously, grow with great energy, hold with great tenacity, and multiply with inconceivable rapidity, so that one variety of thistle might from the fifth successive harvest of a single seed, supply seeds sufficient to plant every square foot of soil in the solar system, from Mercury to Neptune! But let the Divine Husbandman come, and with incredible swiftness the whole moral aspect of human nature is changed. In the soil of society, the vile and vicious and virulent growths of sin, that no effort of man has been able to extirpate, are surely eradicated. Forms of evil, of crime, of rebellion against God and revolt against humanity, that generations have vainly sought to destroy, or even reduce, disappear; and, in their place, are found beautiful characters, with charms that never fade or fall, as does the foliage of deciduous trees, symmetrical lives, fruitful and fragrant, like the bowers of paradise. "Thy people also shall be all righteous;" and it is surely no marvel if in such a transformation God says men shall see God's husbandry—"that they might be called Trees of Righteousness, the planting of the Lord that He might be glorified." *

And now let us note that, of such results of the

* Isaiah lx. 21, lxi. 3.

going forth of His word out of His mouth, God says, "And it shall be to the Lord for a NAME," *i.e.*, a reputation or fame—establishing His glory —" for an EVERLASTING SIGN *that shall not be cut off.*" This is the only sign that is called everlasting, and " that shall not be cut off." Reverently, let us add, this is perhaps the only sign that is in its nature fitted to be everlasting. The progress of human discovery and invention has gone far toward ameliorating, relieving, and removing the ills to which the body is heir. Modern medicine and surgery have, by methods ʼpurely scientific, caused the blind to receive their sight, the lame to walk, the lepers to be cleansed, the deaf to hear, and even the apparently dead to be raised. What future medical, surgical, and sanitary art and science may do, like Pharaoh's magicians, to imitate with their enchantments certain miracles of God, we cannot say. But there is one point at which all competition is at an end, viz., the *transformation of moral and spiritual character.* The soul of man and the soil of society, even under the most careful culture, never lose *sin.* There is a strange sinfulness even in our nature that crops out everywhere, and at all times. Its forms of manifestation change from coarser and grosser, but are more subtle and dangerous even under their refinement. Education has never yet eliminated sin from man's nature or society. Here is a sign of divine power that cannot be counterfeited by science or art or culture, or even reform. Between moral reformation and spiritual regeneration there is still a great gulf fixed, and man cannot bridge it. The seven golden ages—of Egypt under the Ptolemies, Greece under Pericles, Rome under Augustus, Italy under Leo the Great, France under Louis the Magnificent, Russia under Ivan IV., England under Elizabeth,—were ages of awful profligacy, infidelity, and immorality. God has never given to man the key of life, though He may have given him the key of knowledge. Only He who is the Alpha and Omega has the keys of hell and of death, and can release the soul held in chains of hellish habits and deadly vices. And here is God's "everlasting sign which shall not be cut off."

Those who have the widest acquaintance with the history and progress of missions, are rather oppressed with the sense of comparative ignorance, inasmuch as so much remains to be known, and the very vastness of the field baffles the industry that investigates it. But the further these studies are carried the deeper is the impression left on the mind, that the story of missions is, as the Bishop of Ripon finely intimated, a continuation of the Acts of the Apostles: yes, of the Acts of the Apostles, with all its essential supernaturalism. No exhibition of a Power unmistakably divine, or a Presence unmistakably divine, has ever presented to mankind proofs more obvious than those found

in these new chapters in this modern Book of the
Acts. The devout student of missions, but most
of all the devoted worker in missions, bows before
these evidences of a providential and spiritual intervention which to his mind defy doubt, not to
say denial.

These proofs need only to be put before the
candid and conscientious observer, to compel
conviction. We read how, in the days of Christ,
" the multitude wondered when they saw the dumb
to speak, the maimed to be whole, the lame to
walk, and the blind to see ; and they glorified the
God of Israel." * Corresponding marvels are to
be found in the history of missions, and, when the `
doubting disciple, or even the sceptical unbeliever,
is confronted with them, wonder is excited, and if
there be a readiness to be convinced by evidence,
conviction becomes irresistible, and God is again
glorified. Would that all who profess to be disciples would diligently read this new Book of the
Acts, which is the book of facts of modern missions ! There may be seen features correspondent
to all the most distinctive and distinguishing marks
of the apostolic era. The same Pentecostal outpouring ; the same marvellous opening of doors,
great and effectual ; the same call of God separating the modern apostles to the work of evangelization ; the same grace, converting the Gentiles,
purifying their hearts by faith, and anointing con-

* Matt. xv. 31.

verts for service; the same transformation of
individuals, and even communities, by the power
of the Word and the Spirit; the same overcoming
of obstacles and triumph over difficulties ; the same
supernatural answer to believing prayer. That
great world's conference in London in 1888—
what was it but another gathering of the Church
to hear the missionary laborers rehearse all that
God had done with them ? etc.

What a new epoch of missions will begin when
the Church of God will but read with open eyes
these new chapters in the history of grace, and see
how God is yet present and powerfully working in
the world, to honor the witnesses to His Gospel!

John Williams' progress through the South Seas
was a triumphal march.   Even in the career of
Paul as, from Antioch to Athens, and from the
Golden Horn to the Pillars of Hercules, he went
on his great errand of evangelism, there are not
more convincing signs of God's power than in
John Williams' voyages, from the shores of Eimeo
to the fatal coast of Eromanga!   His missionary
career covers but twenty-two years, from 1817 to
1839.   Yet, like a flying messenger of Jehovah,
with a flaming torch, he sped from island to island,
and group to group, Aitutaki, Atiu, Raratonga,
Mangaia, Raiatea, Samoa, and one unbroken
series of successes crowned his work, till not only
islands, but groups of islands, came in rapid succession under the sway of Christ's golden sceptre;

and until, in 1834, five years before he fell, he could calmly say: "At the present time, we do not know of any group, or any single island of importance, within two thousand miles of Tahiti, in any direction, to which the glad tidings of salvation have not been conveyed! " In some cases he saw the spears, which a year before were used in desolating warfare, serving as pulpit balustrades; and the wooden images of the great god of war, ONO, and other similar deities, turned into supports for the roof of common wood-sheds, and other inferior buildings! The inhabitants of these islands turned with unparalleled rapidity from the worship of idols and the practice of cannibalism, burned their Maraes, and laid their false gods at the missionaries' feet as trophies of Gospel triumph.

When Rev. Jas. Calvert was asked to give in one sentence a proof of the success of missions, he said, "When I first arrived at the Fiji group, my first duty was to bury the hands, feet, heads, and bones of the arms and legs of eighty victims whose bodies had been roasted and eaten in a cannibal feast. I lived to see the very cannibals who had taken part in that inhuman festival gathered about the Lord's Table."

The cannibalism of Fiji was not simply the result of an impulse of passsionate hate or revenge, but an institution inwoven with the very fabric of social life, and even religion. It was not the resort of, hunger, for with plenty and variety of food, human bodies were regarded as a delicacy to be preferred. Rev. S. McFarlane, LL.D., has suggested that the Fijians regarded cannibalism as an act of supreme revenge upon a fallen enemy; a kind of vindication of the national honor, which patriotic pride demanded; and to devour a slain enemy might also imply the transfer of his strength and prowess to him who ate him. But, more than this, Dr. Seemann suggests that cannibal feasts belonged to the ceremonies of *religion*. The ovens are never used for any other purpose, and whereas fingers are the only forks used in eating ordinary food, for human flesh a peculiar fork, with three or four prongs, made of hard wood, and each fork known by its peculiar name, is used. These forks are evidently regarded as sacred, and as profaned by the touch of a foreigner. Under the great banyan-tree, the sacred Akautabu, cannibal feasts took place, and certain parts of the bodies of victims were hung on this tree. Here the famous cannibal chief, Thakombau, kept his abominable revels.*

Where this practice of cannibalism was thus associated with social custom, appetite, revenge, patriotism, and even religion, we might expect that the higher the rank the more indulgence there would be in this revolting practice; and the fact is, that many of the chiefs gloried in the number of human bodies they had eaten, and kept a regis-

* "Among the Cannibals of New Guinea," 100–102.

ter by making a line of stones, one stone being added for each body eaten. The stones thus placed by two chiefs, Wangka Levu and Ra Undre Undre, were counted by a native teacher, and found to number *nearly nine hundred;* and as many as fifty bodies have been cooked for a single feast. What a dynamic power must be found in a simple Gospel message that could eradicate customs so deeply rooted in the very soil of society!

This story of Fiji it would be difficult to surpass, either for the depth of cruelty, iniquity, and idolatry there confronted by the Gospel, or for the rapid, radical, and revolutionary changes which that Gospel wrought. Human life was held in reckless disregard. An Englishman named Jackson was witness to the sacrifice to earth spirits. A chief was building a new hut, and deep holes were dug to receive the main posts on which the house was to rest. To propitiate the gods to uphold the dwelling, men were forced to stand in these holes and clasp these posts while the earth was filled in and buried them alive. At the launching of a war canoe, living human bodies were used as rollers, and they were crushed to a *shapeless mass* beneath the weight. The sacrifice of human life was wanton, as though, instead of crime, it implied merit.

In 1835 there was not a single disciple. When, fifty years later, in 1885, the Jubilee was kept, not an avowed heathen was left in all the large group of eighty inhabited islands; and the returns of that year show a total of 1,322 churches and other preaching places, 3,021 missionaries, catechists, and teachers, only ten of whom were *white* missionaries, and, out of a population of 110,000, 104,585 attendants at public worship. To-day not a vestige of cannibalism, widow-strangling, infanticide and like cruelties, exists, and the Fijian Church sends native evangelists to other distant shores to preach Christ in other tongues. Mr. Calvert himself testifies: " We had no night of toil. God was with us from the beginning, and all along, even to the present time, and he Has ever confirmed His Word with signs following."

That same chief, Thakombau, who, under the sacred Akautabu, cut out the tongue of a captive chief who with it was begging for a speedy death, and jocosely ate it before his face, afterwards built a chapel at Bau, and at his own death-bed preached to his attendants faith and salvation. Ten days after the big death drums had summoned the people to a cannibal feast, in 1854, those same drums were by his orders sounded as a signal for the assembling of the people for divine worship ! * The last act of Thakombau, in October, 1874, was to cede Fiji to Queen Victoria, and, through Sir John B. Thurston, his Prime Minister, present his *war club* to her Majesty, with the significant

* Jas. Calvert, 111.

confession that, "until of late that war club was the only known law of Fiji." That club, with his yanggona bowl, may be seen in the British Museum.

How little would Canon Taylor's and Mr. Caine's criticisms of missions affect minds that were familiar with the great facts of missionary biography and history! For example, when Captain Cook touched at Tahiti, he wrote: "This island can neither serve public interests nor private ambition, and will probably never be much known." About the close of the eighteenth century, William Carey and his fellows so aroused the dormant missionary spirit in the churches, that the London Missionary Society sent missionaries to this island. There was a long "night of toil." Sixteen years went by without a sign of blessing. One day a missionary, with a group of savages about him, read, from a manuscript copy of the Gospel according to John, the third chapter. As he came to the sixteenth verse, which Luther called "the Gospel in miniature," a rude warrior in the group asked him to read that verse again and again. Then he said, "This, if it be true, is for *you* only, not for such as *me.*" But the missionary repeated that wonderful word, "*Whosoever*," and dwelt upon its meaning. "Then," said the warrior, "your God shall be my God; for we have never heard such a message as this; our gods do not love us so."

It is not yet seventy-five years since that first convert, who was also the first-fruits of all Polynesia, was brought from darkness to light; yet now in Polynesia there are about eight hundred thousand converts; and the work has spread till it has reached New Guinea. A band of not less than one hundred and sixty young men and women, going from Tahiti and the neighboring islands, as evangelists, seek to carry the life-giving Gospel to other benighted tribes; and, of all these native workers, not one has ever proved recreant or faithless. Yet these are the people who, at the beginning of this century, had lost all idea of God save that, somewhere afar off, some strange being dwelt, who exercised sovereignty as a tyrannical despot; and at the graves of their ancestors, they were wont to go and beseech them to plead with this unapproachable Deity!

No more expressive and laconic tablet is to be found in the world than that raised by grateful native converts to Dr. John Geddie on Aneityum, one of the Loyalty Islands, or New Hebrides. It bears in their language the now famous but unique parallelism:

"WHEN HE LANDED HERE
IN 1848,
THERE WERE NO CHRISTIANS;
WHEN HE LEFT HERE
IN 1872,
THERE WERE NO HEATHENS."

On most of the islands of Western Polynesia a similar tablet might be erected, a brief epitome of the wonderful work of God within less than a century. And in these lands, where missions have had their modern triumphs, some of the most heroic converts and evangelists have been found. Who has not read the story of Lugalama, the first martyr of Uganda! The cruel Mwanga seized him and Seruwanga and Kakumba, his companions; and, apparently from no other cause than because these lads had found their way to firm faith in Jesus while yet the king was halting between two opinions, he determined in a rage to put them to death by torture. Mujasi, the cruel wretch who wreaked upon these poor boys the hate of Mwanga, mocked them. "O, you know Isa Masiya (Jesus Christ), do you? . . . . You believe you will rise from the dead, do you? Well, I shall burn you and see." The lads answered the mockery by a sacred hymn:

" Killa siku tunsifer !"
(" Daily, daily, sing the praises," etc.)

A dismal swamp, Maganja, was the chosen Golgotha for these young martyrs. The jeering crowd build a rude frame-work and heap fuel beneath. First they mutilate Seruwanga and Kakumba, and fling their bleeding bodies upon the frame-work for the agony of the flame. Then the executioners approach Lugalama, and he cries, " O do not cut off my arms: I will not struggle nor fight—only throw me into the fire!" What a sad prayer: "Only throw me into the fire!" But cruelty insists on butchery, and the armless trunk is flung upon the frame-work for slow fires to finish what the sharp blade has begun. But, until their tongues are crisped in the flame, those martyrs continue to sing praises. Cranmer and Ridley and Huss and Jerome did not honor the Lord more truly; and when Musali, standing by, was threatened with a like fate, he boldly said to Mujasi, "I am a follower of Isa, and I am not ashamed of Him."

A young Sunday-school teacher, a poor seamstress, one Sunday gave to a rough street arab a shilling to go to Sunday-school. That boy, Amos Sutton, was converted, went to India as missionary, and led the American Baptists to begin work among the Telugus. How little they knew the stupendous results that were to hang on that mission! In 1853, the American Baptist Missionary Union, meeting at Albany, seriously considered whether it would not be best to give up that work altogether—so unfruitful had it been. It was on that occasion that the poet, Dr. S. F. Smith, wrote the now famous verses, "Shine on, Lone Star." The mission was continued and reinforced. Twenty-five years after, that mission gathered ten thousand converts in one year—a result of Christian labor which probably surpasses in magnitude any other ever known in Christian history.

The work of the American Baptist Missionary Union covers seventy-seven years (1814–1891). Their first station was begun in 1814; six years of sowing passed before they had one convert to baptize, in 1819. At the end of ten years they had but one small church of eighteen, to reward a decade of trial, self-denial, persecution, imprisonment, and delayed fruit. Now, looking back over the whole period, and including that first decade, on their mission fields they have organized one church for every three weeks, or about seventeen a year, and baptized one convert for every three hours, day and night, or about three thousand a year—over two hundred and twenty-five thousand in all.

In 1819, one baptism; in 1886, 9,342. In 1824, one church of 18; 1886, 123,580 members. In 1814, $1,230.26 income; 1886–7, $351,889.69. In 1814, Mr. and Mrs. Judson the whole force; 1887, 1,986 laborers. In 1814, Burmah the one field; 1886, sixteen fields.

When Adoniram Judson found that some of the friends of foreign missions were beginning to lose heart, he exhorted them to "wait twenty or thirty years, and then perhaps," said he, "you will hear from us again." Once, while sick, he occupied the empty cage of a lion which had just died. After the lapse of years, the King of Burmah, at his own expense, built a Christian church, a parsonage and a school-house, near the very spot where the lion's cage had stood. And the king's sons were pupils in the school taught by the Christian missionaries.

In Turkey the missionaries have made seven new translations of the Word of God within one generation; there are in Constantinople twenty-one sets of electrotype plates for as many editions, and over two million copies have been distributed. Rev. Charles Wheeler's work on the Euphrates is another example of the fruits of missions, and of the peculiar fruit of that field. All along that ancient river he planted little Christian churches of an apostolic sort. He taught the converts to give a tithe of their small income to the Lord, and so out of *ten* converts he would organize a church—a self-supporting church; for over such a little flock he could set a native pastor, who could live on the average level of his own people, since their ten tithes would assure him a support equal to their own. Probably no such self-supporting churches are to be found elsewhere except among the *Unitas Fratrum.*

In the Mumahassa, or North Peninsula of Celebes, Riedel and Schwarr were the means, after 1829, of turning to Christ more than half the population of one hundred and fourteen thousand.* John G. Paton went to Aniwa, that little island where every atrocity and iniquity had a home, and in three years and a half saw a transformed com-

* George Smith, " Short History," p. 180.

munity, the chief himself leading the way both in the espousal of Christ and the public confession of Him; and no book of modern missions has more fascinated every lover of missions than the story of Aniwa. Wm. A. B. Johnson went to Sierra Leone in 1816. He found there the accumulated refuse of slave ships, thirty African tribes represented, horrible crimes of lust and drink and violence, holding Satanic carnival. He lived only seven years; but before he died he saw that whole community transformed into a model state, like Duncan's Metlakahtla among North American Indians; in fact, before eighteen months had passed, Mr. Johnson saw a revival so wide-spread and deep-reaching that it could be compared only to Pentecost.

"Comparative theology," says Dr. Flint, "is a magnificent demonstration, not only that man was made for religion, but what religion he was made for." It is true that results have come slowly at the first in most cases, like the most valuable harvests. In the Hawaiian group, five years passed by before the first convert, the Regent Kauhumanu, yielded to Christ; six years in Burmah, before Moung Nau, and as many years among the Karens, before Kho-Thah-Byu, rewarded the toil. In India, it was seven years before Krishna Chundra Pal was baptized; and in Siam it was twelve before Nai Chune became the first-fruits. Mr. Henry and Mr. Nott waited at Tahiti sixteen years before

Pomare II., the king, took the lead in conversion, and at New Zealand Samuel Marsden lived on hope alone for twenty years. In Australia, in 1860, Nathaniel Pipper was the first convert, after thirty-six years; and so great was the event that a public meeting was called to celebrate it, with the governor in the chair; and in the mountains of Na Vita Leva, in the Fiji group, paganism survived for more than fifty years after the first missionaries had landed. Notwithstanding the fact that the Fijians had, as a nation, long since renounced idols, paganism survived in this mountain district till about ten years ago.

But all this waiting has had its reward. The Hawaiian Islands more than twenty years since took their place among Christian nations; where Adoniram Judson toiled there are now more than thirty thousand converted Burmese; where Mr. Boardman baptized Kho Tha Byu in 1828, in 1878, when the Memorial Hall was built to keep the Jubilee of that event, there were thirty thousand Christian Karens who had fallen asleep beside as many more who were living for Christ. Sir Charles Bernard recently stated that the Christian Karens number two hundred thousand, or fully one-third of the Karen people. About five hundred congregations are practically self-supporting. They tithe the produce of their land for the support of their pastors. They also send missionaries to Siam and furnish all their support.

Where Carey and his colaborers sowed in tears, there are not less than eight hundred thousand baptized East Indians, and Christian communities numbering four or five times as many. That first convert of all Western Polynesia was the leader of a host now numbering eight hundred thousand living disciples in the South Seas. Samuel Marsden's twenty years of patience has its reward: in 1842, twenty-eight years after he landed in New Zealand, a bishop was sent from Britain to take charge of a diocese which included the whole nation; and among the Fiji group not one professedly heathen village can be found since that last mountain citadel yielded to Christ.

These are but a few examples among many. We might multiply them indefinitely, showing that, even where the laborers have been called to exercise long patience, the latter rain has come though the early rain was withheld, and the harvest has proved abundant.

Mission work proper began in China with the cession of Hong Kong in 1843. Then the laborers were very few and the converts in all, seven; in 1888, 34,555. The rate of increase is noticeable: in the twenty-five years from 1863 to 1888, the rate was eighteen-fold; at the same rate, the next quarter century would show over 850,000, and a half century more would show fifteen million, or one in every twenty-five inhabitants a professed disciple. This increase of ratio is one of the com-

mon facts of missionary history: the progression
is not "arithmetical," but "geometrical"—not
along the slow lines of addition, but by the rapid
process of multiplication; not, like a line, in one
direction of length only, but like an expanding
cube, in breadth and depth and height also.   Let
the Church but do her duty and God will show
greater wonders still; thirty-fold shall become
sixty, and an hundred-fold.

The fruit of missionary toil must be judged *nega-*
tively as well as *positively*—by what it has *displaced*
as well as by what it has *created*.

Rev. William Ward gives the testimony of a
Hindu Pundit, that in the province of Bengal
alone, ten thousand children were every month
put to death by their own mothers.   On the coast
of Malabar evil spirits have for centuries been
worshipped by all classes except Brahmins, all
other Hindus paying them homage.   To the lowest caste, that of slaves, is attributed the power to
let loose upon men the evil demon, and exorcists
are called in with noisy native drums, charms, and
incantations, to drive out the malignant spirit.   In
the district of Canara alone were 4,041 temples
to evil demons, beside 3,682 to other fanes, only
as long ago as 1842; and it was emphatically
"Satan's seat."

Claudius Buchanan, in 1806, knew his approach
to Juggernaut, when yet fifty miles off, by the
human bones which paved the way.   He called

it "the Valley of Death," likening it to the valley of Hinnom, and Juggernaut, to the ancient Moloch. He found the temples of this hideous monster decked with the symbols of sensuality, walls and gates bearing indecency, wrought in massive sculpture as in the buried city at the foot of Vesuvius. Two kindred idols, Boloram and Shudubra, brother and sister, were borne along with Juggernaut in festive procession. The priests taught the people that the great weight of the huge car would be moved only as they, the devotees, pleased the hideous god with lascivious attitude, gesture, and song. The green slime of the leprosy of lust and the red stains of blood covered the worship of Juggernaut. And yet a quarter century ago the crowds were so great at his festivals that "one hundred thousand attendants would not be missed."

For two hundred and fifty years England seemed blind to Divine Providence in British occupation of the *East Indies*, and her rulers fought against the evangelization of India. Up to the time of the new charter of the East India Company, in 1813, the opposition was open, systematic, and often malignant and violent. Tongues and pens were used, and ignorance united with virulence against missions. The arguments employed were so absurd that Dr. Duff has compared them to curious " fossil reliques of antediluvian ages."

When, in 1793, in a bill pending for renewal

of the Company's charter, clauses were introduced meant to encourage the propagation of the Gospel, they were promptly and peremptorily *negatived*. A learned prelate in the House of Lords, a champion of orthodoxy, too, argued against any interference with the religion, laws, local customs of the people of India, alleging that upon Englishmen rested " no obligation to attempt the conversion of the natives," even were it possible—which he denied; and that " the command to preach the Gospel to all nations did not in this case apply ! "

In 1813, in the British House of Commons, Mr. Charles Marsh likewise protested against the introduction of Christianity into India:

" When I look at the peaceful and harmonious alliances of families, guarded and secured by the household virtues ; when I see amongst a cheerful and well-ordered society the benignant and softening influences of religion and morality ; a system of manners founded upon a mild and polished obedience, and preserving the surface of social life smooth and unrufled, I cannot hear without surprise, mingled with horror, of sending out Baptists and anabaptists to civilize and convert such a people, at hazard of disturbing or deforming institutions which appear to have been hitherto the means ordained by Providence of making them virtuous and happy." *

This was seventy-eight years ago ; and while

* Exeter Hall Lectures, 1850-1.

Mr. Marsh was indulging his philippic against missions, a class of Hindu procurers, called "Panwas," made it their profession to provide victims for a hideous human sacrifice in the Meriah groves. These victims, or "Meriahs," might be selected without regard to age or sex, bought or stolen from the poorer classes; then conveyed from the plains to the hills, they were *sold* for so many *lives, i.e.,* cattle, sheep, pigs, or fowls,—the medium of exchange where there is no metallic currency. As a life unbought would be an abomination to the gods, a price must be paid.

In all the villages young persons were reared and kept in readiness for this slaughter, and within a comparatively small district four or five hundred such sacrifices have been annually offered for probably two or three thousand years. Human blood enriches the soil in the spring-time, and in the autumn must sanctify the harvest; and meanwhile drought, dearth, disease, and other crises call for similar sacrifices.

Dr. Duff has described these horrid orgies of death: "In the centre of the sacred Meriah grove is an open space. The festival lasts three days, the first of which is consumed in riotous excess of drink and other abominations; on the second, amid the clang of many instruments, the victim, in gay attire, is borne to the centre of the grove, fastened to a post, and there remains while lust and superstition revel in nameless indecencies. The victim,

smeared with oil, butter, and turmeric, is the object of homage and worship. The third day is
the climax of horror and cruelty. The victim
must neither resist nor be bound, so his arms and
legs are usually broken to insure passiveness. A
large tree or branch is brought, with a rift or slit
up the middle, into which the neck is inserted, the
ends being bound with cords; and thus held fast,
the poor creature is ready for the last rites. The
hatchet of the priest strikes the shoulders as a
signal, and then, with the swiftness and the fury
of madmen, the whole multitude pounce upon
him, tear every shred of flesh from the bones,
and fling these bloody fragments over the fields,
an offering to the deity." These are a part of
those "means ordained by Providence of making them virtuous and happy,"—those beneficent
"institutions," the "hazard of disturbing or deforming" which filled Mr. Marsh with surprise
and horror.

It need not be said that, notwithstanding Mr.
Marsh and his coadjutors, the Christian sentiment
prevailed, and the new charter gave sanction to
the efforts of missionaries, though, until the East
India Company ceased, in 1858, to control, it was
always the secret or open foe of missions. The
teaching of the Gospel was a hindrance to greed
and lust and all injustice and robbery; and we
can understand why one of the directors should
have frankly declared that he would rather a band

of devils, than of missionaries, landed in India.* We can also account for the spirit that led some, even amid the horrors of the mutiny and massacre of 1857, to throw up their hats and cry, " Hurrah ! We shall get rid of the saints." But instead, the saints got rid of them.

Before the transfer of the Company's possessions in 1858, noble men led the way in the reformation of India. In 1829, Lord William Bentinck, governor, decreed that all aid, assistance, or participation in any suttees should be construed and punished as murder. The Brahmins replied that their conscience dictated that the widow ought to be sacrificed, and asked whether Englishmen did not teach all men to obey conscience. Bentinck replied : " Obey your conscience: but the Englishman's conscience dictates the hanging of every one of you that is a party to such religious murder. Follow your conscience, and I will follow mine ! " Infanticide has been similarly suppressed ; the last link between idol fanes and state patronage was broken in 1863, and Sir John Lawrence's utterance justified, that " Christian acts done in a Christian way will never alienate the heathen."

Dr. John Wilson, of Bombay, enumerates as follows some of the benefits of British rule in India :

Horrors and iniquities removed :

I. Murder of parents by suttee, exposure on river banks, and burial alive.

* Exeter Hall, Lectures, 1850–1, pp. 90-92.

II. Murder of children, by dedication to the Ganges, to be devoured by crocodiles, by Rajpoot infanticide.

III. Human sacrifices, in temples, by wild tribes, and in the Meriah groves of the Khonds.

IV. Suicide; by crushing under idol cars; by devotees drowning themselves in rivers and casting themselves from precipices; widows leaping into wells; by Trága.

V. Voluntary torment: by hook-swinging, thigh-piercing, tongue-extraction, falling on knives, and austerities.

VI. Involuntary torment: by barbarous executions, mutilation of criminals, evidence under torture, bloody and injurious ordeals, cutting off women's noses, etc.

VII. Slavery: hereditary, predial, domestic, importation of slaves from Africa.

VIII. Extortions: by Dharaná, by Trága.

IX. Religious intolerance: prevention of propagation of Christianity; requiring Christian soldiers to fire salutes on heathen festivals, saluting gods on official papers, managing affairs of idol temples.

X. Support of caste by law: exclusion of low castes from office, exemption of high castes from appearing in evidence, disparagement of low caste.

These results indicate the effect of British occupation of India, only in one direction; and in spite of all the unfavorable impressions left by the administration of the British East India Company and by all the disastrous mistakes of British residents and provincial governors and their subordinates.

When Dr. Duff began work in Calcutta he looked upon female education as an impossibility. "You might as well try to scale a wall five hundred yards high, as attempt female education in India." To-day there are in the province of Bengal alone probably not less than 100,000 receiving instruction, and into the higher education not only the lower castes, but many of India's most gifted daughters, are pressing forward. What half a century since was the missionaries' despair has now become their brightest hope: the far-off goal of fifty years ago, so remote as to be invisible, is the starting-point to-day, and will be left far behind in the new starting-point of to-morrow. The keenest observers of India's condition, even the natives themselves, frankly confess that the future of that country is to be Christian; and many of them have said that, while they cannot change, their children will forsake the gods of India.

In 1834, Mr. Abeel, of China, moved the women of Britain by his appeals to carry the Gospel to women in India and China. This attempt was the parent of zenana missions. At that time even Christians and missionaries held it to be impracticable—it was attempting to force one's way through gates of steel and walls of stone, to seek access to harems, etc. In 1884, the Jubilee year of the "Society for Promoting Female Education in the East" found one hundred and sixty lady missionaries enrolled, and pupils in zenanas numbering thousands and, in day schools, tens of thousands. In prominent and populous cities, Bible women were entering the richest homes, and enlightened Hindus were clamoring for the education of their wives and daughters. At the Jubilee meeting Shaftesbury said: "The time is at hand when you will see the great dimensions of the work you are doing: not only in India, but throughout the East, great changes are in the future."

At that Jubilee year zenana missions were established in Japan, Africa, Egypt, Ceylon, Persia, etc. A prominent Hindu says: "If these women reach the hearts of our women they will soon get at the heads of the men of our country."

The way in which, the key by which, these long-shut zenana doors were actually opened, is interesting and suggestive. Mrs. Elizabeth Sale, of Helensburgh, Scotland, writes me: "As soon as I knew enough of the language to make myself understood, I began going into the villages of India among the women, in 1852. In 1856, I got the first entrance into a zenana proper. In 1858, I began work in Calcutta, and worked more than a year in my first house before I got any one to take anything out of my hand. It was very difficult to get one of the ladies to look at a book, as they feared being made widows if they desired to know anything of the outside world. As soon as some little bits of work were finished, a little pair of shoes and a bit of canvas work, I had them made up, which so delighted the husbands and brothers that the "wonderful work" was taken to other houses, when invitations came to teach there also. The needle-work had to be made the *bribe* to learn to read. I had been so far blessed that the ladies in their zenanas were daily hearing the Scriptures read, and some had so far broken through their fears that they were learning to read.

"In 1860, my husband was ordered to Europe. When I heard of the arrival of Mrs. Mullens and her daughters, I wrote to her of this opening, when she came and was introduced to the ladies of the three zenanas; and from that time the work rapidly spread. Now there is no need of work as a bribe to learn to read, so anxious are the women for instruction."

It is perhaps worth while to compare the conditions of woman's work in India in 1851 and 1881, and see the growth of thirty years.

	1851.	1881.
Female workers, foreign and native .	1,390	2,485
Boarding Schools	91	171
" Pupils	11,549	49,550
Zenanas accessible	1,300	9,506
" Pupils	1,977	9,288
Total under Christian Instruction, male and female	77,850	234,790
Sunday Schools	none	83.321

In thirty years the workers multiplied nearly twofold, the boarding-school pupils over fourfold, the number of open zenanas over sevenfold, and zenana pupils about fivefold, and total number taught, threefold. But as yet this work is but begun. The walls of age-long prejudice are but just giving way; and what astonishing results may now begin to appear!

In such a stronghold of Satan as India, results cannot be estimated by the number of professed converts. Within the Madras Presidency, in the thirty years from 1851 to 1881, churches multiplied eighteenfold, Christian adherents fourfold, communicants sevenfold, and lay preachers fivefold; but the *Indian Witness*, in 1889, makes the public confession: "Secret believers are rapidly multiplying. For every convert avowing faith are hundreds withholding confession for fear of their kin and caste. Thousands are ready when a break shall come."

We, who live amid Christian institutions, cannot understand the almost impenetrable barriers through which a convert in India must force his way. Here are 260,000,000 of people, sunk in poverty so deep that a hungry man will pray for tigers because they do not completely devour their victims, and he may, from what they leave, appease his hunger; and in idolatry so low that a human being will pray to a hole in a rock; and these millions are bound together in the iron bonds of a caste system which is a "cellular structure of society, with isolation so complete that the cells never interpenetrate," and yet to break through whose arbitrary restraints is to meet a penalty worse than death. What chance for woman in a land where two propositions form the unit on which all sects and classes agree: "The cow is a holy animal, and entitled to divine honors;" "Woman is a wicked animal, entitled to no respect!"

A native Hindu paper thus summarizes the work of Carey, Marshman, and Ward, at Serampore : " They created a prose vernacular literature for Bengal; they established the modern method of popular education; they gave the first great impulse to the native press; they set up the first steam-engine in India; in ten years they translated and printed the Bible, or parts thereof, in thirty-one languages."

Hear another witness: "Missionaries come from Britain at a great cost, and tell us that we are in heathen darkness, and that a bundle of fables, called the Bible, is the true Vedanta, which alone can enlighten us. They have cast their net over our children by teaching them in their schools, and they have already MADE THOUSANDS OF CHRISTIANS, AND ARE CONTINUING TO DO SO. They have penetrated into the most out-of-the-way villages and built churches there. If we continue to sleep as we have done in the past, not one will be found worshipping in our temples in a very short time; why, the temples themselves will be converted into Christian churches! Do you not know that the number of Christians IS INCREAS-ING, and the number of the Hindu religionists DECREASING every day? How long will water remain in a well which continually lets out, but receives none in? If our religion is incessantly drained by Christianity without receiving any accessions, how can it last? · When our country is turned into the wilderness of Christianity, will the herb of Hinduism grow? We must not fear the missionaries because they have white faces, or because they belong to the ruling class. There is no connection between the Government and Christianity, for the Queen Empress proclaimed neutrality in all religious matters in 1858. We must, therefore, oppose the missionaries with all our might. Wherever they stand up to preach, let Hindu preachers stand up and start rival preaching at a distance of forty feet from them, and they will soon flee away. Let caste and sectarian differences be forgotten, and let all the people join as one man to banish Christianity from our land. All possible efforts should be made to win back those who have embraced Christianity, and all children should be withdrawn from mission schools."—*From a Tamil Hindu Tract.*

"At a recent missionary meeting in Bombay, Sir Charles Elliot, fearing they might be forgotten,

restated the interesting facts presented two years
ago, as to the numerical progress made by Christianity in Hindustan from 1870 to 1881, which
showed that, while the general population of India
increased by eight per cent. during the ten years
closing with the year 1881, there was an increase
of thirty per cent. during the same period in the
number of Christians. In some portions of India
there was a still larger relative increase. In the
province of Bengal, while the increase in the number of Hindus in ten years was thirteen per cent.,
and that of the Mohammedans eleven per cent.,
that of native Christians was sixty-four per cent.
In the province of Assam, in the extreme north-
east of India, while during the decade already
mentioned the general increase of population was
eighteen per cent., there was an increase of one
hundred and fifty per cent. in the number of
Christians in the eight valley districts, and in the
Khasia hills, where a devoted band of Welsh missionaries are doing a grand work, the increase had
been at the rate of two hundred and fifty per
cent.! What may have been the comparative
results of missionary labors during the decade just
closed, and according to the census recently taken,
will be known in due time. It will undoubtedly
present a greater relative percentage in the increase
of native Christians in the sections now named,
and also in others. In the face of such facts, he
who assumes to say that missions are a failure,

only shows his own ignorance or a perverse determination not to recognize the truth." *

Eighty-five years ago, says the *Missionary Herald*, the Directors of the East India Company placed on solemn record: "The sending of Christian missionaries into our Eastern possessions is the maddest, most expensive, most unwarranted project that was ever proposed by a lunatic enthusiast." A few months since, Sir Rivers Thompson, Lieutenant-Governor of Bengal, said: "In my judgment, Christian missionaries have done more real and lasting good to the people of India than all other agencies combined."

And yet there are some who persist in belittling the work of evangelization. The London *Times*, of 1863, accounted for "prevailing apathy as to the propagation of the Gospel by the lack of satisfactory results"; and yet, already in 1863, missions had left on record some of the most apostolic biographies and histories ever written. Already the new book of the Acts of the Apostles had recorded the modern miracles wrought under William Carey, Robert Morrison, and Robert Moffat, William Johnson and Adoniram Judson, John Hunt and John Williams, Justin Perkins and Peter Parker, Latimer Neville and Dr. Krapf, John Geddie and Charles Gutzlaff, William Goodell and Charles Wheeler, Jonas King and Eli Smith, Henry Martyn and David Brainerd, Eliza Agnew

* Correspondent of *New York Evangelist.*

and Fidelia Fiske, Rosine Krapf and Mrs. Grant, and Melinda Rankin, Dober and Nitschman and John Wilson and William Burns, and Chamberlain and Lansing and Hogg and Butler and Coleridge Patteson. "Truth against the world" is the motto on encaustic tiling in Tennyson's vestibule.

Again, at the very time of the great World's Conference of Missions at London, the London *Times* gave the same challenge as that of a quarter century before, as though a Rip-Van-Winkle sleep had meanwhile buried its editor in oblivion. On June 15, 1888, referring to the appeals for more men and money, the editorial thus closes: " Before the promoters of missionary work can expect to have greater resources confided to them, they will have to render a satisfactory account of their trust in the past. Their progress, it is to be hoped, is sure ; indisputably it is slow. A congress like the present would be better employed in tracing the reasons for the deficiency in quantity of success than in glorifying the modicum which has been attained. The cause it advocates has vanquished the obstructions interposed at home to the accomplishment of its aims. It enjoys a sufficiency which, according to ordinary estimates, might seem an abundance of good-will and funds. Still it marches at a pace which, unless it be registered by the enthusiasm of Exeter Hall, appears little more than funereal. If Carey could have foreseen the magnificence of the means which his successors were destined to command, and the removal as if by magic of all the barriers which hemmed him in, he would have supposed that the foes were beaten and the harvest was being reaped. Exeter Hall says it is, and that the only thing now to be done is to hold the conquered forts and to push on to fresh conquests. For eyes, not endowed with the second sight of the platform, the principal citadels of heathendom continue to flaunt their banners as before. If some people profess to believe, as one speaker deplored the other day, that they hear too much of foreign missions, the explanation is that they see too little of their results." The writer, who was a delegate to that World's Conference, was moved to say in answer to this challenge, that, whatever the editor of the *Times* might know of human Empires, he evidently knew very little of the progress of the Kingdom of God.

It behoves not Christian nations, which owe all their civilization to Christianity, brought to them by missionaries, to depreciate missions. St. Jerome states that when "a boy, living in Gaul, he beheld the Scots, a people of Britain, eating human flesh; and though there were plenty of cattle and sheep at their disposal, yet they would prefer a ham of the herdsman or a slice of the female breast as a luxury." *

* "Among the Cannibals," 100.

The Scots then were once cannibals. When
Julius Cæsar landed at Deal, he found the Britons
a mere horde of half-naked savages, living in rude
huts, and clad in skins, sunk in ignorance and
degradation. What has lifted Great Britain from
barbarism and savagery to the foremost place
among the Christian nations of the world, and the
leadership of a world's missions?

From the middle of Elizabeth's reign to the
long Parliament the British people were the people
of a book, and that book the Bible. Elizabeth
might silence or tune her preachers, but not the
prophets.* And, while those who prepared the
English Bible for the people were burned at˙
the stake or treated with indignity, there was one
martyr who prayed, " O Lord, open the King of
England's eyes ; " and that king introduced, without knowing it, that very Bible among the common
people, as a mere stroke of state-craft ; and to that
Bible, and to the missionaries of the cross, every
nation that takes rank among the enlightened
leaders of the world owes to-day all its lofty level
of national life. That man in a Christian nation
who ridicules missions is like the cub who kicks
the dam by which he was born and suckled !

Yes, even modern missions have their "critics."
As Oscar Wilde found fault with the Atlantic
as monotonous, and with Niagara as wanting
variety of line, there are those who stand and look

* Green's Short History.

on the marvellous work of a century, whose results, considering all the hindrances, and the feeble
force employed, can be compared to no other ever
wrought in human history, and find only occasion
for blame !

Mythology tells us how Pan, the god of shep-
herds, opposed his rude reed music to Apollo's
wondrous lyre; and how Mt. Timolus pronounced Pan defeated in the contest. Only
Midas dissented from the decision, and, as a reward
for his obtuseness and obstinacy, his ears were
lengthened to the dimensions of an inferior animal.
Midas tried to hide the ass's ears, and his attendant, when he discovered the secret and could not
keep it, dug a deep hole and whispered it to
the mother earth. But the reeds that grew, moved
by the wind, whispered : " King Midas has ass's
ears ! " Let these critics who set their judgment
against not only the verdict of wiser men, but the
very facts of the age, beware lest the very soil of
society bear witness to their stupidity, "preten-
tious inaccuracy " and " presumptuous ignorance."

Mr. Darwin, though the apostle of materialism,
was still too honest to withhold a tribute when it
was due. In his recently published " Life and
Letters," he has recorded his impressions of Tierra
del Fuego, when he visited that land in 1833–4 ;
he wrote :

" The Fuegians are in a more miserable state
of barbarism than I had ever expected to have

seen any human being." He describes them as absolutely naked, in primitive wildness; he says that, as they were seated on a rocky point, throwing their arms wildly about, yelling, they seemed the troubled spirits of another world, the expression of their faces inconceivably wild, and their tones and gesticulations far less intelligible than those of domestic animals." *

To Admiral Sir Jas. Sullivan, Mr. Darwin often expressed the conviction that, "to send missionaries to such a set of savages, probably the very lowest of the human race, was utterly useless."

Subsequently, in 1869, and still later, up to 1880, he bore witness that the recent accounts of the mission proved to him that he had been wrong in his estimates of the native character and of the possibility of doing them good through the missionaries; as an expression and testimony of his interest in the Society's work he enclosed his check for £5. He pronounced the success of the mission so wonderful that only the proof that it was fact made it to him credible. And he says, "I certainly should have predicted that not all the missionaries in the world could have done what has been done." †

Similarly this same impartial unbeliever records his impressions of the work at Tahiti and New Zealand. "It is admirable to behold what the missionaries (both here and at New Zealand) have

* Life of Darwin, i., 227.   † Idem ii, 307, 308.

effected; I firmly believe they are good men working for the sake of a good cause. I much suspect that those who have abused or sneered at them have generally been such as were not very anxious to find the natives moral and intelligible beings. They forget, or will not remember, that human sacrifice and the power of an idolatrous priesthood; a system of profligacy unparalleled in any other part of the world; infanticide, a consequence of that system; bloody wars, where the conquerors spared neither women nor children; that all these things have been abolished; and that dishonesty, intemperance, and licentiousness have been greatly reduced by the introduction of Christianity. In a voyager to forget these things is a base ingratitude; for, should he chance to be at the point of shipwreck on some unknown coast, he will most devoutly pray that the lesson of the missionary may have extended thus far." "The lesson of the missionary is the enchanter's wand."

After Rev. William Robertson, of Edinburgh, had made an address on missions, a man accosting him said, "I was captain of the *Ruby*, that bore Bishop Sterling to Tierra del Fuego, and it was Bishop Sterling's reports of the work there that made Charles Darwin a convert to missions. There, where Allen Gardiner found the most debased savages, a society is now organized to rescue shipwrecked mariners."

We reluctantly bring to a close this brief survey

of the fruits of missions. Where the field is the world, it is impossible to bring even one blade from all its various harvests to show a specimen of what the seed of the kingdom yields. We have culled here and there what suffices to exhibit the proofs that in no part of the world have such fruits been lacking as prove that it is God's husbandry. In the islands of the sea, the Fiji and Hawaiian groups, Tahiti, Aneityum, and in the South Seas generally; in the most ancient and colossal kingdoms, like Turkey, China, and India, where the most gigantic and stubborn growths of evil were found, and deep-rooted as the ages could make them; where an iron caste system and the imprisoning law of zenana life and harem seclusion made all work seemingly fruitless; again, among comparatively degraded and low caste tribes and peoples, like the Siamese, Burmese, and Karens; even where the "habitations of cruelty" seemed to have their stronghold, as in Malabar and Calabar; where the people seemed, as Charles Kingsley thought, meant to show that it was possible to sink too low for even the Gospel to reach them, like the Australian aborigines, or the Maoris of New Zealand, or the Fuegians; everywhere, among high and low, the Gospel has been the same power and wisdom of God to salvation.

And now what is the grand conclusion? God has not only fulfilled His promise to His missionary band, but His royal challenge is, in the very successes of a century, thundering in our ears: "Go ye into all the world—preach the Gospel to every creature"—in every part of the field which is the world sow the good seed of the kingdom. And the fruit of the handful of grain shall yet shake like the forests of Lebanon.

VII.

THE DIVINE CHALLENGE OF MISSIONS.

AMONG the attractions of the famous museum at Marseilles, the foremost is the great painting by Auguste Barthélemy Glaize, of Montpellier, which is known as LE PILORI. It fills the entire end of the saloon, and is one of the most suggestive paintings in all France. Theophilus Gautier has described it in language scarcely less artistic than the picture.

Occupying the central place in this group, is the figure of the Saviour, in whose stead Barrabas was preferred; Jesus, who was scourged, bound to a pillar, spit upon, crowned with thorns, and hung upon the cross of slaves. Behind Him an angel unrolls a little scroll, on which we read: "Father forgive them; for they know not what they do."

At the bottom of the scaffold are four huge allegorical figures, symbolizing *Misery*, *Ignorance*, *Violence*, and *Hypocrisy*. These figures, placed back to back, and arranged in two groups like those of the tombs of the Medici, are a monumental and Michael-Angelesque combination of sculpture-like forms.

Misery is a dismal looking female, wrinkled and ghastly, from whose dry breast an infant is vainly seeking to suck nourishment. Ignorance sinks beneath his flabby flesh in a careless attitude, and makes to appear conspicuous his shallow skull crowned with hairy ass's ears, like the head of King Midas or of Bottom. Violence swells his bloated muscles, contracts his knotted sinews, arches his athletic back, with the stolid indifference of a murderer or hangman. The neck of a bull joins his huge shoulders to a bestial head which lacks brain. Hypocrisy holds a painted mask, with which to conceal at will her livid visage, and the feet, which fold beneath her, end in the claws of a demon. These four monsters, are they not the persecutors of these great men, and is not their proper place at the base of the pillory ?

We see standing on the right of the central figure, Christ, Socrates holding the cup of hemlock and pointing heavenward ; beyond him Æsop the fabulist, who was made a slave, and hurled from the rock, Hyampea, by the angry Delphian priests, in spite of the divine wisdom that dwelt in his distorted frame ; still further on, the beautiful and learned Hypatia, whom fanatical ecclesiastics, becoming in their turn persecutors, dragged from her chariot, tore in pieces, and whose palpitating members were drawn through the streets of Alexandria and burned. Beyond her, Kepler, who discovered the laws of the celestial mechanism, and died unable to procure from the imperial assembly his arrears of 8,000 crowns; Galileo, recanting in presence of the Inquisition, and whispering the famous words, "*E pur si muove.*" There is Bernard de Palissy, the maker of the king's rustique pottery, and the predecessor of Cuvier, burning all his furniture for lack of wood for his furnace; Correggio, selling his painting for sixty crowns and succumbing beneath the heavy sack in which he bore the copper coins received in payment.

At the left of the Saviour stands Homer, whom seven cities claimed after he was dead, but who, during life, poor, blind, wandered about, his lyre hung about his neck, chanting his immortal poems to obtain a meagre alms; Dante, the exile, out-
· lawed, showing to mankind the golden ladder to Paradise, and then mounting the staircase of a stranger at Verona.*   Cervantes is further on, the illustrious cripple who was maimed at Lepanto's battle, the "Captive" of Algerine Corsairs, sad, imprisoned for debt, burdened with infirmities, and buried in the convent of the nuns of Trinity without any tombstone until 1835, more than 200 years afterward, forgotten even by his own countrymen.   Joan of Arc, whom the funeral pyre of Rouen recompensed for the heroism that made her the savior of France; Christopher Columbus,

* A reference to Can Grande *della scala*, with whom he took refuge at Verona, 1313-1318.

receiving fetters as the price of unveiling the New World; Salomon de Caus, locked up in the insane hospital of Bicêtre, and with the grimace of a fool, showing the first outlines of the steam-engine of which Arago counted him the true inventor; Denis Papin, the physicist and machinist, forerunner of James Watt and Fulton, in a moment of despair breaking the model of the paddle-steamer which he had invented; Etienne Dolet, the free-thinker, hung and burned in Paris in 1546, who, marching to his death, and seeing the impatient multitude clamoring for his torture exclaimed: "*Non dolet ipse dolet, sed pia turba dolet.*" *

The picture bears at the extreme right-hand corner the name, GLAIZE, with the date, 1855. And beneath is the inscription, fit companion to such a work of art:

They are persecuted;
They are hidden in oblivion;
Until, after a long time elapses,
They have a monument, inscribed;
" TO THE GLORY OF THE HUMAN RACE."

'The critics and deriders of missions have often attempted to make out Christian missions a failure, but they have succeeded only in making themselves appear ridiculous; and those whom they have put in the pillory of their derision are now beginning to be recognized as the heroes of the human race,

* It is not himself whom Dolet bewails,
But the pious mob that seeks his blood.

and the far-seeing sages who beheld the true future which is to dawn on the world. The story of the successes of Christian missions is from many witnesses, and their testimony is unimpeachable. However "limited their knowledge, it cannot be set aside on account of the ignorance of others, however extensive."

The contest between Christianity and paganism has been waged with all the advantage on the side of the powers of darkness. And yet,—notwithstanding we have sent out less than six thousand men and women to meet a thousand millions; notwithstanding the little band have to master foreign tongues, and often create a literature in those tongues; have to overcome difficulties of climate, caste, customs, superstition, bigotry, depravity; have had even to face death by martyrdom for the truth's sake; notwithstanding it was less than one hundred years ago that the Church of Christ began the organized movement in this direction, and has never given over ten or eleven millions of dollars a year even in these days of ample resources,—there is scarce a land into which the missionary has not gone; and, wherever he has gone he has planted the cross, and about it the Christian home, school, church, college, theological seminary, printing-press, hospital, dispensary, and every characteristic institution of Christian lands. The work of modern missions, begun a hundred years ago amid innumerable obstacles and discouragements—the very leaders in this grand enterprise being put in the pillory as the objects of derision, scorn, and ridicule—that work has compelled from all intelligent and impartial observers the candid confession that, for the men and means invested, no success has ever been so great !

The Reformation period was a sort of signal gun in modern history ; and, if ever God unfolded a purpose of His own to men, He did it then. He sounded the signal for a rapid advance all along the lines.

Dr. Croly,* in an admirable sermon, preached in St. Paul's, before the Bishop of London, nearly a half century ago, called the Reformation the *" third great Birth of Time."* There was a wonderful conjuncture of events and inventions, all indicating the opening of a new era of world-wide evangelism. The magnet, guiding all vessels over hitherto untraversed seas, opened the whole world to commercial intercourse. Then the steam-engine became the great motor, propelling vessels on the sea and carriages on the land, and shortening time of transit, so that where Ziegenbalg took seven months to reach Zanguebar, and Carey five months to reach Calcutta, we can go in three weeks. Then came the printing-press, which threw open the mind of the world to European literature, as the mariner's compass and the steam-

* Exeter Hall Lectures, 1846-7.

engine had thrown open the gates of empires
and the ports of the sea! And now, while
these three greatest inventions or discoveries of
modern ages afforded all these facilities for missions, behold three of the miracles of *history*
standing side by side, in their combination and
culmination more wonderful than in their succession and accumulation. In the midst of this period
comes the *Fall of Constantinople*, 1543. The
storming of the Turks humbled the Queen City
of the Golden Horn, but scattered Greek learning
through the West. Then followed the *passage to
India*, the solution of that problem of ages which
was to find afterward a happier solution by the
Isthmus than by the Cape, and all the quickening
of opulent commerce was added to the contact of
remote nations. Britain and India, the very
centres of European and Asiatic civilization, were
brought together, and permanently linked. And
at the same great signal hour of history the curtain rose that unveiled *a New World.* God gave
mankind a new hemisphere in which to exercise
all the accumulated power of five thousand years
—a new treasury of wealth, a new granary of
food, a new arena of civilization and Christianity.
" Never before was there such a series of brilliant
excitements heaped upon the human race." All
society felt the thrill, and the amazing combination of events dazed the very eyes that beheld
them. Constantinople fell in 1453, Vasco de

Gama turned the Cape of Storms into the Cape of Good Hope in 1497, and Columbus touched the shores of the West Indies in 1492. These three events thus occurred within less than half a century!

The mariners' compass appears to have come into general use about 1400; the first book printed with movable types was brought out by Gutenburg about 1450, and the steam-engine seems to have begun to attain to practicable form under Blasco de Jaray in 1543. And now let us remember that just *at this time*, and in the very centre of this brilliance, Luther nails up his theses. Scarce twenty years before America was discovered, Luther preached his first sermon at Wittemberg; and, scarce twenty years after he startled all Europe by his beating a hole in Tetzel's drum, the Barcelona engineer is said to have propelled a vessel by a water boiler.*

Thus the Church, after a sleep of a thousand years, awoke once more to the sense of duty and debt to the lost race of man. If there be a divine providence—if the end of all history is Redemption, and the goal of all redeemed life is the restoration of man to the image of God,—we should expect to see the most wonderful developments of history side by side with these awakenings in the Church. We should look to see at least *three* developments: first, the *wide opening of doors*, mak-

* Appleton's Encyclopedia.

ing the whole world accessible; secondly, the *provision of new and more perfect facilities* for universal contact and communication; thirdly, the *more thorough organizing of the Church itself* for the work. The first is a question of *opportunity*, the second of *equipment*, and the third of *activity and advance*. What are the facts? Precisely in the line of these expectations have come the interpositions of God, only, as usual, when He does anything, it was on a scale of majesty, might, and overwhelming grandeur, the like of which man never saw, exceeding abundantly above all we could ask or think. Let us stop in our hurry and cast a backward look.

Some of our readers may have thought it extravagant language to affirm that the modern age, like the Apostolic, has abounded in the supernatural. But the marvellous developments and coincidences of history in the world and the Church admit no explanation without God. The undevout historian, like the undevout astronomer, must be mad, if he is not overwhelmed by these miracles of intervention.

Another wonderful age has come to *us ;* may we not call it the *Fourth birth-hour of human history ?* Gladstone says that the first fifty years of this century marked more progress than the previous five thousand, in art, science, invention, and discovery; the next twenty-five, more than the previous fifty; and the next ten, more than the previous twenty-five.

Probably the statement is not an exaggeration. God never sounded a louder signal-gun than now, and no combination of events ever startled the attentive observer like the present. William Carey led the way in the organization of the Church for modern missions in 1792. In rapid succession followed the organization of the great missionary societies and the sending forth of missionaries, until now between two hundred and three hundred societies are represented by 6,000 laborers.

At this present time, we seem to have reached not only *a* crisis, but *the* crisis of missions. The whole world is open to missionary labor, but there are not enough workmen to occupy the field; and again there are many workmen offering to go to the field, and there are not enough means at our disposal to secure them a support in the field. And, still worse, the missionary boards of most of our Churches are so crippled by debt or by insufficient funds, that, at a time when every voice of God or need of man cries "Expand" and "Advance," the only course apparently open to us is to contract the work and retrench the costs!

Nothing is more calculated to awaken surprise than to see how mistaken and short-sighted are the views of many intelligent members, and even ministers of the Church, as to the existing crisis.

For example, it appears to occasion alarm and awaken hostile criticism. It is said, there is something wrong in the Church's work when its demands exceed the supply; that our Boards ought to lay out no more expenditure than the receipts warrant—that the work should be cut down to meet the income, etc. One would suppose that the present aspect of missions is one of disheartening *failure*, and that those who have charge of our missions are seriously to blame for allowing the demand for men and money to be so imperative, and increase so fast. But let thoughtful men and women reflect, whether this is not an entire misapprehension of the existing state of things. Like Elisha's servant, we need our eyes opened to see that, where some behold only cause for discouragement, God means an incentive to joy and praise.

Such a crisis in missions is sign and proof not of failure, but of *success.* Our keynote should not be set to the minor strain of despondency, but the major key of thankfulness. All this means *growth*, and growth always brings a demand for new conditions, provisions, accommodations. The growing plant must have more space, more room to grow; the old pot must be discarded for a new and more spacious one. The growing boy must have new clothes; he cannot wear the same suit that he wore a year ago; the cripple who has no growth, and perhaps cannot move a foot or lift a hand, may wear one suit for years; but not so the stalwart, growing lad. Who finds fault with these demands of growth? and who would exchange such a healthy boy for a cripple?

The growing family must have a larger house, a more ample board. A growing business needs new shops and factories, a larger stock and heavier outlay : no merchant complains when, because he has double the custom, there must be more care and cost, and more clerks and goods.

Now, how comes it to pass that, when the work of the Lord outgrows all past provision for its successful prosecution ; when its very successes call for more room to grow, more men and money, more churches and schools and colleges, more preaching stations and evangelists, more books and Bibles, more medical missions ; and, in a word, more of everything that goes to supply the wants of an awakening community, we should begin to be heavy-hearted because what was inadequate ten years ago is absolutely and hopelessly unequal to the demand to-day ! This is certainly a paradox and anomaly. There is but one place where there is no new necessity created by growth ; and that is where there is no longer life. In a sepulchre or a cemetery, death is regnant. A mummy wears the same wrappings as when, 3,000 years ago, it was embalmed. But Lazarus, when loosed from the sepulchre, left his grave clothes behind him, and it was the price of his resuscitation that he must henceforth have food and raiment. Life is costly, and growth adds to the cost even of life. And, because the work of missions is a growing child yet in its infancy, and not a cripple without a future; because it is a living form and not a mummy, the conditions change and the demands increase every day.

This crisis of missions is in fact an *answer to prayer.* It is not one hundred years ago since the whole world stood over against the Church, like a gigantic fortress with double-barred gates of steel. Devout disciples who, like Simeon, looked and waited for the Kingdom of God, were earnestly beseeching God that the doors of the nations might be opened and the way be prepared for the Church to carry out her great commission. It was because God heard that strong crying, and so marvellously answered, that, within the past fifty years, pagan, papal, and heathen territory which a century ago defied the approach of Protestant missionaries with an open Bible and a pure Gospel, now admits, if it does not welcome, the message of life.

So rare and exceptional is it that any nation like Thibet should yet lock itself in hermit seclusion, that we may now say, with almost literal truth, that the whole world is now accessible, and that the Gospel herald may go where he will. A great door and an effectual is opened, though there are many adversaries; and that door opens upon a domain that is world-wide.

No student of political history needs to be told that changes in the attitude of governments toward questions involving popular customs and

religious faith are effected very slowly. Centuries
are the hours upon the dial of national life. To
move a whole people is a process that often requires the leverage of ages, so that we have been
wont to think of Oriental peoples as petrified in
their immobility.

The rapidity with which these doors of access
were thrown open, the keys whereby they were
unlocked, the singular preparation for the entrance
of the Gospel which they revealed, the fitness and
fulness of times which marked these new and startling developments, have impressed the writer's
mind as nothing else ever has, in a life largely
given to historic studies.

One example might be cited in detail, as an
illustration. The year 1858 is the "Annus mirabi-
lis" of modern missions. Probably no one year
in human history has been marked by changes
more stupendous and momentous, as affecting the
evangelization of the world; and it is the more
appropriate that it here have due emphasis, inasmuch as, so far as he is aware, the writer has been
the first to set in array the wondrous events that
marked that pivotal year of missions.

First of all, the winter preceding had been distinguished by one of the most remarkable outpour-
ings of the Spirit known in modern times. In all
parts of Christendom there was an almost simul-
taneous blessing, which suggested a gigantic tidal-
wave that moves from equator to pole, that washes

with its giant swell the coasts that border the ocean's bed, all along the shores of vast continents, and sweeps over those continents themselves. Churches in every part of the world were quickened into new life; converts sprang up like willows along the water-courses; hundreds of thousands were gathered into the Churches, and to this day the grand results are visible.

One special result of the revivals of that autumn and winter of 1857-8 was a new spirit of *prayer for missions.* As yet a large portion of the earth's vast population was shut out from Christian labor, and the awakened Church besought God to make bare His mighty arm and burst open the barred gates, that all the ends of the earth might see the salvation of our God.

Behold the marvellous and majestic movements of a prayer-hearing God! Great Britain approaches Japan, which, from 1640 to 1854, had closed her ports even to the commerce of Christian nations. The Earl of Elgin, on August 26, 1858, concluded that new Treaty which broke down the barriers of two centuries between the Sunrise Kingdom and the foremost Protestant nation of Europe. About the time of the conclusion of this treaty, the reigning Tycoon died, and left the throne to his son, the present emperor, a young man of great intelligence and singularly liberal sentiments touching both commerce and politics. Here, by one master-stroke, the Island Empire, with nearly 40,000,000, became accessible to British ships and the Gospel loved by British Christians, while at the same time governmental changes took place which doubly assured progress. What was the consequence? No nation has, for eighteen centuries, moved at such a pace toward Christianity. Ten years later, a vast number of Buddhist temples were confiscated for public uses, chiefly educational, and the Mikado pledged himself to promote complete religious toleration. How well he kept his word will appear from the decree of July 11, 1884, that thenceforth there should be no official priesthood, and that all religions, Shintôism, Buddhism, and Christianity alike, should be impartially protected and occupy the same platform of legal equality! Four years later there were reported 28,000 church communicants in the Reformed or Protestant churches, and church buildings, Christian schools, theological seminaries, Young Men's Christian Associations, religious newspapers, and all the distinctive features of a Christian community, were to be found. With a swiftness that reminds us of the rapidity with which dawn advances to full day, this empire has earned its right to its proud title—that of " the *Rising Sun.*" Where in 1853 there was only an impenetrable wall of· exclusion, we have now, less than forty years later, a whole land penetrated and permeated by occidental influence.

During that same memorable year, changes

almost as great took place in *China*. We have seen what occurred in Japan, August 26. The *day previous*, the Atlantic Cable flashed across the Atlantic its first news dispatch that, after nearly a year of war, peace had been concluded between the allied forces and the Middle Kingdom. The famous Treaty of Tientsin, signed June 26, enlarged the provisions of the Treaty of Nankin, of 1842, which opened five ports to foreign trade. British subjects are henceforth allowed to travel for business or pleasure to all parts of the interior,* under passports issued by their Consul ; and, what is most significant, the Christian religion is to be protected by Chinese authorities.† The language is as follows : " The Christian religion, as professed by Protestants and Roman Catholics, inculcates the practice of virtue and teaches man to do as he would be done by. Persons teaching or professing it, therefore, shall be alike entitled to the protection of the Chinese authorities ; nor shall any such, peaceably pursuing their calling and not offending against the laws, be persecuted or interfered with."

Thus, to one quarter of the population of the globe, access was given, in one diplomatic document ; and the Church of Christ may now preach the Gospel through the Celestial Empire. It is difficult to apprehend or appreciate what such a step means : it is not a step, but a stride—the stride

* Art. ix.   † Art. viii.

of a giant in seven-league boots, from mountain-top to mountain-top. China is in itself a world, containing a population larger than the whole world at the time of Christ. And yet in one year that world of China was made accessible to Christian missions.

Let us go still Westward. What is, during this same year, 1858, occurring in *India*, itself another great world of many languages and peoples and religions?

The mutiny of 1857, which, in the opinion of godless and greedy men who would make money out of traffic in human bodies or souls, was to rid India of the saints, *opened* India to them. God gave it to such Christian heroes as Sir John Lawrence and Sir Henry Havelock and Sir Colin Campbell, to save the British army from massacre. It was this formidable revolt of 1857 which called attention to the mismanagment of East Indian affairs by the East India Company, whose powers had gradually grown, until, long before its abolition, it had become a court from whose decisions there was no appeal. And the result of investigation was that, not only in this memorable year 1858, but in that same month, August (2d) all the territories previously under the government of the Company became vested in the British Queen, and Victoria became Empress of the Indies. This was a change that can be appreciated only by those who have studied minutely the history of the Company, which from the year 1600 had been growing more and more despotic; who remember how, when the devoted Robert Haldane, in 1796, sold his estate at Airthrey and proposed to establish a new mission at Benares, the centre of Brahminical idolatry, at his own expense, the Company defeated his scheme, one director remarking that he "would rather a band of devils than a band of missionaries landed in India"; who remember how Wm. Carey and Henry Martyn had encountered the bitter hostility of this same East India Company, so that the flag of Britain, now the symbol of a Christian civilization and the pledge of both civil and religious liberty wherever it floats, was in India the signal for hatred and jealousy of mission work.

But now the 300,000,000 of India were brought under the sway of the British sceptre and made accessible to the mightier sceptre of the King of kings. Surely it was a momentous epoch in history which opened on the day when British courts, laws, and judges, churches, schools, and colleges, presses, books, and Bibles had freedom to plant over those wide domains the institutions of a Christian state! Here opened another world, almost as large and populous as China, and some think that an accurate census would show India to be the more populous, as it is undoubtedly the more important of the two—the pivot of Oriental life. Meanwhile, in that same India, another transformation was taking place, scarcely less important.

We all know how heathen and pagan institutions have shut women out from all contact even with the uplifting influence of knowledge. The zenana, like the harem and seraglio, has stood for thousands of years as the polite name for a domestic and social Bastile, in which, without cause, at the will of a domestic despot, in India alone one hundred millions of women and girls have been effectually imprisoned.

Now that the zenana work has grown to such dimensions, there are more claimants for the honor of its origination than for the honor of cradling Homer; but, as near as can be traced, it was in 1858 that Mrs. Elizabeth Sale, of Helensburgh, Scotland, began work in Calcutta among the women, using needle-work embroidery as the key that unlocked these long-shut doors.* From that first attempt at organized work among women in the zenanas, the harvest has already become wonderfully fruitful.

And now, to the marvellous events already noted which make 1858 the Year of the Open Doors, we must add three more. In that year the revolutionary changes in Papal Europe prepared the way for Free Italy and Protestant missions; in that same year the revolution in Mexico under Benito Juarez paved the path of the Gospel in Central

* *Miss. Review*, July, 1890, p. 554.

America; and in the same year David Livingstone sailed a second time for Africa to complete his explorations and pioneer a road into the interior for the missionary. Thus in Japan, China, India and its zenanas, Italy and papal Europe, Central America, and even Africa, 1858 was the great year when doors were unlocked for the Gospel.

Thus, at risk of tediousness, we have expatiated on the providential interventions in answer to prayer which show that the crisis in missions, which is the result and the sign of growth, is also the direct proof of a prayer-hearing God. And what follows? That what appears to be an emergency to which we are unequal, is in fact a *divine challenge* to renewed prayerfulness, consecration, dependence on God, and confidence and courage such as faith inspires. Such crises have occurred at various turning-points of Christian history; and everything depends on *how the Church meets the exigency.*

From the voluminous records of missions we select *two* representative instances of how everything hangs upon the spirit in which *critical* and *pivotal* conditions are met by the people of God, in hopes that we may learn the lesson of the hour.

The only way to meet such a crisis in missions is to appeal to God in believing prayer, and then take new courage. Even discouragements are thus transformed into incentives and incitements to duty. Where we have our Lord's plain command, especially when backed by such providential openings and leadings, the apparent hopelessness of our task is only designed to try our faith and develop our courage.

First, we may find a representative and impressive example of this principle in the story of Tahiti. The missionaries seemed for fourteen years to have labored in vain and spent their strength for naught. Their zeal, their toil, their long journeys and faithful exhortations, did not even awaken interest or inquiry on the part of the natives. Not one instance of conversion had yet rewarded them. Not only so, but the missionaries, driven away from the island by war, their houses burned, were actually cut off from all communication with it. The first missionaries of the London Missionary Society had landed in 1797, and so many years had passed in fruitless effort that, about 1813, the directors, disheartened, proposed to abandon the mission altogether. A few firm friends of the work resolutely resisted all such proposals. Dr. Haweis, for example, added to his former donations another of two hundred pounds, and pressed the society to new efforts and more earnest prayers. Rev. Matthew Wilks, John Williams' pastor, joined with Dr. Haweis in remonstrance against such unbelief and abandonment of the Lord's work, and with his peculiar vehemence said, " I will sell the garments from my back before I will consent to give up this mission," and instead, proposed that a special season of prayer for the mission be observed. The suggestion was accepted, and in place of letters of recall, letters of encouragement and hopefulness were despatched to the discouraged laborers in the South Seas.

Thus they vanquished Satan by the shield of faith and the rod of prayer. Nothing in human history is more remarkable as a proof of a prayer-hearing God than the events which now transpired. The vessel which bore from England to Tahiti these letters of inspiration and encouragement crossed in her passage another ship from Tahiti, bearing letters from the missionaries, announcing the entire overthrow of idolatry, and bearing likewise the rejected idols of the people brought by them to the missionaries and by them sent to London, where they now stand in the museum of the society. God had literally fulfilled His word : " Before they call I will answer, and while they are yet speaking I will hear."

His set time to favor the work had fully come, and He chose a way to do it which would both glorify Himself and stimulate confidence in prayer. The missionaries had been compelled to seek refuge in the New South Wales, and Mr. Nott, at Eimeo. Reports suddenly reached Mr. Nott, and others who, in 1811, had returned to Eimeo, that remarkable changes were in progress at Tahiti. Messrs. Scott and Hayward, by request, went to the island,

and to their astonishment found praying men there, and two of them, Oito and Tuahine, the first natives that had ever prayed to the true God, returned with them to Eimeo, where the first great meeting was held in 1813.

It appeared that these two natives, formerly servants in the families of the missionaries, had, unknown to them, received impressions which led them to pray to God after the expulsion of the missionaries; so that on the return of the latter they unexpectedly found a people prepared of the Lord. From this time one unbroken series of successes followed, in fact *attended*, the labors of the missionaries, so that island after island and group after group received the Gospel with a rapidity unknown before or since.*

Another conspicuous example may be chosen from the later annals of missionary enterprise.

Ongole, about 200 miles north of Madras, has been the scene of an in-gathering which perhaps exceeds any other ever known for the display of God's power. In the close of 1853 and the beginning of 1854, Dr. Lyman Jewett, a missionary from Nellore, still living at Madras and connected with the American Baptists, was touring in this desolate though densely populated district, and upon the summit of a mountain near Ongole he prayed God to send a missionary there. But let

* "Missionary Enterprises in the South Seas," John Williams.

us enter more fully into details which deserve a permanent record.

The first mission of the American Baptist Missionary Union had been planted in the Telugu country in 1835, at the suggestion of Rev. Amos Sutton, an English Baptist; Rev. Samuel S. Day and wife sailing Sept. 22, 1835, for this field. In 1837 Mr. Day made a tour of some 120 miles and back from Berhampore, visiting forty villages, of which one-half had probably never before seen a missionary, or even a Christian. In 1840, he, with Rev. and Mrs. S. Van Husen, were found at *Nellore*, which was regarded as a good centre for the work, being in the midst of a dense Telugu population and about midway from Cape Cormorin to the upper boundary of the Telugu country.

In 1853, the thirty-ninth annual meeting of the American Baptist Missionary Union was held at Albany, N. Y., May 17. The moment was so critical that the very destiny of the Telugu mission hinged on the decision then reached. Mr. Day and Mr. Jewett and their wives were now at this Nellore station. Mr. Day had been in India eighteen years, and Mr. Jewett five, having sailed in 1848. As early as 1846, the executive committee had discussed the propriety of abandoning the work, but were prevented by the vigorous protest of Mr. Day, then in this country for his health. But now again, in 1853, the question of abandoning this field was raised, no results that seemed to justify the expenditure having been attained. No more than *three* persons had been baptized since the mission was recommenced in 1849 ; there were no native helpers in training or in prospect, and the annual expense was over $2,600.

At the evening session at Albany, the great question to be considered was "*Shall the Telugu work be abandoned ?* " and one of the speakers, pointing to Nellore on the map, the only station in the Telugu country, gave it the name which has since clung to it—"*The Lone Star.*" That epithet inspired Dr. S. F. Smith, the poet, and his pen put on paper the following prophetical verses, which we here place on permanent record :

> Shine on " Lone Star " ! Thy radiance bright
> Shall spread o'er all the Eastern sky ;
> Morn breaks apace from gloom and night ;
> Shine on and bless the pilgrim's eye.
>
> Shine on "Lone Star " ! I would not dim
> The light that gleams with dubious ray ;
> The lonely star of Bethlehem
> Led on a bright and glorious day.
>
> Shine on, " Lone Star " ! In grief and tears
> And sad reverses oft baptized :
> Shine on amid thy sister spheres :
> Lone stars in Heaven are not despised.
>
> Shine on, " Lone Star " ! Who lifts a hand
> To dash to earth so bright a gem !
> A new " lost pleiad " from the band
> That sparkles in Night's diadem !

Shine on, "Lone Star"! The days draw near
When none shall shine more fair than thou;
Thou, born and nursed in doubt and fear,
Wilt glitter on Immanuel's brow.

Shine on, "Lone Star"! Till earth, redeemed,
In dust shall bid its idols fall;
And thousands, where thy radiance beamed,
Still crown the Saviour Lord of All!

Those verses proved so prophetic that the very details of the prediction, ventured by the poet, have been accomplished.

Notwithstanding all discouragements, it was resolved that the *Telugu mission be continued and suitably reinforced.*

Toward the close of this eventful year another turning-point was reached in the mission's history. Mr. and Mrs. Jewett, with Christians, Nersu, Julia, and Ruth, touring northward, reached Ongole about the end of December, and on January 1, 1854, before sunrise, this little band, as stated in previous pages, mounted the hill which overlooks Ongole and the surrounding country. They saw the large, populous town with its mosques and temples, and counted fifty villages dotting the plains—and all, like Athens, "wholly given to idolatry." There, kneeling, each in turn besought God to send to Ongole a true missionary, and en-joyed assurance that they were heard.

For a time Mr. and Mrs. Jewett were the only active laborers among the millions of Telugus.

But the Union had, at Albany, settled the question that the Lone Star Mission should live, and Mr. Jewett earnestly pleaded in 1855 for a missionary to be located at Ongole, with its 10,000 people.

Mr. Jewett's health compelled his return to America in 1862, and finding that again the question of abandoning the Lone Star Mission was before the Board and Churches, he emphatically insisted it should not be deserted, and declared that he would go back, if only to die there.

In 1865 he returned, with Rev. and Mrs. J. E. Clough, and arrived in the Telugu country. Of Mr. Clough one word ought to be said: he was trained as a civil engineer, and, not until his third application, was he accepted by the Baptist Union and sent to the field.

The work went on for another twelve years, with slow progress; the wail of disappointed hope went up to God, like Isaiah's cry—"Lord, who hath believed our report ; " The "lone star" had shone for twenty years, but how few had by it found the Light of the World!

In 1866, in September, the new station was opened at *Ongole*, seventy miles north of Nellore, and Mr. Clough took charge. Another feeble luminary was added to the "Lone Star" of Nellore; and in March, 1867, *two* converts were baptized. Mr. Clough undertook a tour among the villages around, sending out word that he had come to tell the people of Jesus. The next day

after arriving at Tula Conda Padu, he found from
thirty to forty persons, who had come to his tent
in the tamarind grove—had prepared to stay for
days, and brought not only provisions with them,
but *a change of clothes to put on when they were
baptized*, for they had come to learn of Christ, with
the expectation of confessing Him! On Sunday,
January 20, twenty-eight were baptized, and a
Pentecost seemed begun. Native preachers visited more than eight hundred villages lying about
Ongole, and in 1867–8 the little church had swelled
to seventy-five members. Meanwhile, the Canada
Auxiliary, organized in 1866, had sent A. V.
Timpany to Nellore, and the arrival of this new
laborer and wife, in 1868, was the signal for a
new era in the history of the mission.

Mr. Clough had been singularly impressed that,
if he could join Mr. Jewett in labor among the
Telugus, 10,000 souls would be given them in one
harvest. This, which was regarded as the sign
of excessive enthusiasm, if not of unsound mind,
by the members of the Baptist Board, was in fact
a prophecy of coming triumphs.

Many a time, when far away among the jungle
villages, in 1869, would those words come to him :
" Be still and know that I am God. I will be
exalted among the heathen, I will be exalted in
the earth." In December, 1869, three hundred
and twenty-four more were baptized; and, suddenly, from one of the most unpromising, the

Telugu field became one of the most inviting. And already, in 1870, the little church of seventy-five had grown to seven hundred and nine. In 1871, Ongole had 1,200 members; in 1872, 1,658; in 1873, 2,092; and the number of baptisms was limited only by the inability of the missionaries to visit the villages and examine and baptize converts. At Ramapatam, where, four years before, a missionary had preached the first Sabbath in his own sitting-room to a congregation of his own servants and a few others, there were, in 1873, 500 communicants, and a theological school for native ministry with fifteen students! The field, of which Ongole was the centre, and over whose area of 7,000 square miles a million of people were scattered in 1,300 villages, was then divided into eight parts, and over each was placed a native preacher and assistant, to go from village to village telling the Gospel story.

In 1873–4, 1,026 Telugus were baptized; in 1875, Ongole reported 2,642 members; and in 1876, the " Lone Star " mission, at Nellore, which in 1845 had not a missionary, and whose utter abandonment was so often considered; which in 1865, when the veteran Jewett was returning with his new recruit, Mr. Clough, had but thirty-eight living members; had now 4,000 members, six stations, and twenty missionaries!

The famine of 1877 exposed hundreds of thousands to starvation, and just now it became obvious why God had chosen a *civil engineer* for that field. Mr. Clough obtained a government contract for completing the Buckingham Canal, and on this work he employed thousands of natives, to whom the Gospel was preached after the day's work was done; gangs of men, successively employed, heard the Word of Life, and the next year, thousands came forward to ask baptism. On one day 2,222 were baptized; between June 16 and July 7, about three weeks, 5,429 were baptized by Mr. Clough and his assistants at Ongole. And Mr. Clough adds: " Perhaps not one hundred had ever received from me, directly or indirectly, the value of a pice (one-quarter of a cent) from the famine fund, or ever expected to receive from me any financial aid." Up to July 31, in less than seven weeks, 8,691 had professed faith and received baptism. In twelve years, a church of eight had thus grown to one of 12,000! The wild dream of John E. Clough, and the long waiting prayer of Dr. Jewett, had been fulfilled. Within less than twelve months the number of baptized converts had swelled by 10,000; and to this day the revival work goes on, without interruption; the last reported year is one of abounding fruitfulness, and one of the largest in the in-gathering of converts.

This Telugu field furnishes another marked illustration of the answers to prayer. Mr. Clough, on coming to Ongole, was waited upon by high-caste citizens, who gave him support and placed sixty-two of their sons in his school and furnished the funds for carrying it on, without restricting his religious teaching. One day three low-caste men presented themselves as converts, and were made welcome; but at once an indignant committee informed him that if he had anything more to do with Sudras and Pariahs, the high-caste scholars would be at once withdrawn. Two more low-caste converts applied for admission. The crisis had come—the school was likely to be wrecked against this Gibraltar of caste, and the social sea was in a wild tumult.

Mr. Clough and his wife went at the same time to different apartments to pray for divine guidance. Each cried for direction in this great extremity, and each took up a Testament to seek in the Word of God guidance. In the hand of each the Testament of its own accord opened to the same passage—I. Cor. 1, 26–29: "Ye see your calling, brethren, how that not many wise men after the flesh, not many mighty, not many noble, are called: but God hath chosen the foolish things of the world to confound the wise; and God hath chosen the weak things of the world to confound the things which are mighty; and base things of the world, and things which are despised, hath God chosen, yea, and things which are not, to bring to nought things that are: that no flesh shall glory in His presence."

"Ah, yes," said Mr. Clough, "I see it—I have

not been building on God's plan: it must tumble down, and I must begin anew." And he left the room to go and tell his wife, whom he found coming into the study with her hand on the same Scripture. By this striking coincidence God led them henceforth to build from the broad bottom of the social pyramid, where the many are found. They at once announced their purpose, and every scholar left! But, though the upper classes at once changed from friends to foes, God on this new basis built the greatest single Church of modern times, and the greatest revival since our Lord's ascension; and of the thirty thousand Ongole communicants, more converts from the upper castes have been gathered than Mr. Clough ever would have hoped under the previous plan.

These two instances have been previously referred to in these pages, but are here given somewhat in detail that they may stand as representative examples of what blessing would have been forfeited had the Church of God at these critical times deserted her post and abandoned her work! God had in store the greatest blessings known since Pentecost—one in the South Seas, the other in the East Indies. He allowed the faith and patience of His people to be sorely tried, and when they proved faithful He poured out a blessing. And so it will be to-day, if this new crisis be met in the true spirit.

The great signal-gun of God is sounding out

the call to ADVANCE! Those old Greeks—
princes in the wisdom of this world—showed their
sagacity in the Olympic games. Three pillars
were reared in the ancient stadium, respectively
at the starting-point, the midway-point, and the
turning-point, or goal. Three Greek words were
inscribed upon these pillars respectively: on the
first αριστευε, "Do your best"; on the second,
σπευδε, "Speed you"; and on the third, καμψον,
"Stop." When the racer was starting, the first
pillar incited him to show himself a man; when
he reached the third, he was reminded that he had
reached the goal, or turning-point; but it was at
the middle pillar that he met the caution, "*Speed
you!*" "*Make haste!*"

There was philosophy in that. No risk is so
great as the risk of over-confidence in a success
but half attained. He, who at first outran the rest
and at the middle of the course found himself
ahead, would be tempted to relax his efforts; and
so some other racer, who had reserved his strength
for the supreme effort at the end of the race,
would pass him by and get first to the goal.

Paul was in the spiritual sphere a trained
athlete. His law of life was, "Forgetting those
things which are behind and reaching forth unto
those things which are before, I press toward the
mark for the prize of the high calling of God in
Christ Jesus." Spinoza wisely said, that there is
no foe more fatal to progress than self-conceit and

the laziness which self-conceit begets. To think and feel that we have already attained, or are already perfect, is the narcotic and sedative that brings on the sleep of the sloth and the sluggard. At the present critical hour of missions the banners of God's hosts should bear one word emblazoned in capitals: FORWARD!

The motto of the great Apostle to the Gentiles was, "THE REGIONS BEYOND." Satisfied with no work already done, content with no other man's line of things made ready to hand, he yearned to evangelize the regions beyond, where Christ had not been named.* That motto of Paul is the true watchword of this new age of missions. After all the work of a century, we have only just begun, and are not even at the midway pillar. God says, "Speed ye! Make haste! Forget what is behind, reach toward, press toward what is before! Push for the regions beyond!" Our work is not done—in a sense is not fully begun—so long as there remains one country or people or family where the Gospel has as yet not been proclaimed. A salvation provided for all and free to all must be at least announced to all.

The other signal word for this supreme hour of missions is PRAYER. In the Pantheon at Paris is a superb painting of the death of St. Genevieve, the patron saint of the city. And the picture sug-

* II. Cor. x. 16.

gests the marked contrasts of history. Above is a triumphal procession entering the gates with all the pomp and pageantry of victorious war—the legions of soldiery, the captives in golden chains, the spoils of priceless value, all suggest the imperial glory of human power in the insolent boastfulness of conscious success. Beneath, in a dimly-lighted chamber, Christians gather about the rude couch of the dying saint. It is but a convent cell, and a little band of praying disciples; yet in gazing you feel that this is the far grander scene —and that, in the circle of prayer, and not in the march of battalions, lies the secret power which is yet to overturn the empire of the Cæsars and make the banners of the Church more victorious than the silver eagles of Rome!

The autobiography of Charles G. Finney is confessedly one of the most remarkable narratives in the English tongue. At a time when the American Church was well-nigh enwrapt in a dead orthodoxy, and vital godliness was in peril, this wonderful man swept like a flaming evangelist through the churches, kindling into a fierce fire the smouldering embers on God's altars. Tens of thousands of formal Christians were quickened into life, and converts sprang up like willows along the water-courses. The power of that whole movement was the power of believing prayer. Mr. Finney himself, from the very hour of conversion, had his hand on the throne of God. His principal co-workers were men and women of marked power in intercession. Rev. Daniel Nash, familiarly known as "Father Nash," had inflamed eyes, and was for weeks at a time shut up in a dark room; but that room became a holy of holies, in the secrecy, solitude, silence, separation of which he communed with God at the mercy-seat. His closet was the throne-room of God, and as he could neither read nor write, Father Nash gave himself up almost entirely to prayer. From that hiding-place he went forth with a double black veil on his face to work for souls, full of the power which only prayer can bring. He had a "praying list" of persons for whom daily, and in some cases, many times in a day, he prayed. And his faith was so marvellous that the hardest hearts yielded when he began to beseech God for them. The bar-room of a low groggery would become a prayer-meeting room and the blasphemous bartender the leader of the meeting. When the devil reared especially high bulwarks against the truth, and impassable walls seemed to defy progress, Mr. Finney and Father Nash would simply overcome all obstacles by this one resort: they would go together to some retired place, a grove perhaps, and give themselves up to prayer until they *knew* that God heard and would answer; and often, while Mr. Finney gave himself to the preaching, his brother Nash would pray without ceasing, and the most brazen-faced and stiff-necked opposers

would give way. Such mighty praying gave
Father Nash the power of a prophet. For ex-
ample, when at Governeur, N. Y., a band of god-
less young men joined hand in hand by ridicule
and every other means to resist the revival, Father
Nash, coming forth from his closet with awful
solemnity, as if he were striking chords from
Ezekiel's iron harp, thus solemnly warned them :
" Now, young men, mark me ! Within one week
God will break your ranks, either by converting
some of you or by sending some of you to hell !
He will do this as certainly as the Lord is my
God !" Down came his hand on the pew before
him, and the very house seemed to · shake with
the presence of God. He sat down, dropped his
head, and groaned with agony for souls.

Even Mr. Finney was startled at the boldness
of the prediction. But two days had not passed
before the leader of those young men, in the
deepest distress, came to Mr. Finney and, broken
down with contrition, submitted himself to God ;
and at once went back to his companions, besought
them to turn unto the Lord, and prayed with
them. Before the week was out that band of
mockers were rejoicing in hope.

Abel Clary, of Rochester, was another of these
praying saints to whom more than to his own
pungent and powerful preaching Mr. Finney traced
the mighty revival tide that swept over the Eastern
and Middle States. Though he was licensed to

preach, such were his hunger for souls and his thirst after God, that he forsook the pulpit for the closet, and gave to prayer his time and strength, night and day. The absorption of his soul was often such that he could not stand, but would writhe and groan as he travailed in birth for souls. He never appeared in public, but gave himself wholly to the secrecy of divine communion. Is it any marvel that the whole city was moved as it never was before or since? How slow are we to learn that from the secret springs of the closet flow the rills and rivers of grace, by which the deserts are transformed into gardens of paradise!

In his revival lectures Mr. Finney tells of another man in New York State, whose name he does not give—a consumptive, poor and sick, unable to do anything but pray. Yet his intercession brought answers to one soul and one community after another, and even to distant fields in pagan and heathen soil. Revivals sprang up as if spontaneously and unaccountably; but after his death his diary revealed the secret cause. Daily he set apart certain hours for certain ministers, churches, communities, and mission stations. Often in these pages would be found such an entry as this: "To-day I have been enabled to offer what I believe to be the prayer of faith for the outpouring of the spirit on ——, and I trust in God that there will soon be a revival there." And not long after would follow the record of the answer, even in

places as distant as Ceylon. What is more remarkable, the revivals followed in the *order* named,
as though to defy any explanation but that found
in prevailing prayer.   During his sickness, as death
drew nigh, he was specially engrossed with prayer
for the town he lived in.   After he *died*, his works
followed him, and that last prayer found gracious
and abundant answer in the place of his residence.
The prayer was recorded on high and his tears
put into God's bottle; and, though the praying
lips were dumb, and the holy tears were wiped
from his eyes, the prayers he had offered came back
in converting grace, and the tears he had shed
descended in abundant showers of blessing.   That
the Church of God can neglect a motor like prayer
is a sure sign of apostasy !   Were it possible for
one man to speak in a voice of thunder, that
should peal around the world and reach every
Church and every Christian believer, it would
be my desire to sound, as the motto of the present hour, these two words, viz. : " FORWARD ! "
" PRAY ! " or they might both be included in the
counsel given by that Japanese preacher, Dr.
Neesima, lately deceased : *"Advance on your
knees !"*

Could the whole Church just now determine in
God's strength to allow no retrenchment, surrender
no station, withdraw no workman, but rather multiply her laborers, enlarge her gifts, and at once
vigorously push for the regions beyond—could

the Church but resolve that within this generation every human soul shall hear the Gospel proclaimed, there would come, as we solemnly and confidently believe, a new era of blessing, of which even Pentecostal outpouring was but a forecast and first-fruits! All prophecy and promise paint a glorious future for the Kingdom of God.

The visitor at Florence enters that grand apartment in the Museum of Natural History known as La Tribuna Galilei. The walls are inlaid with precious stones and the ceiling is glorious with elaborate frescoes. Around are the master achievements of sculpture, each in its own little shrine. In the centre of a large and semicircular window, at the extremity of this temple of science, stands the colossal statue of the man who first with telescopic eye penetrated to the arcana of the heavens. And around that central figure all else is clustered, and toward that all else in this costly Cabinet of the Medici seems to point. The surrounding busts of great men all face toward him who was greater than they all, and the very glories of that ceiling, which sets forth the leading events in the career of the famous Florentine, rains down on his head its lavish splendors.

All history is the Tribuna of Jesus of Nazareth. He is the central glory of the ages. The very universe was built to be His temple. The greatest of prophets, priests, and kings, the foremost of poets, philosophers, and statesmen, the leaders in

art, science, and invention, turn toward Him who
is greater, wiser, and mightier than all. The ages
move about Him, and the very heavens shine for
Him. His supernal glory a stable could not dim
nor a manger hide. A hating world nailed Him
to a cross of shame, but they were only lifting
Him up to draw all men unto Him. His very
crown of thorns became a diadem of royalty, and
His death destroyed death and turned the grave
into the gateway of paradise. The cross was not
the symbol of defeat and shame, but of conquest
and glory.

By the cross of that Nazarene, the Church is to
conquer. Missions represent, not a human device, but a divine enterprise. Its thought was a
divine idea, and its plan, a divine scheme; the
work is a co-labor with God; the field is a divine
sphere; the spirit of missions is a divine inspiration, and the fruit of missions a divine seal, an everlasting sign that shall not be cut off.

There are some watchwords which, as with
trumpet tongue, should peal out all along the lines
of the Church; our great motto should be, "The
world for Christ and Christ for the world, in this
our generation." The Fulness of the Times has
come. The cup of God's preparation overflows.
The open door of the ages is before us. The
whole world invites and challenges occupation.
Facilities, a thousandfold multiplied, match the
thousandfold opportunities. If it is the open door

of the ages, it is also the crisis of the ages. Some one will enter these open doors; if an inactive, indifferent Church delays, the arch adversary is always on the alert. Satan never yet lost his opportunity. He was in the garden of Eden as soon as man was; he not only occupies, but preoccupies; with sleepless vigilance he watches while even disciples sleep. His missionaries are everywhere; his synagogues and seats throng the great centres of population and plant their subtle influences through the hills and valleys; his pioneers go before the boldest and bravest who pierce the unknown lands; he sets up his printing-presses long before the Christian literature scatters its healing leaves.

Christ is waiting for His final Coronation. The Kremlin, that island in a sea of domes, is the sanctuary of Russia. But, in all this maze of temples, towers, ramparts, and palaces, nothing impresses one more than that singular Treasury where are seen the many crowns worn by the rulers who swayed their sceptres over the kingdoms of Poland, the Crimea and Kasan, before they were absorbed in the ever-encroaching gulf of Russian conquest.

The structure of the future has its Throne-room; there lie the crowns of empire, waiting for Him to whom by right they all belong. And, when He shall return to mount His throne, these crowns shall be all laid at His feet. He waits for the grateful suffrages of a redeemed people, brought out of every nation, before He assumes His rightful dominion. What can you and I do to hasten that consummation!

Let my closing appeal be to young men. Some of us have passed middle life and our sun is declining; with others of us the sunset hour already reddens the horizon. With you the dawn has yet to climb to its noontide. History is dense with its events. Every year, every day, every hour, is the prolific parent of opportunities that might make angels rejoice, and responsibilities that might make even angels tremble! These pages are now bringing to a conclusion a series of appeals which have been written as with my heart's blood, and in them the energy and enthusiasm of the inmost life have found utterance. And now let the last words be put in capitals, as their emphasis demands:

GOD IS MOVING ON.

HIS MARCH IS SWIFT, AND OUR TIME IS SHORT.

NO SUCH AGE HAS EVER BEFORE SHONE ON THIS PLANET.

NO SUCH DOORS EVER BEFORE OPENED TO HIS CHURCH.

WHO WILL FALL INTO LINE WITH GOD,

JOIN IN HIS MAJESTIC MARCH,

AND IN THE SURE ADVANCE OF HIS PLAN

REACH THE GOLDEN FRUITION OF THE AGES

INDEX.

PUBLICATIONS OF

THE BAKER & TAYLOR CO.

Publishers and Booksellers,

740 AND 742 BROADWAY, NEW YORK.

Mailed to any address, postpaid, on receipt of price.

BEHRENDS — SOCIALISM AND CHRISTIANITY. By A. J. F. BEHRENDS, D.D. 12mo, paper, 50 cents ; cloth.................................... $1 00

"Uniting to the uncompromising honesty of a catholic mind a large endowment of practical constructive ability, he (Dr. Behrends) is not only able to give his readers a comprehensive grasp on the rather intricate subject of Socialism in all its schools, but, better than this, to offer some sound, sensible, and, above all, practical remedies for the sores on the social body."—*Providence Journal.*

BLAKELEE—INDUSTRIAL CYCLOPEDIA. By GEORGE E. BLAKELEE. 8vo, cloth, 720 pages, 200 illustrations.. $3 00

This book is stored from cover to cover with thoroughly simple, practical, and easily understood directions for making and mending every conceivable article of use or ornament, for performing every process that could be of service in the workshop, the kitchen, about a village home, or on a farm, and for the application of a thousand and one clever expedients to the task of best accomplishing every variety of every-day work. Its abundant illustrations put matters so clearly before the reader that doing is nearly as easy as seeing.

"This book has a department for everything, and is worth its price every year to every family."—*Rural New Yorker.*

"A blessing to mankind. A book everybody should have. It is the only practical and comprehensive work on simple mechanics in the world."—*N. Y. Tribune and Farmer.*

BUNYAN—THE PILGRIM'S PROGRESS. From this World to that Which is to Come. By JOHN BUNYAN. Being a Fac-simile Reprint of the First Edition, published in 1678. See "Fac-simile Reprints." 16mo, antique binding, with Renaissance design, gilt top, $1.25 ; imitation panelled calf, $1.25 ; full morocco, basket pattern, $2.25 ; Persian, $2.25 ; levant.......................... $2 50

BRANCH—NATIONAL SERIES OF SPEAKERS.
By O. E. BRANCH, author of "Hamilton Speaker." I. Primary Speaker; boards, 50 cents. II. Junior Speaker; cloth, 75 cents. III. Advanced Speaker; cloth.......... $1 25

These entirely new books contain the very freshest and most unhackneyed selection of good speakable pieces now accessible to seekers after new subjects for declamation and recitation. They are graded to meet the needs of persons of all ages.

CALKINS — KEYSTONES OF FAITH; OR, WHAT AND WHY WE BELIEVE. By WOLCOTT CALKINS, D.D. 16mo, cloth.............. 75 cts.

This book is designed for young Christians and busy people who need a brief outline of the great doctrines of grace in which *all evangelical denominations agree.* In the body of the work, Chapters I.-VIII., this is given in popular language, free from all technical phrases of theology. In Chapters IX. and X. another outline is given in the language of the Catholic and evangelical confessions, and in Chapter XI. still another short but complete outline is given, in the exact language of Scripture.

COOPER — LEATHER-STOCKING TALES. By JAMES FENIMORE COOPER. A New Library Edition, in large type, from new plates. 5 vols., 12mo, green cloth, gilt top.. $5 00

CO-OPERATION IN CHRISTIAN WORK. Common Ground for United Inter-Denominational Effort. By Bishop HARRIS, Rev. Drs. STORRS, GLADDEN, STRONG, RUSSELL, SCHAUFFLER, GORDON, KING, and HATCHER, President GILMAN, Professor GEO. E. POST, and others. (Uniform with "Problems of American Civilization.") 16mo, paper, 30 cents; cloth.................... 60 cts.

This book contains a series of selected addresses delivered before the General Christian Conference held at Washington, D. C., December 7-9, 1887, under the auspices of the Evangelical Alliance.

CRANE — VIRGIL'S ÆNEID. Translated literally, line by line, into English Dactylic Hexameter, by Rev. OLIVER CRANE, D.D. 4to, cloth............... $1 75

This translation is probably the closest reproduction of the original extant in any language. It retains the metre and, with remarkable smoothness and aptness of language, gives the English of the great poem in the same number of lines, and almost in the same number of syllables, as the epic itself.

DEUTSCH — LETTERS FOR SELF-INSTRUCTION IN THE GERMAN LANGUAGE. By SOLOMON DEUTSCH, Ph.D. 2 vols., 8vo, cloth, $5.00. Each volume also sold separately. Vol. I. First Course, Grammatical; 8vo, cloth, 480 pages, $2.50. Vol. II. Second Course, Idiomatic and Literary; 8vo, cloth, 364 pages. $2 50

DEUTSCH—LETTERS, Etc.—*Continued.*

This is an elaborate work which perfectly accomplishes the task of making it possible for an English student, entirely without other aid, to master every detail of the pronunciation, grammar, and idioms of the German language, and at the same time to become familiar with its conversational forms, its proverbs, and classical sayings.

MR. CHARLES DUDLEY WARNER fitly characterized the book when he said of it : " *The method is scientific, but is perfectly intelligible. The author is thorough : in order to be easy he cannot be brief; he explains carefully.*"

DEUTSCH—DRILLMASTER IN GERMAN. Based on Systematic Gradation and Steady Repetition. By SOLO-MON DEUTSCH, A.M., Ph.D., author of "Letters for Self-Instruction in German," etc. 12mo, cloth, 469 pages. $1 50

A perfect instrument for the complete mastery of German.

The subject-matter of the book is divided into twenty-four sections, consisting of numbered paragraphs containing German sentences on the left page, and the exact idiomatic English equivalent on the right page. Each of these sections of fifty paragraphs is followed by the same number of paragraphs in English, containing Drill Exercises for Oral and Written Review. In these no new terms are employed, but merely modifications and variations of the sentences already given, and these have been selected with a view to practical usefulness. The grammatical rules deduced from the model sentences which form the bulk of the book appear in copious foot-notes and in the appendix. The latter also contains synoptical tables, giving a general view of the inflections, and an alphabetical list of the prepositions, with their idiomatic use. An index, alphabetically arranged, directs the student at once to the resources of the book on any given point.

FAC-SIMILE REPRINTS of Walton's "Compleat Angler," Bunyan's "Pilgrim's Progress," and Herbert's "Temple." Being reproductions of the First Editions of these books. Each 16mo, antique binding, with Renaissance design, gilt top, $1.25 ; imitation panelled calf, $1.25 ; full morocco, basket pattern, $2.25 ; Persian, $2.25 ; levant $2 50

" These immortal works are here presented, as nearly as possible, in the precise form in which they were first issued."—*The Literary World*, London, England.

GASPARIN — UNDER FRENCH SKIES ; OR, SUNNY FIELDS AND SHADY WOODS. By Madame DE GASPARIN, author of "Near and Heavenly Horizons." 16mo, cloth $1 25

" Daudet's windmill sketches are not more delicately drawn. It is a book to be devoured before an open grate, or under green apple boughs."—*Philadelphia Press.*

" Done with great delicacy and finish."—*Springfield Republican.*

GODDARD—THE ART OF SELLING. With Hints on Good Buying ; also, Changes in Business Conditions

GODDARD—THE ART OF SELLING.—*Continued.*

and Methods ; Salesmen's Compensation, Opportunities, and Prospects ; Commercial Travellers ; Retail Merchants and Salesmen ; Saleswomen ; How to Read Character, and the Most Important Legal Principles and Decisions Governing Sales. By F. B. GODDARD. 12mo, flexible cloth.. 50 cts.

In this book the author lets the reader into the secrets of the accomplished and successful salesman, illustrates his tact and finesse, and tells how he masters men.

" We doubt if anything better of its kind has ever been published. Any one with this handbook as a guide might easily develop into a skilful and successful salesman. To many it will be worth its weight in gold."—*Christian at Work.*

HERBERT—THE TEMPLE. Sacred Poems and Private Ejaculations. By GEORGE HERBERT, late Oratour of the Universitie of Cambridge. Being a fac-simile of one of the Gift Copies printed for circulation by Nicholas Ferrar, before the publication in 1633, of which only one copy is known to exist. See " Fac-simile Reprints." 16mo, antique binding, with Renaissance design, gilt top, $1.25 ; imitation panelled calf, $1.25 ; full morocco, basket pattern, $2.25 ; Persian, $2.25 ; levant............ $2 50

JANES—HUMAN PSYCHOLOGY. An Introduction to Philosophy. Being a Brief Treatise on Intellect, Feeling, and Will. By E. JANES, A.M. *New and Revised Edition*, 12mo, cloth $1 50

" This book is intended for use in Schools and Colleges by classes beginning the study of Philosophy, and is also adapted to the wants of the general reader. Its definitions are clear and concise. Its treatment of the subject is such as to impart to the student who goes no further an adequate knowledge of the elements of Psychology, and to lay a solid foundation for the future work of the student of Philosophy."—*Christian at Work.*

LIGGINS—THE GREAT VALUE AND SUCCESS OF FOREIGN MISSIONS. Proved by Distinguished Witnesses. By Rev. JOHN LIGGINS, with an Introduction by Rev. ARTHUR T. PIERSON, D.D. 12mo, 249 pages, paper, 35 cents ; cloth......................... 75 cts.

A powerful presentation of overwhelming evidence from independent sources, largely that of Diplomatic Ministers, Viceroys, Governors, Military and Naval Officers, Consuls, Scientific and other Travellers in Heathen and Mohammedan countries, and in India and the British Colonies. It also contains leading facts and late statistics of the Missions.

LOOMIS—MODERN CITIES AND THEIR RELIGIOUS PROBLEMS. By SAMUEL LANE LOOMIS. With an Introduction by Rev. JOSIAH STRONG, D.D. 12mo, cloth $1 00

LOOMIS—MODERN CITIES, Etc.—*Continued.*

" The author has reached more nearly to the true cause of the difficulty and the proper manner to remove it than any other author with whose works we are acquainted."—*Hartford Post.*

NATIONAL NEEDS AND REMEDIES. The Discussions of the General Christian Conference held at Boston, Mass., Dec. 4-6, 1889, under the auspices and direction of the Evangelical Alliance for the United States. 8vo, paper, $1.00 ; cloth $1 50

The important subject of causing, by means of inter-denominational effort, Christian principles and feeling to thoroughly permeate our whole civilization, was elaborately discussed by Phillips Brooks, Josiah Strong, Richard T. Ely, Howard Crosby, Bishop Huntington, Joseph Cook, and many others who are giving direction to the thought of to-day.

" This Boston Conference is the most important event in the American religious world which we have been permitted to chronicle in a very long time."—*The Churchman.*

NATIONAL PERILS AND OPPORTUNITIES. The Discussions of the General Christian Conference held at Washington, D. C., Dec. 7-9, 1887, under the auspices and direction of the Evangelical Alliance for the United States. 8vo, cloth. $1 50

The book is indispensable to every Christian who would keep abreast of current religious thought and effort.

Among the speakers were : Dr. S. J. McPherson, Dr. Arthur T. Pierson, Pres. James W. McCosh, Bishop Samuel Harris, Dr. Josiah Strong, Dr. Washington Gladden, Dr. A. F. Schauffler, and fifty other prominent representatives of all denominations and all sections of the country.

" All the prominent social questions which now confront the churches were discussed, and the foremost men in the churches were present to discuss them."—*Christian Union.*

PIERSON—THE CRISIS OF MISSIONS ; OR, THE VOICE OUT OF THE CLOUD. By the Rev. ARTHUR T. PIERSON, D.D. 16mo, paper, 35 cents ; cloth $1 25

" We do not hesitate to say that this book is the most purposeful, earnest, and intelligent review of the mission work and field which has ever been given to the Church."—*Christian Statesman.*

PIERSON—EVANGELISTIC WORK IN PRINCIPLE AND PRACTICE. By Rev. ARTHUR T. PIERSON, D.D. 16mo, paper, 35 cents ; cloth. $1 25

An able discussion of the best methods of evangelization by an acknowledged master of the subject.

" The book tingles with the evangelistic spirit, and is full of arousement without sliding into fanaticism."—*Springfield Republican.*

PIERSON—THE ONE GOSPEL; OR, THE COMBINATION OF THE NARRATIVES OF THE FOUR EVANGELISTS IN ONE COMPLETE RECORD. Edited by Rev. ARTHUR T. PIERSON, D.D. 12mo, flexible cloth, red edges, 75 cents; limp morocco, full gilt $2 00

Each evangelist furnishes some matter, found, if at all, not so fully in the other records. It has been sought to blend all the various features of the four narratives into one without losing whatever is distinctive in each. Without taking the place of the four Gospels this book will be an aid in their study—a commentary wholly biblical, whereby the reader may, at one view, see the complete and harmonious testimony of four independent witnesses.

PROBLEMS OF AMERICAN CIVILIZATION: Their Practical Solution the Pressing Christian Duty of To-day. By Presidents McCosh and GATES, Bishop COXE, Rev. Drs. PIERSON, DORCHESTER, McPHERSON, and HAYGOOD, Hon. SETH LOW, Prof. BOYESEN, Col. J. L. GREENE, and Rev. SAMUEL LANE LOOMIS. (Uniform with "Cooperation in Christian Work.") 16mo, paper, 30 cents; cloth . . . . 60 cts.

This book contains a series of selected addresses delivered before the General Christian Conference held at Washington, D. C., Dec. 7–9, 1887, under the auspices of the Evangelical Alliance.

ROSS—VOICE-CULTURE AND ELOCUTION. By WILLIAM T. ROSS. New and Revised Edition. 12mo, cloth $1 25

A thorough, practical, and progressive work on the art of vocal and physical expression. It treats of calisthenics and the organs of speech, and covers the whole field of elocution.
"The nearest perfect of any book intended for the use of students of elocution."—*Lois A. Bangs, Packer Institute, Brooklyn.*

RUSSELL—WHAT JESUS SAYS. Being an arrangement of the words of our Saviour, under appropriate headings, with a full index. By Rev. FRANK RUSSELL, D.D. 12mo, cloth. $1 25

" The idea of the book is original; the execution is excellent, and cannot fail to be very helpful to all who desire to know exactly just what our Lord has said. His simple words are so covered up with glosses and commentaries that we are almost unable to consider their natural meaning. In accomplishing this most desirable result of listening to Christ alone, this work is most serviceable to us all."—*J. B. Angell, LL.D., Pres. Michigan University.*

SCOTT—THE WAVERLEY NOVELS. By SIR WALTER SCOTT. Centenary Edition. In 25 vols., illustrated with 158 Steel Plates, and containing additional Copyright Notes from the author's pen not hitherto published, besides others by the editor, the late DAVID LAING,

SCOTT—THE WAVERLEY NOVELS.—*Continued.*

LL.D. With a General Index, and separate Indices and Glossaries. Sold only in sets. 12mo, half calf extra, $68.75 ; half morocco, $68.75 ; cloth extra, gilt top.. $31 25

" A handsome and convenient set, neatly bound in dark blue cloth. Each volume has a special glossary and an index, and the illustrations are numerous."—*N. Y. Nation.*
" The edition is an admirable one. It is one of the best editions available for comfortable reading."—*N. Y. Tribune.*

STRONG—OUR COUNTRY. By REV. JOSIAH

STRONG, D.D. 140th thousand. Enlarged and revised with reference to the census of 1890. 12mo, paper, 30 cents ; cloth................................... 60 cts.

This revision shows the changes of the last ten years, and pictures the religious, social and economic condition and tendencies of our country to-day.
The present edition has been printed from entirely new plates, and enlarged by the addition of more than one-third new matter. Diagrams have also been employed to forcibly illustrate some of the more startling facts and comparisons. In its new form it adds to its original worth the merit of being the first general application of the revelations of the recent census to the discussions of the great questions of the day.

THOMPSON—SONGS IN THE NIGHT WATCH-ES, FROM VOICES OLD AND NEW. Compiled

by HELEN H. STRONG THOMPSON, with an Introduction by Dr. JOSIAH STRONG. 317 pages, cloth, full gilt. $1 25

This is a collection of religious verse designed, in the words of the compiler, " to pierce with a joyous note the darkness of the night."
" Nothing lovelier than your ' Songs in the Night' has ever come into my way."—*Margaret E. Sangster.*
" The sweetest songs ever sung this side of Heaven."—*North-western Presbyterian.*

THWING — THE WORKING CHURCH. By

CHARLES F. THWING, D.D. 16mo, cloth. Revised and enlarged................................... 75 cts.

A careful treatise by a successful church administrator on the best methods of making the church organization an efficient instrument. Its topics are : I. The Church and the Pastor ; II. The Character of Church Work ; III. The Worth and the Worthlessness of Methods; IV. Among the Children ; V. Among the Young People ; VI. Among Business Men; VII. From the Business Point of View ; VIII. Two Special Agencies ; IX. The Treatment of Strangers ; X. The Unchurched ; XI. Duties towards Benevolence ; XII. The Rewards of Christian Work ; XIII. The Country Church.

TODD — INDEX RERUM. By JOHN TODD, D.D.

Revised and Improved by Rev. J. M. HUBBARD. 4to, cloth................................... $2 50

TODD—INDEX RERUM.—*Continued.*

The index is intended to supply to those who are careful enough readers to make notes of what they may wish to use again a book especially adapted to that purpose by a system of paging by letters, each page having a margin for the insertion of the word most expressive of the subject of the note. It contains 280 pages of quarto size, ruled and lettered. With the minimum of effort it secures a lasting record of every reference that may be thought worthy of preservation in the course of the widest reading.

" An indispensable part of every literary man's equipment."— *Chicago Interior.*

TODD — THE STUDENT'S MANUAL. By JOHN TODD, D.D. 12mo, cloth.................... $1 00

As a formative book for the college period of life, it is unequalled in our literature. It has received the universal approbation of those who are interested in the best education.

" I know of no better guide for young men seeking to obtain a liberal education. It ought to be in the hands of every student."— *James S. Rollins, President of Curators, State University, Mich.*

WALTON — THE COMPLEAT ANGLER ; OR, THE CONTEMPLATIVE MAN'S RECREATION. By IZAAK WALTON. Being a *fac-simile* Reprint of the First Edition published in 1653. See " Fac-simile Reprints." 16mo, antique binding, with Renaissance design, gilt top, $1.25 ; imitation panelled calf, $1.25 ; full morocco, basket pattern, $2.25 ; Persian, $2.25 ; levant $2 50

WOODBURY—TALKS WITH RALPH WALDO EMERSON. By CHARLES J. WOODBURY. 16mo, cloth, gilt top, with a hitherto unpublished portrait.......$1 25

The poet's opinions, freely and spontaneously expressed in conversations on current thought, literature, philosophy, and criticism, and his thoughts about contemporary writers and workers. The book is at once an epitome of his philosophy and a commentary upon the time and society in which he lived.

" No lover of Emerson can afford to overlook this book. He pervades it. The man himself is there."—*New York Sun.*

" Mr. Woodbury is the one man who has caught Emerson as Boswell caught Johnson ; caught him in his utterance ; caught the accent of his sentences ; caught the very impulse which Emerson felt himself in the act of speaking."—*Chicago Interior.*

ADDITIONS TO THE LIST OF

THE BAKER & TAYLOR CO.

CUYLER.—THE EMPTY CRIB. By THEODORE L. CUYLER, D.D. 24mo, cloth, full gilt, with two steel portraits .... 75 cts.

" Those who have lost little children by death, will read this book with moist eyes."—*Lutheran Observer.*

" A real gem ; the outpouring of a stricken parent's sorrows into the very bosom of the Saviour."—*Christian Advocate.*

CUYLER.—GOD'S LIGHT ON DARK CLOUDS. By THEODORE L. CUYLER, D.D. 16mo, cloth.... 75 cts.

" To thousands of disconsolate hearts these pages are fitted to carry just the comfort which they crave."—*Congregationalist.*

" These are words of sympathy and cheer to the desponding and bereaved—utterances clear, tender, and comforting, out of a suffering heart to suffering hearts."—*Presbyterian.*

CUYLER.—HOW TO BE A PASTOR. By THEODORE L. CUYLER, D.D. 16mo, cloth, gilt top .... 75 cts.

" If any man living understands the subject of this little book, it is Dr. Cuyler."—*Independent.*

" Ought to be read by all pastors, young and old."—*N. Y. Tribune.*

" Its beauty and its power are precisely in this, that it is eminently simple, its teachings so obvious that their mere statement carries conviction of their entire adequacy. Their statement is full of charm."—*N. Y. Evangelist.*

" This book will be read by thousands of teachable and conscientious ministers. It ought to be. Dr. Cuyler is a noted example of success in this branch of work. Nobody's pen can write wiser words than his."—*Mich. Christian Advocate.*

CUYLER. — POINTED PAPERS FOR THE CHRISTIAN LIFE. By THEODORE L. CUYLER, D.D. 12mo, cloth, with a steel portrait of the author $1 50

" Dr. Cuyler holds steadily the position which he reached years ago, as the best writer of pointed, racy religious articles in our country."—*Presbyterian.*

" We know of no better volume for the stimulation and guidance of the Christian life in all our reading, nor one more likely to attract and hold readers of widely varying culture and character."—*Evangelist.*

CUYLER.—STRAY ARROWS. By Theodore L. Cuyler, D.D. 18mo, cloth .... 60 cts.

" A collection of brief, pointed religious articles. They are very suggestive, and arrest the reader's attention by their pointed manner as well as their striking and impressive thought."—*Evangelist.*

MORELL.—AN HISTORICAL AND CRITICAL VIEW OF THE SPECULATIVE PHILOSO- PHY OF EUROPE IN THE NINETEENTH CENTURY. By J. D. Morell. 8vo, cloth, 752 pp $3 50

" The late Dr. Chalmers said in the *North British Review*, that he had seldom read an author who makes such lucid conveyance of his thoughts, and these never of light or slender quality, but substantial and deep as the philosophy in which he deals. In similar terms the leading reviews and writers abroad have spoken of him, and his philosophical history has taken rank among the very best productions of the age."—*N. Y. Observer.*

RYLE—EXPOSITORY THOUGHTS ON THE GOSPELS. By Rev. J. C. Ryle. 7 vols., 12mo, cloth, in a set.. $8 00

Matthew, 1 vol. Mark, 1 vol. Luke, 2 vols. John, 3 vols. Each volume......................... $1 25

" It is the kernels without the shells."—*Christian Union.*
" It has a sure place in many families, and in nearly every minister's library."—*Lutheran Observer.*
" The work of a ripe scholar. These expository thoughts have met with the heartiest welcome from the press of the leading Christian denominations in this country."—*Inter-Ocean.*

THORNE—FUGITIVE FACTS. An Epitome of General Information, obtained in Large Part from Sources not Generally Accessible and Covering more than One Thousand Topics of General Interest and Frequent Inquiry. By Robert Thorne, M.A. 8vo, cloth.............. 2 00

" It answers hundreds of such questions as are addressed to our Department of Replies and Decisions, and will be found invaluable in the family, in the office, in the school-room, and wherever else there is an inquiring mind."—*New York Journal of Commerce.*
" It is as full of information as an egg is of meat, and, from the composition of Absinthe to the politics of Zululand, all interests are provided for."—*The Nation.*

The above books will be mailed postpaid to any address on receipt of the price by the publishers.

THE BAKER & TAYLOR CO.,
740 AND 742 BROADWAY, NEW YORK.

WORKS BY ARTHUR T. PIERSON.

THE CRISIS OF MISSIONS;
Or, THE VOICE OUT OF THE CLOUD.
16mo, paper, 35 cents; cloth, $1.25.

" One of the most important books to the Cause of Foreign Missions, and, through them, to Home Missions also, which ever has been written. It should be in every library and every household. It should be read, studied, taken to heart, and prayed over."—*Congregationalist.*

" We do not hesitate to say that this book is the most purposeful, earnest, and intelligent review of the mission work and field which has ever been given to the church."—*Christian Statesman.*

EVANGELISTIC WORK IN PRINCIPLE AND PRACTICE.
16mo, paper, 35 cents; cloth, $1.25.

" If our pen could become as fervent as fire, and as fluent as the wave, we could not write either too warmly or too well of this book. Dr. Pierson has given us a real book—a thunderbolt—a cataract of fire. These flame-flakes ought to fall in showers all over Christendom, and set every house on fire."—*C. H. Spurgeon.*

" The book tingles with the evangelistic spirit, and is full of arousement without sliding into fanaticism."—*Springfield Republican.*

" A stirring trumpet blast to every earnest soul it reaches."—*Christian at Work.*

" Every page is filled with the evangelistic spirit. . . . . Dr. Pierson is full of facts, arguments, incidents, illustrations, and pours them over his pages in a molten stream."—*N. Y. Evangelist.*

THE ONE GOSPEL;
Or, THE COMBINATION OF THE NARRATIVES OF THE FOUR EVANGELISTS IN ONE COMPLETE RECORD.

Edited by Rev. Arthur T. Pierson, D. D. 12mo, flexible cloth, red edges, 75 cents; limp morocco, full gilt, $2.00.

Without taking the place of the four Gospels this book will be an aid in their study—a commentary wholly Biblical, whereby the reader may, at one view, see the complete and harmonious testimony of four independent witnesses.

" Dr. Pierson has done his work with excellent judgment and fidelity to the spirit and letter of the evangelists."—*Christian Union.*

" To ministers, Sunday-school teachers, and all Bible students it is of great value, presenting, as it does, the gospel story without break, and the events in chronological order."—*Presbyterian Observer.*

The above books sent, postpaid, on receipt of the price,
by the publishers,

THE BAKER & TAYLOR CO.,
740 AND 742 BROADWAY, NEW YORK.

www.ingramcontent.com/pod-product-compliance
Lightning Source LLC
Chambersburg PA
CBHW021802110726
47902CB00006B/1611